NIGHTFALL

NIGHTFALL

JAKE HALPERN AND PETER KUJAWINSKI

HOT
KEY
BOOKS

First published in Great Britain in 2016 by
HOT KEY BOOKS
80–81 Wimpole St, London W1G 9RE
www.hotkeybooks.com

A CIP catalogue record for this book is available from the British Library.

ISBN: 978-1-4714-0573-0
also available as an ebook

This book is set in Mercury.

Printed and bound by Clays Ltd, St Ives Plc

MIX
Paper from
responsible sources
FSC® C018072

Hot Key Books is an imprint of Bonnier Publishing Fiction,
a Bonnier Publishing company
www.bonnierpublishingfiction.co.uk
www.bonnierpublishing.co.uk

For Sebastian and Lucian, you are the lights of my life
—J. H.

For Blaze, Alina, and Sylvie—may you see clearly,
and write of what you see with courage
—P. K.

Shiprock Point

Southerly Bay

Fishing Depot

Graveyard

The Arch

Dwarf
Oak
Islands

Home
Bay

Deep Well

Hourglass

Town

BLISS

CHAPTER 1

MARIN WALKED INTO THE WIND AND FELT IT GENTLY PUSH back. A few more steps and she'd be at the edge of the cliff. Her focus was on the thistle, the prickly green plants that crunched beneath her feet. What would happen to these plants during the years of Night? Would they wither and die, or would they simply lie dormant, waiting for the first rays of sunlight to peek up from the horizon? She had asked those who had been through this before, but they refused to discuss it. No one talked about the Night, even though it was almost upon them.

She stopped near the precipice. The water below was dark, almost black, and it stretched everywhere, like a liquid version of the sky. In the last year, as the sun had begun its final descent, the water had gone from blue-green to iridescent blue, and from there it grew steadily darker. A hint of its fluorescence remained, but now it provoked a shiver instead of a smile.

Marin took a deep breath of the cold sea air. When the sun vanished, it would get even colder. Everything would freeze—at least that's what people at school said. In any case, by the time that happened, she'd be long gone, along with everyone else in

Bliss. Only the buildings would remain, silent and empty, entombed in ice.

The wind flung Marin's wavy black hair into her face. She was smaller than other girls her age, but she was stronger than most. Her arms and legs were long and well-muscled, the product of years spent climbing, hiking, and sailing. She had honey-colored eyes, long lashes, and bronze skin—a striking combination, which she inherited from her mother. Her clothing, however, was plain and purely functional: waxed canvas pants, a raw denim shirt, and leather boots.

"Has the tide turned yet?"

Marin spun at the unexpected voice. She had been waiting for her friend Line, but instead she saw Palan—a frail man with paper-thin skin and a bald head marked with brown sunspots. Palan had lived through several Mornings and his skin bore the proof. His cobalt-blue robe rippled in the wind, revealing a left arm that ended in a stump just above his wrist.

"I'm not sure about the tide," Marin replied. "What do you think?"

The old man faced Marin, his watery eyes looking past her, into the distance. "This is my fourth Evening," he said quietly. He tightened the heavy wool scarf wrapped around his neck. "The sun seems to be moving faster and faster with the years."

Marin followed his gaze. The sun had almost disappeared below the horizon. Only a sliver remained visible. The entire western sky was ablaze in magnificent shades of orange and red. A few degrees more and the sun would vanish completely, plunging the island into darkness for the next fourteen years. They said this would happen soon, perhaps in a matter of days.

2

It sounded a bit like the end of the world to Marin, and she still found it hard to believe.

The wind blew gently and Palan sighed. "It saddens me that I will never see this place again. When I leave here—I expect I won't return."

Marin reached out and touched his arm. The old man turned away from the sea, back toward the island's interior, and grasped her hand. "I've heard movement in the forest," he whispered.

"What do you mean?" asked Marin, worried that Palan may have become lost in his mind.

Palan gripped her hand tighter but did not reply.

A muffled shout rang in the distance.

"MARIN!"

They looked up and watched a teenage boy moving toward them. It was Line. If Palan hadn't been there, she would have run to him, but now she just waved back.

When he arrived, Line appeared slightly confused. Palan studied them both, arched an eyebrow, and smiled.

Line's dark brown eyes twinkled as he approached Marin. He was handsome in the way that few boys of fourteen are. He was tall and broad-shouldered, with an unkempt shock of reddish-brown hair, high cheekbones, and a cleft chin.

"Elder Palan," said Line. "Any news of the boats?" A gust of wind pressed his curly hair flat against his head.

Palan straightened, as if the use of the honorific—Elder—reminded him of his role and station. "Sorry, my boy, I've heard nothing of the boats," said Palan. "But I am not here for that. Come—I'll show you."

3

He approached the cliff's edge and pointed downward. Marin and Line followed close behind him and peered over. The face of the cliff was shrouded in shadow, but they could make out several thick white veins coming out of the cliff and running down its side, like a hardened trail of wax from a giant candle.

"It's *ice*," said Palan. It was colder at the edge of the cliff, and his shoulders began to tremble. "My father brought me to this place as a boy. The ice always begins here. It squeezes out of the rock and then, they say, it spreads . . . until it covers everything. The island turns to ice."

Marin and Line stood close together, near Palan. Line's fingers grazed Marin's.

Palan leaned over several inches more. "Somewhere down there is the hag." His voice turned hoarse. "At times, when the waves break just right, you can see her."

He took a step back from the cliff and smiled with great contentment, as if recalling a particularly fond memory. Marin and Line looked down at the water. It seemed no different than before. Palan often spoke in riddles, in the manner that those of such age do.

"I'd like to get a better view of that ice," said Line, taking off the coil of rope slung across his shoulder and pushing up the sleeves of his sweater. His forearms and biceps were tan and muscled from years of rock climbing.

"As you wish," said Palan. "But be careful. Ice is much slicker than rock."

Suddenly impatient, Marin and Line said good-bye. As Palan shuffled back to town, Line set up the rope, tying it securely to a small brass ring jutting from the rock. Marin and Line had been climbing the cliffs that formed the island's perimeter their entire lives, and recently, it had been just the two of them. Going off unchaperoned was frowned upon, but at the moment, the town was too consumed with other matters to pay them any mind.

Just before beginning, they checked to make sure they were each securely fastened to the rope. Marin faced Line. She tucked a lock of hair behind his ear so it didn't dangle over his eyes. "You were late," she said, scowling as if she were cross with him.

"Just a minute or two," he said with a grin. Line shook his head so that his hair fell back over his eyes. "It won't happen again."

They descended steadily until the ocean spray began to mist their legs. The rays of the setting sun could not reach this area, and it was darker than they expected. Still, they were able to see the veins of ice glowing in the murky twilight.

Line continued down several feet, until the ocean spray wet his heavy canvas pants and wool sweater. Marin heard him mutter in surprise.

"What is it?" she called.

Line looked up. Marin was standing comfortably on a tiny ledge two body lengths above him. "The tide's turned," he said.

"Just now?"

She climbed down to get a better look.

"You're right," she said. "Look, you can see it." She pointed to a thin band of white that clung to the cliff wall near their feet.

5

Line nodded. "That dried salt is the high-water mark."

They hugged the cliff wall. After all the anticipation, it was happening. During the fourteen years of Day, the waters around their island remained at high tide. Then, just before the sun vanished, the tide reversed itself suddenly and rapidly, rolling out hundreds of miles and leaving exposed seabed where once there had been crashing waves. And the sea stayed away until Sunrise—some fourteen years later—when it returned just as fast. The timing of all of this was crucial for the islanders, who migrated with the tide. Once it turned, they had just a few days to depart.

"Do you think anyone else knows?" she asked.

"I bet the okrana know." Line adjusted his hold on the rock and shivered. The nearby ice emanated cold with a surprising intensity. "We should go."

He was beginning to climb back up when Marin saw something brown and green poking out of the frothy water.

"Line!" she called. Her voice was sharp against the muffled thump of the waves.

Line stopped. His foot was jammed into a tiny crevice in the rock, and one of his fingers curled around a slight nub. He leaned out and looked down, using his free arm and leg for balance. To Marin, it looked like his finger and foot were glued to the wall. Marin shook her head and smiled. *Show-off.*

"What is it?" he asked nonchalantly.

"Just come look," said Marin. Her eyes were wide and brimming with excitement. "There's something in the water."

Line climbed back down to join her on the ledge. He followed her gaze and, over the next few minutes, they watched a human form emerge from the receding tide. It jutted out at a strange angle, but still they could tell that it was a statue of a woman. The head was carved in simple lines, yet her expression was surprisingly intricate. Her mouth was gaping open, as if she were screaming or expressing great terror. The statue was big—three or four times the size of an average person.

"Palan's hag," whispered Line.

The water level was dropping steadily, and soon they saw her upper torso. The hag brandished a shield and wore a simple cloak wrapped tightly around a lean, muscular body.

"I see writing!" Marin called. "There—on the shield!"

They waited breathlessly through several waves, until the trough of one large wave revealed the following words in huge block letters: THE HOUSES MUST BE WITHOUT STAIN.

Marin tried to suppress an uneasy feeling. The island was littered with old ruins—crumbling foundations, broken pillars, old stone walls. This statue was just another relic of the island's past. A vestige of ancient peoples. Still, the phrase seemed strangely relevant. *The houses must be without stain.* Now that the tide had turned, everyone in town would be cleaning their homes, preparing to leave. It was an ironclad rule—the last task before departure.

"Why is this statue here—in the ocean?" Marin asked.

Line said nothing at first. "It's curious," he finally replied. "It looks very old." He frowned as if an unpleasant thought had crossed his mind, then turned to Marin. "I'm ready to head back. All right?"

"What's the matter?" Marin asked. The sea had left a fine mist on their exposed skin and hair.

7

Line smiled, but it was forced. "I'm just cold, that's all."

"Let's go," she said, nodding. Line was more her brother's friend than hers, and she still didn't know him that well. They began ascending the shadowy rock face. Marin was about to urge Line to climb faster when his foot rolled off the rock. It was shocking—he might have fallen backward if he didn't have a rope to grab onto. Line was one of the best climbers in Bliss. He'd never slipped before.

"What happened?" called Marin.

"Ice," said Line, almost as a curse. "It's in the crags."

Together they climbed as quickly as they could, back toward the sunlight.

CHAPTER 2

EVEN THOUGH MUCH OF THE ISLAND WAS COVERED IN shadow, there were still places that caught the light. The trail that led back to town was such a place. It was perfectly situated along a hill, facing the nearly disappeared sun. As a result, everything—from the garnet pebbles on the ground to the swaying remnants of wheat and grass—shimmered.

After their cold, dark climb, even this small amount of sun warmed Marin. It made her think of the Desert Lands and of her mother, who was born in that distant place. The ice had appeared so suddenly—and the cold coming from it still seemed to grip her. All of a sudden, following the sun to the Desert Lands didn't seem like an entirely bad idea.

"It'll be chaos in town," said Line as they walked up a hill dotted with clumps of fragrant, blue-tinged bushes. He shook his head and shrugged, as if this would be more an annoyance than anything else. "Pure chaos."

Marin frowned, trying to imagine their orderly town in a state of chaos. "They send the envelopes out after the tide turns—right?" Of course, she knew this to be true. *How many times has my father said as much?* But still, now that the moment had arrived, she felt a compulsion to repeat it—just to be sure.

Line nodded. "I bet they're doing it right now," he replied. "And after that, everything will shut down—the markets, school, even the fall wheat harvest."

Marin thought about this. "I figured we'd have at least two more weeks." She paused for a moment and then added, "I guess that means we've just had our last climb together."

Line sighed, hoping that wasn't true.

"I knew this was going to happen," he said, glancing at the sea. "Anyone who sails could see the tide was going to turn sooner rather than later. I don't know why the mayor uses that stupid lunar calendar."

They continued on, walking single file along the narrow path. Marin picked up her pace, both to match Line's longer strides and to warm herself up. Was she cold from the climb, or was the wind turning sharper? Probably both. The path widened again, and Line drew up next to Marin. Although she didn't look over, she could sense that he was close to her. "What are you going to do now?" she asked softly.

Line massaged his palms to release the tension from climbing. "Well, classes for the children will have ended now that the tide's turned—so I have Francis to look after. I'd like to forage for some mushrooms, too—maybe even a bit of lekar."

"You think you'll be able to find lekar so close to Nightfall?" she asked.

"Maybe," he replied. "Francis and I could really use the extra money."

Line lived with his younger brother. Their father died just

after Francis's birth, and two years ago, their mother had suddenly taken ill and died, too. The doctor said it was pneumonia, an illness that often came with Dusk. After that, the two boys lived with their uncle for a while, but it hadn't worked out—he was foul-tempered and spent most of his time drunk. For over a year now, fourteen-year-old Line and seven-year-old Francis had been on their own. It was unusual, to say the least, but Line managed.

Line grabbed at a clump of dead wheat stalks and started shredding them. He glanced at Marin. "With the tide turning, I have a lot to do. I haven't really packed up the house yet."

Marin's eyes widened. Her family had been doing this for weeks. Line's house was much smaller, but still. "I'll help," she said quickly.

It was Line's turn to look surprised. "Really? What if your parents find out?"

"Don't be stupid," she retorted. "I'll help a bit—that's all." Marin was suddenly embarrassed, and she wondered if Line could tell. Luckily, they'd crested a hill and were heading down the other side, into shadow. Of course, Line was right. It would be risky going to his house. Marin's mother, Tarae, didn't like the idea of her spending time alone with a boy—especially Line, who lived without parents.

They continued along the footpath, crested a small bluff, and took in the view, surveying their town's collection of evergreen gardens, neatly manicured walls, timber-framed houses, and slate rooftops. It was a bucolic place. Theirs was a town of five hundred people, but from this vantage point it looked small. And compared to the massive forest that covered the island's interior, it *was* small—just over a hundred buildings, nestled together.

Delicate trilling noises suddenly filled the air. Moments later, a mule appeared pulling a cart. It was decorated with dozens of silver bells, which jingled rhythmically as the cart rolled down the dirt road that led toward Bliss.

In the driver's seat was a figure clad in a black robe; he was the town's vicar, a stony-faced man whose eyes stared purposefully ahead. In the backseat sat a fragile-looking elderly woman who held an infant in her arms. The woman was the matriarch of a band of widows who scaled fish to earn their keep, and she claimed to be 107 years old. No one had the temerity to dispute this. She looked so frail, it was surprising that she was able to sit up straight *and* hold the baby.

Marin and Line came to an abrupt halt. This custom—the so-called Pageant of Life and Death—occurred as soon as the tide turned; because this was their first Sunset, it was also the first time they'd witnessed the ritual. They stood in place, watching the cart pass, until the sound of its bells grew faint. The noise, however, was soon replaced by a number of distant, high-pitched screams. The sounds were not human, but they were bloodcurdling all the same.

"What *is* that?" asked Marin. She put her hands to her ears. "It makes my skin crawl."

"They've started slaughtering pigs for the journey," said Line. "Things are moving faster than I thought. We'd better hurry."

CHAPTER 3

THEY TOOK A WINDING GOAT PATH THAT LED THROUGH the abandoned fields surrounding Bliss. With the sun so low and the weather turning cold, their previously fertile farmlands had gone barren. Only a few fields still produced food, but it was nutritionally poor fall wheat and stunted potatoes. In recent weeks, even these were hard to find—the fields suddenly teemed with bugs, mites, and strange biting worms. And so the people of Bliss lived mainly off their supplies while waiting for the ships that would take them south.

Line's home was a small farmhouse at the edge of Bliss, notable for its round stained glass windows. Just beyond his farmhouse, the houses were built closer together, and the cobblestone roads of the town appeared.

As they neared Line's home, they could see that foot traffic in town had picked up dramatically, and the usually quiet streets were filled with people chattering and pushing past one another. Bells began tinkling, and people stopped what they were doing to stare at the main street, which cut Bliss neatly in two. The Pageant of Life and Death had arrived in town.

Parents drew their children close, while others muttered devotions and averted their eyes.

Line slowed down and frowned. "Why is Kana in that tree?"

At the mention of her brother's name, Marin looked around eagerly. "Where?"

Line pointed to a bare apple tree that stood near his house, overlooking Bliss's main street. Like most apple trees, this one had stopped bearing fruit almost a year ago. Now a slender, fine-boned boy watched the pageant from its topmost fork.

"Kana!" Marin yelled.

The boy flinched but did not acknowledge her, not even with the slightest turn of his head.

"Kana!"

Again he ignored her.

Kana was Marin's twin. He was about Marin's size, but where Marin was dark-skinned, with black wavy hair, Kana's hair and skin were pale—"snow-kissed," as they called it. The only physical feature they shared was their long pitch-black eyelashes. They made Marin's eyes unusually expressive; for Kana they served as a spotlight, drawing attention to his pale blue eyes.

Until recently, though, his eyes hadn't seemed to work. Kana had been born blind. Or at least that's what the family had believed. At around ten years old, as the sun started dipping lower in the sky, Kana began perceiving shapes and shadows. When he squinted he could see better, so the town's glass blower made him a bizarre pair of spectacles, which were essentially wire frames with eye patches on them. Each patch had a tiny hole in the center, allowing in only a pinprick of light. Within the last year, however, as it grew darker, Kana no longer needed the spectacles at all.

"Kana!" shouted Marin again, betraying more than a touch of irritation. Nearby townspeople turned toward her voice. Kana looked at her, revealing the other side of his face, which was marked by a jagged scar that began at the top of his right cheekbone and continued down to his jaw. Kana eyed Line and his sister coldly for a moment, then turned away.

Line put a hand on Marin's arm. "Don't force it," he said. "He'll come around."

Marin just furrowed her brow.

"Come on," said Line.

A short while later, they found Francis waiting at the farmhouse where he and Line lived. He was wearing green overalls, a buckskin vest, and a gray flannel hunting cap. This was his favorite outfit, and Line let him wear it every day—until the smell became too ripe. As soon as he saw Line, Francis jumped to his feet and raced toward them. Line ruffled Francis's thick brown hair, which probably should have been cut months ago.

"Were you waiting long?" asked Line.

Francis shrugged. "Some okrana came for you a few minutes ago."

"Now what?" said Line. The okrana were the town's volunteer police. They patrolled the coastline, looking out for the raiders and thieves who occasionally preyed on towns. Most were farmers with a desire for something more exciting, but Bliss—up to now—had provided little opportunity for action. Lately, they had been checking in on Line often—urging him to pack up and get his house in order. This drove Line crazy.

Marin wasn't so sure he didn't need the reminders, but she never admitted as much.

"They gave me something," said Francis. He dug into his pants and extracted a crumpled envelope. "They said it's for the master of the house. What does that mean? Are you the master?"

Line ignored his brother and eyed the envelope. "I guess the letters are here," he said to Marin. "I wanted to get to the bakery before this. We need bread."

"Don't worry—there's plenty at our house," said Marin. "My mother's been hoarding it. Let's open the envelope. May I?"

"Might as well," said Line.

Francis began fidgeting, unable to contain his excitement. "I'll do it!" he exclaimed. He tore awkwardly at the seal, ripping the paper in several places. Impatient now, Francis thrust it at Line, who promptly gave it to Marin.

She felt the envelope's weight in her palm. It was heavier than she expected. Carefully, she pulled out two sheets of thin paper. The first page contained a detailed floor plan of the house. The second was filled with notes describing where each carpet, piece of furniture, and picture was to be stored.

"What's this?" she asked, pointing to a diagram of a wall in the front room. It was marked with an arrow and the words RAT, SNOUT, AND TEETH.

Line peered at the pages. Marin looked inside the envelope again, and saw a skeleton key encrusted with verdigris.

Francis's eyes grew wide. He snatched the key but fumbled it, and it fell to the ground with a metallic clang. In an instant, he'd crouched down and picked it up.

"Can I keep it?" he said, face beaming with excitement.

Line took the key from Francis and turned it over several times. "Later," he said as he pocketed it. "I don't want to lose this before I know what it opens."

Francis frowned and gave his brother a shove. "I'm old enough! I won't lose it."

Line glanced at Marin and smiled. At least several times a day, and in a variety of situations, Francis claimed to be *old enough*. It was his favorite thing to say.

Line grabbed Francis and lifted him up. "Let's get inside," said Line. "I'm starving."

He opened the door, walked inside, and unloaded Francis, who rushed away. Marin paused on the doorstep to look behind her. The Pageant of Life and Death was still occupying everyone's attention, and Kana was no longer in the tree.

Line reappeared at the doorway. He held the door open for her and smiled. "Coming inside?"

Marin nodded and quickly followed him, shutting the door behind her.

CHAPTER 4

THE FIRST FLOOR OF LINE'S HOUSE WAS A LARGE OPEN space with whitewashed walls, which appeared a murky green in the glow of the many stained glass windows. The walls were bare except for a number of crudely fashioned pegs where the family hung its cloaks and hats. Line lit a few candles so they could all see properly. During the brighter years of Late Morning and Noon, the stained glass helped mute the ever-present glare of the sun. Nowadays, it was so gloomy that Francis refused to enter the place alone, which is why he'd been waiting outside.

Even in the dim light, however, there was no mistaking how little packing Line had done. Farm tools—spades, hoes, and buckets—were still caked with dirt. The corners were thick with cobwebs made by strangely industrious spiders that emerged in the recent months of Twilight. Dirty plates and dishes, crusted and flaking from previous meals, lay on the kitchen table and counters. Bearing mute witness to the dirt and grime was an army of toy soldiers, perched on every ledge and in every crevice.

Line waved a hand at the mess. "I may have mentioned that I haven't packed up the house yet."

"You may have mentioned that," Marin said dryly. It was strange to be in Line's house without an adult present. And yet this was how Line lived—on his own—with no one to answer to. She imagined, for a moment, what it would be like to live here, too, with Line, spending her time with her own rules, rather than those of her parents.

Line led Francis into a small alcove at the back of the house, which served as the kitchen. He pushed a small wooden panel in the wall, triggering a copper pipe to splash cold water into a cast iron pot that sat in the jade washing basin. Marin stood nearby, fidgeting with a toy soldier that she'd picked up.

Just then, Francis screamed.

A monstrous apparition was staring at them through the front window. Its face was long and blackened, except for its eye sockets—a pair of cavernous, bloodred tunnels through which two green serpents protruded. The face quickly disappeared, and then there was a knock on the door. Francis cowered behind Line.

"It's okay," said Line, lifting his brother into his arms. "I was expecting something like this—they're a little early, though."

He swung the front door open. A nine- or ten-year-old child stood in the doorway, wearing the gruesome mask they'd seen in the window. Marin considered ducking out the back door, but it was too late; the child had already seen her. *Will he tell anyone?* It probably didn't matter. People had bigger things to worry about these days than who was unchaperoned.

"Take off your mask," ordered Line. "You're scaring my brother."

"We're not allowed to," said the boy. He turned his head, as if looking for confirmation, and a second figure emerged in the doorway. This was a grown man, wearing a yellow mask emblazoned with flame-shaped metalwork.

"Who are they?" whispered Francis, his face half buried in Line's neck.

"I am the Specter of Night," the boy with the serpent eyes intoned. His deep voice was clearly forced. "And he is the Specter of Day."

The man in the golden mask nodded.

"The tide has turned," continued the boy with the serpent eyes. He spoke solemnly and deliberately, enunciating every word, as if reciting the lines from a poem. "The cycle of the stars has begun. The sun is gone. Darkness shrouds the island. We are to leave."

Line took a step forward. "We have the envelope," he said. "And we're in the middle of preparing the house." He paused. "Are you done here? Like I said, my brother is scared."

"He *should* be scared," the boy said. "I am the Specter of Night and there are other spirits, much more gruesome than I, waiting in the woods. My face was made in their likeness."

"Is that true?" asked Francis, looking up at his brother.

"He's repeating the lines from an old poem," said Line. "It's just a silly game."

"You should show more *respect*," interjected the man with the golden mask. He pointed an accusing finger at Line. "These customs are sacred. Prepare your house before the furriers arrive." He looked around. "You have work to do here, *boy*."

Line's jaw tightened. He set his brother on the ground and stalked toward the door. Marin, sensing a possible confrontation, stepped in front of Line and addressed the man with the golden mask.

"Specter of Night," she said, inclining her head respectfully. "You have something for this house, do you not?"

The man nodded, appeased. The boy with the serpent eyes reached into his coat, pulled out a small paper bag, and gave it to Marin. *"Cover your scent."*

Francis pushed his way toward Marin. "What is it?"

"Lime," replied the boy with the serpent eyes, using his regular pitch now. "It's what they put on dead bodies. You need to sprinkle it around the house before you leave."

Marin bowed. "I'm sure there are other houses awaiting your arrival."

"Blessed be the Day," said the man with the golden mask.

"Save us from the Night," said the boy with the serpent eyes.

And then, much to everyone's relief, they departed.

No one spoke at first. Francis kept his large brown eyes fixed on his brother.

"Was that the silversmith?" asked Marin, finally breaking the silence.

"It sounded like him. He's a friend of my *uncle's*," Line said with a roll of his eyes.

Line sent Francis to play with his soldiers, then returned to the kitchen. Eager for something to do, Marin began to clean, starting with wiping down the windows. As she rubbed a cloth across the dusty panes of glass, she thought again of the hag in the ocean. *The houses must be without stain.*

Line cooked up a generous amount of dandelion greens, sprinkling in salt, pepper, and dried cod. When the food was ready, he served three large plates and they sat at a rickety wooden table. They were hungry, and ate in silence.

Francis finished first. He dashed to a worn-down armchair and picked up an oversize leather-bound book embossed with flowing gold script across its cover: *Tales of the Desert Lands*. It told the story of a little girl named Shiloh who was born along the equator, where the sun rose and set in a shorter cycle: seventy-two hours of Day followed by seventy-two hours of Night. Children from all of the northern islands were given this book, in order to prepare them for life in the desert. Once there, the islanders would spend fourteen years in a small city of sandstone buildings, situated on a crescent-shaped beach hemmed in by the Desert Lands on one side and the ocean on the other.

Marin stood up from the table and walked over to the chair where Francis was sitting. She eyed his book and recalled how Shiloh rode a two-humped horse across the dunes, befriended the desert nomads, and found wādīs where treasures were buried. Most memorable of all was the story of Shiloh's time at the Cloister—a forbidding stone tower rising from the sand—where she spent a year isolated with other girls her age. It was a rite of passage for natives of the Desert Lands and their daughters. During this time, the "women-to-become" meditated together and used scalpels and ink to etch markings across their bodies and faces.

Francis looked up at Marin. "What's it really like in the Desert Lands?" he asked. "Your mother lived there, didn't she?"

Marin nodded. "She did."

"And that's why she has those marks on her wrists?"

Marin nodded again. "The markings aren't only on her wrists," she explained. "They go all the way up her back, too."

"Can I touch them one day?"

"Francis—it's late," said Line, eager to change the subject. "You need to get to bed."

Francis shook his head. "I don't want to go by myself. And I'm not tired."

"Go with him," Marin told Line. She felt a sudden pang of sadness for Francis, this little boy with no parents to tuck him in. "I'll clean up, and we can move the furniture when you come down. And don't forget, we also have to deal with the key."

CHAPTER 5

LINE WALKED FRANCIS UP THE NARROW, CREAKING stairs that led to the second floor, holding his hand so he wouldn't trip in the dark stairwell. At the top of the stairs was a small landing and three doorways. One doorway led into Line's room, another into Francis's room, and a third into the room his parents had shared.

"Can I sleep in your room tonight?" asked Francis.

"Okay," said Line. He was too tired to argue. Francis walked over to Line's bed and climbed into it. Line crawled in next to him and pulled a huge comforter over them. It was used only in Twilight, when the weather became uncomfortably cold. Francis was quiet, and for a moment, Line wondered if he'd fallen asleep. That hope was dashed when Francis turned and asked, "Did Mother know about the spirits who live here at Night?"

Line paused. Francis did not talk about their mother often.

"Nothing lives here at Night," Line replied, patting his little brother on the shoulder. "It's too cold. The island freezes."

"But the spirits are dead," persisted Francis. "So it doesn't matter how cold it gets."

"There's no such thing as spirits," said Line gently. "Adults think that telling kids to get ready before the spirits come will make them pack up quickly. But we live on our own, so we're kind of adults already and don't need to play. Understand?" He kissed his brother on the cheek. "Now close your eyes."

"But I'm not tired."

Line sighed. "Do you want me to sing?"

"Yes," said Francis with a yawn.

Line cleared his throat and began to sing "Hand Over Hand," one of the ballads that old men and women sang as they scaled the island's cliffs. It was a slow, sad melody—perfect for chanting in rounds, with each climber on a rope singing in intervals. Line sang for a while, then hummed the tune.

Some time later, Line woke with a start. *How long have I been asleep?* It could have been minutes or hours—he was too disoriented to tell. He stood and walked downstairs. Marin was gone, and the house was in tip-top shape. She had done a great deal of work—the dishes were cleaned, the toys put away, and the tools returned to the shed. Much of the furniture had been moved, too. Marin was incredible.

They had grown up alongside each other, part of a group of children who'd been born at Sunrise. Throughout their early childhood, Marin and Kana had kept to themselves, as twins often do. In fact, one of Line's earliest memories was watching Marin lead Kana along the cliffs. For years, Line had thought her beautiful—her brown skin, her smile, her confidence, even with the elders. Yet it was Kana whom Line befriended first— the two boys became close around the time that Line's mother died.

Together, they explored the darkened edges of the forest, where Kana helped Line gather mushrooms and a medicinal plant called lekar. Lekar always fetched a good price at market, but it was hard to find so close to Night, so he mainly sold mushrooms now. This, and a little farming, was how Line supported himself. It was only within the last three months or so that Line and Marin started spending time together—and this, unfortunately, had been the beginning of things souring between Line and Kana, *and* between Kana and Marin.

Line walked into the kitchen. The old windup clock by the stove read midnight. He had been asleep for hours. Then, on the counter near the food cupboard, he saw a note.

> *Line,*
>
> *I thought I'd let you sleep.*
>
> *The kitchen chairs are in the living room. The coffee table needed to be rotated by a half turn, so it faced the other way. (Insane.) The end table from Francis's bedroom is in the parlor. I moved the desk by myself. Aren't you impressed? I also cleaned up your parents' room. I hope you don't mind.*
>
> *There were a few notes on the floor plan that I didn't understand, like the bit about the* RAT, SNOUT, *and* TEETH. *And I couldn't find the round tables. I'll bring you some bread tomorrow.*
>
> *Remember the key. It fits that door in the cellar.*

"The key," said Line aloud. He nodded—fully awake now—and set to work. He grabbed a lit candle from the dining room

26

and proceeded to a door at the back of the kitchen. He opened it, cleared away a thick draping of cobwebs, and headed downstairs to the cellar. The stone walls of the cellar were sweating rivulets of water, which had softened the gravel and dirt floor, making it mucky. Line could feel his shoes sticking to the earth as he walked.

At the far end of the cellar, he found what he was looking for: a sturdy wooden door, bolted and sealed shut with an old warded lock. He'd never seen the door open. His mother had told him it was a storage closet, and he'd never been especially curious about what was inside. The cellar was not a place to spend free time.

Line took the key from his pocket, slid it into the lock, and fumbled around until he was rewarded with a click. He opened the door and revealed two round tables and three large wooden boxes. He walked deeper into the closet and leaned in to examine the boxes more carefully. One of them was marked RAT, a second was marked SNOUT, and the third was marked TEETH.

Line sat back on his heels, intrigued. He hadn't expected the arrival of the envelopes to lead to a treasure hunt in his own house.

One by one, he brought the boxes to the main floor and arranged them in a row. Line knelt down over the box marked RAT and pulled out a huge animal head, stuffed and mounted on a wooden slab. It looked like a cross between a rat and a storybook mastodon. The head was twice the size than that of a horse, which meant that the body must have been gigantic. Beneath the head was a brass plate emblazoned with ornate cursive letters written in a strange alphabet.

27

"Wow," said Line. "You're an ugly one." He consulted the floor plan and concluded that RAT was meant to go on the middle peg in the front room. The head fit perfectly. He then walked back across the room and opened the crate marked SNOUT—and removed yet another mounted head. This one had interlocked plates instead of fur, two pointy tusks, and a long snout—almost like an armadillo with an especially big nose. This head hung to the left of RAT. Finally, he opened the box marked TEETH and pulled out a third mounted head. It was almost identical to SNOUT, except for a set of long, jagged fangs.

"What are you?" asked Line quietly, as if he half expected the head to answer his question. "And where in God's name did you come from?"

There'd always been stories that wild boars—and animals even fiercer and more primordial—lurked in the depths of the island's forests. Line never entirely believed such tales, but he never totally discounted them, either. It was a large island, and very few people left the immediate vicinity of town and the coastline.

Line consulted the floor plan again, placed TEETH on the wall, and returned the wooden boxes to the basement. He then moved the two round tables into the front room. Finally, he opened the small paper bag of lime and sprinkled it as he walked around, giving the entire dwelling the air of a disinfected outhouse.

When he was done, he stopped to stare into the lifeless eyes of RAT, SNOUT, and TEETH, wondering what the purpose of hanging these grotesque animals on the walls could possibly be. It was pointless—absurd. *What will I tell Francis at breakfast?*

Line glanced at the small grandfather clock in the corner. It was an hour past midnight. Francis would be asleep for the next six hours. His little brother was the soundest sleeper that Line had ever encountered, and this was a good thing. Line wanted to make a quick trip to the edge of the woods to collect mushrooms for trading. And he knew of a spot that might still have some lekar, though that was probably too much to hope for.

He reread Marin's letter. She'd even cleaned his parents' room—knowing that it had to be done, and that he was reluctant to do it. Marin saw a problem, and she attacked it. They were a good team. But everything would change in the Desert Lands. Line knew this because Marin's mother had pulled him aside recently and said exactly that. She hadn't been unkind about it, just matter-of-fact: *This is the way it must be—she will spend time with other girls her age. In seclusion. And after that, she will be busy with many other things.* Tarae had lingered on those last words as she looked at Line. Her message was clear: the relationship between Marin and Line would come to an end when they left Bliss.

Line never told Marin about this conversation. Maybe she already knew. All this filled Line with a sense of immediacy— the next day, or two, perhaps, was all that he and Marin had.

He stood up straight and looked again at Marin's letter. If he went quickly, there was something he could do for her.

He'd been thinking about this for weeks but hadn't found the time. It wouldn't take long, and he'd be back before Francis awoke. He grabbed a thick wool sweater and rushed out of the farmhouse.

CHAPTER 6

AFTER A RESTLESS SLEEP, MARIN WOKE EARLY AND DE-
livered a loaf of bread to Line's house. She came while the town
was still largely asleep and placed the warm parcel at the front
door. Marin had already been up for several hours, baking the
dark, tough bread—known as *sheet iron* or *tooth dullers*—which
would be their staple for the long journey to the Desert Lands.
The main ingredient was fall wheat, a slender, reedy grain that
grew reluctantly in the dimming light of the last year. For those
who remembered the hearty summer wheat of years past, it was
a poor substitute. Still, Line and Francis probably wouldn't care,
especially since the loaf was still warm. Marin walked away,
smiling at the memory of the three of them eating together last
night. It might be a long while before she spent time with them
like that again. Soon she would be in the Cloister. *What then?
Will Line wait for me—for a full year? And wait for what?*

On the way home, Marin trailed along the cliffs, pausing
for a moment to take in the view. The island and surrounding
water were gripped in shadow. Angry gray-black clouds roiled
above, while only a thin sliver of orange peeked on the horizon.

Marin looked up the shoreline to where the island began to curve inward. Standing here, she felt as if the island were a massive ship plowing through the sea. No matter how terrible the storm, waves would beat themselves into nothingness against the cliff wall.

It was strange to think that the people from Bliss had lived here for only a few generations—just over a hundred and fifty years. Before discovering the island, they sailed the Polar Sea following fishing stocks, as weather and the currents permitted. Then they landed on the island and found a beautiful storybook town, perfectly intact and completely uninhabited. After much prayer and argument, a decision was made. To the sounds of deep bass-toned drums, the oldest person carried a newborn baby into Deep Well House. There they stayed for twenty-four hours, hoping that the house did not contain some trap or curse that would kill them. Eventually, the old lady emerged triumphantly carrying the exhausted baby, and everyone moved into the town.

As a child, Marin loved to hear every detail of this story, and she eagerly looked forward to its retelling during the Pageant of Life and Death. But over the years, she'd grown dubious of the history. She'd recently overheard an uncle repeating the story to one of her younger cousins, and asked him afterward if he really believed it.

"Of course I believe it," replied her uncle with a smile. They were sitting in the parlor of Shadow House and he was sipping his ale contentedly. "Don't you?"

"It makes no sense," Marin had said. "Why were all of these houses in *perfect* condition?"

"It was our destiny to come here," replied her uncle, setting down his ale and leaning in. "This island was a divine gift, and you do not question such gifts. You accept them and humbly express your gratitude." Marin merely shook her head—as she always did when the adults spoke of destiny, and gifts, and unquestioning acceptance. There had to be a better explanation—a fight, a battle, maybe even a plague—but clearly this town had been inhabited, right up until the moment her people had arrived. And the former residents had been scared off, run off, or killed off. She glanced back at the town. No one would abandon such a perfect place without cause. Marin felt certain of this.

For several seconds, she stared at the water and felt the bracing wind curl around her face. Then something in the distance caught Marin's eye. To the left of the disappearing sun, dipping between each curling wave, was a boat. Her heart sank. Only one? Impossible. They needed more than that to evacuate the whole town. Moments later, a few more boats came into view, sailing in tight formation. The clippers that would transport them sailed in the middle, surrounded by sleeker, two-hulled vessels. All the sails were yellow. It was the furriers, no doubt about it. They were right on time, coming with the tide. The furriers were mercenary nomads of the sea who hunted in the Polar North, accumulating furs, then sailed to the Desert Lands to sell their stock. Furs were prized, even in the Desert Lands, where it grew cold when the sun fell. Along the way, the furriers picked up passengers from the northern islands—for a price.

Marin turned and ran back toward town. Was she the first

to spot the ships? She hoped so. It'd be nice to show the okrana how easily a teenage girl could best them at their own job. She followed the old wagon trail back to town, jogging and then running. At a certain point, she was sprinting flat out, and almost crashed into someone heading toward her. She tripped and came to a stop in a cloud of dust.

"What is it, child?" asked the person she'd almost collided with. He was a portly man in a blood-smeared smock—Bliss's fishmonger. He'd seen Marin running and come out from behind his carving table to meet her. "You look like you've seen a ghost."

"The furrier boats," said Marin as she struggled to catch her breath. "They're here."

"How many?" barked the fishmonger, as if he were annoyed that she had failed to specify an exact number.

"Half a dozen," said Marin. "I—I don't know. I didn't count."

"Half a dozen!" he replied. He bit his lip and ran a hand through his matted brown hair. "By God, I hope there are more than that. Otherwise, we'll have riots—families against families, brother against brother. It has happened before."

Marin stared at him, unnerved by the fear on the fishmonger's face.

"What do we do?" she asked.

The fishmonger didn't seem to hear her. So she took a step closer and asked again, almost shouting this time.

The fishmonger looked at the ocean and squinted. "Get home and tell your people," he ordered. He turned abruptly and headed into town, leaving his fish to the flies.

CHAPTER 7

MARIN SPRINTED UP A WINDING DIRT ROAD TOWARD the woods. Her house was about a mile from town, and stood alongside a cold, fast-running stream. It was a grand old mansion called Shadow House, named for its proximity to the forest. Because of their age, the trees in this section of the woods had massive trunks and stretched several hundred feet tall. Over the course of Marin's childhood, as the sun arched across the sky and sank toward the sea, the shadows from these trees had lengthened, like the fingernails on an old man who had lost his clippers. Within the last several months, the shadows had crept faster, nearly erasing Marin's house from the landscape—as if blotting it out in a pool of black ink. This close to the woods, the shadows of the trees were so thick and overlapping that Marin wouldn't have been able to find her house at all if her mother hadn't placed candles in the windows.

As she approached the front door, Marin heard a steady clanking, like someone banging two pieces of steel together. She squinted through the darkness and saw her father kneeling by the front door, banging away with a small hammer. The door was a huge oval-shaped slab of oak, crisscrossed with a lattice-work of blackened metal. Her father was hammering with great concentration at an ornately engraved copper keyhole below the doorknob.

"It won't come off?" asked Marin. She breathed deeply and tried to catch her breath.

Marin's father was so startled that he dropped his hammer. Anton was a stonemason by trade and he looked the part, with broad shoulders, bulging forearms, and perpetual dust in his light brown hair. He wore heavily patched workman's coveralls and a long-sleeved muslin shirt. The only sign of softness was in his dark blue-green eyes, which were unmistakably kind.

"Marin," said her father with a shake of his head. "You scared the wits out of me. It's not wise to sneak up on people like that—especially these days."

She leaned over to peer at the keyhole. "Is it rusted shut?"

"Afraid so," replied Anton. "The other locks came off without any trouble, but this one is stuck."

"I still don't see the sense in it—taking off the locks," she replied.

Anton leaned back onto his heels and stared at her. It was clear that she'd run home and had something to tell him. He smiled expectantly, bringing dimples to each cheek.

"I walked home along the cliffs." She paused for a moment, savoring the news she was about to deliver. "I saw the boats—they're here."

Anton nodded slowly. "How many?"

"Half a dozen."

Her father frowned and stood up. *"Half a dozen,"* he repeated.

"Is that enough?" she asked.

Anton deliberated the question for several seconds. "I suspect more are on the way," he said finally. "Overall, the furriers always come with enough. There have been exceptions, but not in recent times . . ." He picked up the hammer with one hand and ran his thick fingers through his hair with the other. "We'll be fine, I'm sure." Although his voice was confident, he still looked uncertain. "Go on, hurry along and tell your mother." Anton opened the door to let Marin in, and turned back to the lock. "She's looking for you," he said, then began to hammer loudly.

Upon entering the foyer, Marin heard her mother's footsteps before she actually saw her. The footsteps were hurried, frantic, as if she were nearly running. Her mother was frenzied with the prospect of moving.

As far as Marin could tell, Tarae had been eager to leave the island ever since arriving fourteen years ago. "I came here because of love," she was fond of telling her children. "Your father was so charming and so handsome that he lured me to this rock in the Polar Sea." Anton was a native of the island, and had met Tarae during his last stay in the desert. They had married and Tarae had agreed to follow him north, but it had never been an entirely happy arrangement. Now, on the eve of their journey to the south, Tarae was unable to contain her excitement.

"Mother!" Marin called. "I'm back—I saw the ships!"

"I heard."

Moments later, Tarae emerged from the darkness, holding a candle. Marin's mother was tall and darkly olive-skinned, with waist-length raven-black hair that gleamed in the candlelight. Like her daughter, she had honey-colored eyes, a trait that was fairly common in the Desert Lands. Tarae was wearing a sleeveless white gown, cinched at the waist with an elaborately braided belt. Her arms, shoulders, and lower neck were covered with interconnected skin markings that depicted a tapestry of snakes, lizards, and dancing nymphs. They started just above her wrist, then twisted and turned and writhed all the way to the base of her neck. The sight was arresting, even for Marin, who had seen her mother's body many times before. What really surprised Marin, however, was her mother's revealing outfit. Women on the island typically wore pants, silk waistbands, and long-sleeved shirts made from simple muslin. In colder weather, closer to Nightfall, they wore long oilskin coats. No one dressed like this—not on the island.

"I met your father in this dress—he could not avert his eyes. *The poor man is bewitched,* they said." Tarae's cheeks flushed with color as she smiled at the memory. "He fell helplessly in love—and it happened just weeks after I left the Cloister."

Marin had heard many times about her parents meeting and about Tarae's year in the Cloister, where she pierced her eyelids with lizard bones and marked her skin with scalpels and ink.

"Are you going to the boats dressed like that?" asked Marin tentatively, thrusting her hands into the front pockets of her pants. *People will gawk at you.*

"Why not?" asked Tarae, sounding slightly wounded. "Would you mind?"

"Of course not," said Marin, kicking at the floor with her boot. "I was just asking. It's cold out there."

"Marin," said her mother, stepping closer to her daughter. "After fourteen years, I am headed *home*. I know that you love your life on this island, and I don't expect you to share my joy. Just understand that . . ." Tarae's voice cracked as she tried not to cry. "I recognize something of what you feel. I wasn't much older than you when I left the desert."

Marin swallowed hard. She had never really thought about just how scared her mother must have felt coming to Blinn. She was about to say something—what, exactly, she didn't know— when suddenly a breeze blew in from the front door, causing the candle in Tarae's hand to flicker and then go out. They could hear the sound of Anton hammering on the lock downstairs. Tarae muttered in annoyance and turned to get a match.

"Wait!" said Marin. "Don't light the candle yet."

"Why?"

"Because," said Marin. "I want to see your arms again."

Tarae spun around and arched her back proudly.

CHAPTER 8

IT LOOKED AS IF RAYS OF GREEN LIGHT WERE EMANATING from cracks in her mother's skin. Marin had seen these luminescent markings before, but pitch darkness made them look different—bolder, brighter.

"What you see is on every desert woman—they are the arrows of light—and they guide us not only in the Cloister, but throughout our lives." Tarae caressed her daughter's cheek and placed both hands palm down on her hair, as if bestowing a blessing. "You will understand better when we arrive in our new home."

Marin pulled away, almost recoiling. "I'm sorry . . . I have things to do." *I can't think about this—not now.* The idea of moving to the Desert Lands was not particularly appealing, especially when it meant giving up her freedom . . . and Line. Still, she realized belatedly that her voice sounded harsher than she intended.

Tarae's arms fell, and her radiant smile faded. "Yes," she said flatly. "You have chores to do."

"Where's Kana?" asked Marin.

"Working—as you should be."

Marin pressed her lips tightly together. She was determined not to say anything to further provoke her mother. Their relationship had been tense of late, especially in regard to Line. It was better to lie low until they were on the boats.

"Hurry along now," said Tarae. "There are scuff marks on the living room floor. Your brother is working to remove them. You will help. Remember, *the houses must be without stain.*"

Marin paused for a moment. A tingling ran up her spine. Those were the very words that appeared on the statue of the hag. "Why did you just say that?" she asked. "Where does it come from?"

"I don't know it's just an island saying," said her mother, who was now busy herding dust into a pile on the floor.

"But what does it mean?"

"It means you need to start working," said her mother impatiently. "Now go."

Marin found Kana in the living room. He was wearing black wool pants and a matching sweater. The contrast made his skin look paler than usual. At the moment, he was hunched over with his back to her, scrubbing at a stain on the wood-paneled wall.

Thick carpets that ordinarily stretched across the floor were rolled up, ready to be carried into the storage rooms downstairs. Marin was surprised to see that, beneath the rugs, the floorboards were scarred with hundreds of circular indentations—as if someone had walked around stabbing the floor with a spear.

"Have you seen what Mother's wearing?" Marin asked. She

tried to sound lighthearted, in the hopes that she and Kana might enjoy a brief truce. Kana continued working at the stain.

"Kana?"

He finally looked up and stared at her impassively, with neither fondness nor bitterness in his eyes. It was his Kana-as-a-blank-canvas look, and Marin hated it.

"You can start on the other side of the living room—there are some blotches on the wall," said Kana. He turned back to the stain and began prodding at it in a violent, jerky motion. Marin sighed, walked to the far wall, and began to scrub. The excitement of the arriving furrier boats seemed far away; her family was putting her in a very bad mood.

Several minutes later, Marin finished and moved to the parlor, a large room furnished with several upright couches, a stone fireplace, and an old but functional player piano. Currently the piano was playing a nocturne whose forlorn melody echoed down the hallways. Marin found the music unbearably sad, but Kana was fond of it, and he played it whenever he was home. The house had six bedrooms, a parlor, a formal dining hall, and a solarium. Stonemasons like Marin's father wouldn't usually live in such a grand place, but the house's location next to the woods made it less desirable.

Today there was a fire crackling in the fireplace. It was a stark contrast from Marin's childhood, when it had been far too warm for a fire. Now they built one almost every day. The island was cold, and ocean storms appeared more frequently, peppering houses with driving hail. A burning ember cracked in the fireplace, and Marin jumped. She was more on edge than she realized.

Tarae appeared in the doorway, standing so she was in profile. Her back—with its incandescent skin markings—cast a faint glow on the wall behind her, giving her an almost ghostly appearance. "Marin," she said with a kind of forced cheerfulness. "Please get the clock from Kana's room. I meant to ask him, but he's already upstairs. Put it on the mantel in the parlor and make sure it's facing seaward." She paused, then smiled in a way that put Marin on alert.

"I have something for you—wait here." A minute later, Tarae appeared again in the doorway. She was holding a rectangular box, six inches long and three inches wide. It was made of highly polished copper, and the red-brown hues of the metal threw ribbons of color onto Tarae's white dress. She approached Marin solemnly and held out the box. "Your birthright. I have been waiting for this moment . . ."

Marin took the box in her hands. The metal was cold and heavy.

"You will need this in the Desert Lands." Tarae's light brown eyes brimmed with tears. "Keep it safe during the journey." She caressed Marin's cheek with the palm of her hand. "Do you want to open it?"

Marin knew how much her mother wanted her to open the box, but she couldn't. It felt unbearably awkward. She'd do it later, on the furrier boats, when the reality of her life in the Desert Lands was inescapable.

"Mother," said Marin. She drew closer and placed a hand gently on Tarae's arm. Marin's voice was apologetic, sheepish, and so quiet that it was barely audible. "Can we do this on the boats? When there's more time? I just—I feel so rushed."

Tarae pursed her lips and nodded. "As you wish."

Marin mumbled her thanks and headed upstairs. The second floor of the house had seven rooms, but only hers and Kana's were occupied. After they were grown enough to move out of their parents' bedroom, Marin and Kana had chosen these, which were right next to each other.

Recently, however, Marin had begun to wish that their rooms were farther apart. On several occasions within the last few weeks, Kana had woken her with hysterical screaming. She'd run to his room and found him terrified and staring out the window, or sitting upright in bed, one arm across his face, another extended outward, as if pushing something away.

But he wouldn't talk about it. Not to her, anyway. After one of these episodes, Marin heard him and Tarae whispering in his room. The following day, Anton bolted Kana's window shut. When Marin asked why, they told her that Kana was suffering from "night terrors"—nightmares so terrible that they seemed real even after you awoke.

Upon reaching the top of the stairs, Marin continued down the candlelit hallway toward the open door of her brother's bedroom. Kana was studying his reflection in the mirror while rubbing lekar into the scar along his cheek.

Lekar was a powerful remedy against infections of all kinds. It could be eaten or applied to a wound, and it worked quickly. Many villagers claimed it had saved their lives. It came from a bright yellow fungus that appeared on the underside of woodfern, a small, soft plant that grew in the deep woods. It was very difficult to find or even to buy—especially this close to Nightfall—and Kana was lucky to have it. He'd been applying a small amount to his face just once a week, and it was working, though he'd always bear a scar.

Marin knew she had intruded upon a private moment, but she couldn't help but watch. Every once in a while she was reminded of the fact that her brother was actually quite beautiful. People in town said he looked like their father, but it was only recently that she'd begun to see the resemblance. He had grown taller, broader, and stronger from top to bottom during the past few months, and had even developed a dimple on each cheek like their father. He still wasn't as tall as Line, or as thickly built as Anton, but he had undeniably come into his own.

The only blemish on Kana's face was the scar. A fresh wave of guilt washed over Marin. She was about to dart away when Kana set down the jar of yellow lekar, turned his back to the doorway, and approached a large rocking chair in the corner of his room. He looked down at it and began to whisper. At first, Marin couldn't understand him, but then the words seemed to waft through the darkness, like a chant or the faintest of prayers: *It didn't happen ... It didn't happen ... It didn't happen.*

CHAPTER 9

IT DIDN'T HAPPEN. IT DIDN'T HAPPEN. KANA MOUTHED the words as he studied the leather-bound chair that had been torturing him for weeks. *I'm being tormented by a piece of furniture,* he thought. *How tragically stupid.* And yet that was the truth of it. The chair figured prominently in Kana's recurring nightmare. In it, he was lying in his bed, and a woman would call out his name. She sat in the rocking chair, hidden beneath a cloak, and she always said the same thing: "Stay away from the woods, child—don't let them see you." It would have been funny, in a dark kind of way, if it didn't seem so real. And that was the thing—it felt so lifelike that Kana wasn't entirely certain that he was dreaming.

On one occasion, he was positive that the woman leapt from the rocking chair—with astounding speed—landed on top of him, and covered his mouth and eyes with a cold, musty rag. Kana struggled but couldn't shake her off. He gasped for air but couldn't breathe. She was suffocating him. As she did this, she started talking again: "It's better this way, child—better for you." Then, rather inexplicably, as he felt his body go slack, she let him go. He tumbled off the bed and cracked his forehead against the floor. Everything went black. When he opened his eyes, hours later, he was looking into the terrified face of his mother. She'd come to check on him and found him on the floor, his face covered in thick, drying blood. That happened a week ago. Thankfully, he hadn't dreamed since.

Kana continued to stare at the old chair, as if it might start to rock on its own. It was an absurd thought, and yet it wouldn't really have surprised Kana. Not at this point. His great-aunt Malony was a lunatic—everyone knew this—and, apparently, he had inherited her illness. *I have Dad's dimples and my great-aunt's screwy brain.* His aunt had died several years ago, but he could still picture her: Malony had cloudy eyes and hair so thin it revealed her scalp, which was always covered with scabs. She had lived with his father's oldest sister, in a small bedroom in the attic. As a very little boy, he was terrified to be near her.

He'd voiced these worries to his mother as she was cleaning up his bloodied face, but she'd dismissed his concerns. "Kana, my love, it's impossible."

"Is it?" Kana had replied. "Malony threw herself down the stairs, didn't she? And they locked her in her bedroom afterward, right?"

Tarae had shaken her head. "You're fine," she'd told him. "It's the coming of the Night—it's upsetting all of us."

Now Kana continued to stare at the old rocking chair until he heard a wooden board creak in the hallway. He listened for a moment. "Marin—are you just going to stand there?"

There was no reply.

He turned and faced the doorway. "You're not very good at spying," said Kana. "If you want to come in, then do it."

"Sorry," she said. "Mother asked me to bring your clock downstairs." Marin stepped out of the hallway and entered his room. "What are you doing?" she asked. Marin absentmindedly rubbed her hands together and looked around Kana's bedroom.

"Slowly losing my mind," said Kana. He glanced at Marin. "What's that box you're carrying?" Recognition dawned on his face. "*Oh.* That's the box Mother's always chattering about. I'm a little jealous—my going-away gift was a set of bolted windows." He smiled. "Did you two have your talk? How did that go?"

Marin opened her mouth in amazement. It was uncanny how he was able to hone in on what had happened.

"The talk didn't go that well," she replied with a sigh. There was no point in elaborating. Kana clearly didn't want to have an actual conversation about this. "I just came to get the clock. That's all."

Marin took the clock off the wall and left the room.

Alone again, Kana felt drained, as if his brief back-and-forth with Marin had been more taxing than he realized. He eased himself down on the rocking chair. It groaned predictably every time Kana pushed back. It was one of the noises he remembered most from his childhood. He listened for sounds coming from Marin's room but heard nothing.

Marin. My twin sister, Marin. He missed her. That was the truth of it. He missed being closer with her—talking, joking, even just walking to school together. The constant bickering was tiresome. And yet he couldn't stop himself. He was angry—deeply angry—and this emotion had a will of its own.

Kana closed his eyes and envisioned the forest. He could smell the pine, and even with the window bolted shut, he knew a gentle breeze was making the needles shudder ever so slightly. It'd be good to get out.

He stood up and was about to leave, when he heard voices from outside. Kana pressed an ear against the window. Before he knew who it was, he could hear their agitated tone. After listening for several seconds, he called out to Marin.

She appeared at the doorway with a tired smile. Kana studied her face. Even in the poor light, he could see her with startling clarity. Her bronze skin seemed to glow, adding color to her eyes and lips. It was no wonder Line was so taken with her.

"What is it?" asked Marin.

"You have visitors coming," said Kana.

"What are you talking about?" she asked. Her eyes flicked to the window next to Kana. After years of being nearly blind, Kana's hearing was incredibly acute.

"The okrana are heading toward our house," he said. "They're coming from the woods and they want to talk to you."

In addition to monitoring the coastline, the okrana were the only ones in Bliss allowed to range in the woods. And as far as Kana and Marin knew, the okrana never made house calls.

"Are you joking?" asked Marin, narrowing her eyes.

"Do I look like I'm joking?" he replied, face stoic.

Suddenly nervous, Marin stalked out of Kana's room and headed downstairs. As she went, she heard voices in the foyer,

49

followed by her mother calling for her. At the foot of the stairs she met Tarae, who had wrapped a long black shawl tightly around her bare shoulders.

"Oh, Marin," said her mother. "What have you done, child?"

"I did what you told me to do," she protested. "I put the clock away."

"No, something else," said her mother. "The okrana want to speak with you."

"*Why?*"

"I don't know," said Tarae. Her anger was subsumed by a thick layer of motherly worry. Her lips and cheeks were pinched from frowning. "They wouldn't say."

CHAPTER 10

THE LEADER OF THE OKRANA, A MAN NAMED IVO, stood in the doorway. Or, more accurately, he dominated the doorway. His shoulders were so wide that they left only a few inches of space on either side. Marin recoiled. She'd always found him menacing. As a little girl, she remembered staring at the pockmarks along his chin and throat, wondering why his face was so badly scarred.

At the moment, Ivo was deep in conversation with Anton, who was a full head shorter. It took several seconds before Ivo realized that Marin was there. When he did, he stared at her probingly.

"Is this her?" Ivo asked. His black wool sweater was caked with mud and torn at the elbows.

"Yes," replied Anton, placing an arm protectively around his daughter's shoulders. "This is my daughter, Marin."

"I will ask her a few questions."

"Of course." Anton sounded amenable enough, but he was studying Ivo intensely.

Ivo cleared his throat. "Alone—if you please."

Marin's father frowned, but he clearly couldn't think of a suitable reason to object. He glanced inside and saw Tarae waiting in the foyer, biting a fingernail.

"It won't take long," said Ivo.

Marin walked past her father, shrugged at him as if this were a perfectly normal situation, and then closed the front door behind her. She stood alone on the doorstep with Ivo. In the distance, more okrana with wick torches waited by the edge of the woods.

"You know that the ships have arrived?" asked Ivo.

"Yes, I saw them." Marin shivered. It was no longer possible to be outside without a sweater, and she had left hers inside.

"So you know that we are pressed for time," he said.

Marin nodded.

Ivo stared flatly into her eyes. "I am glad you understand." He paused. "There is a problem. Quite serious."

"What is it?"

"A boy has gone missing," said Ivo. "He disappeared, probably within the last twelve hours."

"Disappeared?"

"Yes," said Ivo. He looked at her expectantly.

"I'm sorry," said Marin. "But I don't see how ... I mean what does this have to do with me?"

"You know the boy."

"Who is he?"

"Line."

Marin took a step back. She felt a cry building in her chest, but quickly suppressed it. *Where could he be?*

"You do know him—correct?" asked Ivo.

Marin nodded.

"How?"

"He's my friend," she replied. Her voice felt pinched, as if someone were taking her vocal cords and squeezing them.

"More than a friend, yes?" pressed Ivo.

Blood rushed to her cheeks. "Does it matter?"

"If I am asking, it matters."

"M-more than a friend," she stammered.

Ivo nodded with satisfaction. "When did you see him last?"

"Yesterday," she quickly replied, thinking that the speed of her response might prevent follow-up questions.

Ivo leaned closer. He had a strong, almost animal-like accent. "When yesterday—what time?"

"Just before midnight, I guess." Marin imagined her mother's shocked face.

"Don't guess," snapped Ivo. "Be certain."

"A quarter to midnight."

Ivo nodded and rubbed a hand across his chin.

"What were you doing at his house?"

Marin forced herself to hold his gaze. "The envelopes came. I was helping him get ready. He put his brother to bed and fell asleep. I was downstairs, cleaning, and let myself out."

"Was anybody else with you?"

"No," said Marin in a low voice. She heard her parents whispering behind the door, but neither intervened.

"Did Line mention plans to go anywhere?" Ivo asked.

She paused, recalling more of their conversation. "He *did* mention something about gathering mushrooms in the woods, maybe searching for lekar."

Ivo glanced at an old brass timepiece that hung from a chain attached to his jacket pocket. "It's now three in the afternoon," he announced. He paused to clear his throat and spit on the ground. "The boy's brother showed up at the neighbor's house upon waking and reported him missing. That was over seven hours ago. Do you believe he is still picking mushrooms?"

"I don't think so," said Marin tentatively. She felt sick to her stomach. *What the hell was Line thinking—running off now?* "I doubt it."

"Did he seem upset? Angry?"

Marin shook her head.

"Is there anything else you're not telling me—anything at all?"

"No," she replied.

Ivo took a step closer. He was so close that, when she looked up at him, she could see the stubble growing along the many tiny indentations on his pockmarked face. "There is precious little time left to find this boy. And if we leave without him, may God help him and may God have mercy on our wretched souls." His voice became a snarl. *"Now think hard, girl.* Do you have any idea where he might be?"

Marin struggled to remain calm. She did not want to break down in front of this man.

"I don't know where he is," said Marin. "I don't."

Ivo glared at her for several seconds, then stalked into the darkness. Marin watched as the distant torches of the okrana moved along the edge of the forest.

The door opened. "What did they want?" demanded Tarae.

Anton stood just behind her. Marin could tell that they had both overheard everything.

"It's Line," said Marin. Her body was beginning to shake. "He's missing. They thought I might know where he was."

"Do you?" asked Tarae. She moved in closer, forcing Marin to meet her eyes.

Marin shook her head. "No." But her mind was less certain— *Do I know where he is?* Random conversations with Line began floating through her mind. Was she overlooking some clue, some suggestion?

"Are you sure?" her mother asked. "Think, child. Nightfall is here, and instead of preparing, you're spending time with that boy. *In his house—alone!*"

"All right, all right," said Anton, stepping between them. "There is time later to discuss these matters. On the boats. For now, I will check on Line's brother." He addressed Marin in a voice that brooked no opposition. "Stay here. Help your mother and Kana finish our packing. Understand?"

Marin nodded.

Tarae took Marin's arm and, in a calmer voice, said, "Come along. Everything will be fine. You'll see."

"I should go look for Line," said Marin. She pressed her fingernails into her palms, fighting to keep her panic under control.

"No," said her mother firmly. "The okrana will find Line. In the meantime, there's still work to be done. I need you and Kana to return a box to Deep Well."

CHAPTER 11

TWENTY MINUTES LATER, KANA AND MARIN WERE pushing a small wheelbarrow through the darkness. Inside the wheelbarrow sat a wooden crate they were bringing to the mayor's house, known as Deep Well. The box was old, dusty, and quite heavy. For some reason the mayor had been storing the box at their house.

It was less than a quarter of a mile to Deep Well, but it was slow going. The path skirted the edge of the forest, where shadows formed interlocking pools of darkness. In the distance, where the cliffs dropped off into the sea, the sky still brimmed with a faint glow. But here, Night had already arrived. This was the route Kana took home from school. He favored it precisely because it was so near to the woods.

No one else went that way. Most people in town feared the forest. Kana didn't, but he never felt at ease there, either. During the years of Day, the forest was unnerving because it was still—like the profound silence at the bottom of a well. Even the wind seemed to die at its edge. It was so quiet that any sudden noise—like a snapping branch—reverberated like gunshot.

The forest was different now. Strange, undefined noises had become common. People said that wild boars were stirring, emerging from their lairs deep in the woods. Even more reason, said the okrana, to stay away from the woods while preparing to depart.

As they neared the mayor's house, Kana finally broke the silence.

"Marin, why didn't you tell the okrana about *our* trip into the woods?"

Marin frowned. "What does that have to do with Line?"

Kana slowed his pace for a moment, gestured for Marin to back away, and then carefully navigated the wheelbarrow around a sizable rock.

"Because he was looking for *clues*," said Kana as they continued pushing the wheelbarrow down the path. "You could have told Ivo about our trip. You could've told him going in was my fault. I mean, it *was* my idea."

Several months earlier, Kana, Marin, and Line had taken a forbidden trip into the woods. There were trails, but they were not mapped, and they tended to wind and fork in dizzying patterns. Kana, however, had overheard two older okrana talking about a trail that led to a canyon and a real freshwater pond. They said the trail began close to the old hermit's cottage—*three rights, then two lefts*.

Unfortunately, the plan went wrong from the outset, starting when Line invited Marin to tag along. This irked Kana, but it didn't surprise him, not really. In the weeks leading up to this excursion, Line had repeatedly stopped by Shadow House for one reason or another, just to say hello or ask a question. It was always designed to seem spontaneous, and it inevitably ended with Line and Marin chatting. It was all quite obvious and rather annoying.

On the day of the expedition, when Line showed up—with Marin in tow—Kana decided to play it casual, as if the three of them going had been the plan all along. So they followed the okrana's directions—*three rights, then two lefts*—which got them precisely nowhere. But they pressed on in a northerly direction, and in time, they came upon the pond.

The pond was set at the edge of a great clearing. Nearby was a dark, gaping canyon that cut through the clearing's center— giving the place an ominous feel. The ground here was made of soft white stone, almost like chalk. At that time, the sun had already dropped below the treetops, but the white stone was so iridescent that it seemed to glow. As soon as Kana entered the clearing, he was nearly blinded by the radiant stones. He squinted and looked around for Marin.

"Here," said Marin. "Take my hand." Kana hesitated, as if embarrassed to be guided like a child in front of his friend, but Line didn't seem to notice, and they made their way together to the edge of the pond. The water was crystal clear and much warmer than the ocean. For the next hour or so, Marin and Line frolicked in the pond, jumping off rocks and doing swan dives and cannonballs into their own private watering hole. Kana could barely see, so he lay down on a long, flat rock by the shore and closed his eyes.

"I think we should explore a little," said Line after they'd been swimming for a while.

"We shouldn't leave Kana on his own," said Marin with a sigh. "He can't see a thing."

"He'll be fine," said Line. He eyed Kana, who seemed to be sleeping. "He doesn't need babysitting."

"Actually, he does," said Marin. Her voice wasn't unkind, just neutral, as if she was stating a simple fact. "He's pretty helpless in bright light," she said. "And that's the way it's going to be in the Desert Lands, too."

At that, Kana sat up, wearing a look of barely controlled anger. "Don't mind me," he said tightly. "I don't want to burden anyone." Then he stood up, spun around, and set off into the clearing—half stumbling as he went.

Marin kept calling to him, but Kana pressed onward as if he didn't hear her. It was Line's shouting that finally got through.

"Stop!" screamed Line. "The canyon!" But it was too late. Kana had taken a final step and stumbled on a rock outcropping at the top of the precipice. Then he tumbled down, slamming into rocks as he went, until he landed on a narrow ledge about ten feet down that stopped his fall. It all happened so quickly that it took Kana a moment to realize that he was hurt. His body was bruised, his hands were lacerated, but the real damage was on his right cheek, where a rock had sliced him open like a knife blade. Blood gushed from his face. It was a miracle that Kana hadn't fallen to his death.

Later on, Marin sobbed and said how sorry she was. "You misunderstood me," she said again and again. "I was just trying to make Line realize what it was like for you." Later on, Marin said a lot of things. But these were just words. The simple fact of the matter was that Marin felt sorry for him, and thought Line should, too. There was no pretending it wasn't true. Nor was there any erasing the scar that now marked Kana's face.

This incident was still fresh in Kana's mind as he and Marin made their way to Deep Well. The scar was a painful daily reminder of what had happened. Still, Kana refused to discuss it any further with Marin—and he had simply lied to their parents about it, claiming that he had fallen from a tree. But it was obvious, even to Anton and Tarae, that a rift had grown between the twins. "I don't know what happened," Tarae had said to them more than once. "But you need to move past it." Marin would then look at Kana imploringly, and he would look away, as if they were both performing well-rehearsed parts in a play.

After several minutes of walking along the path to the mayor's house, Marin finally responded to her brother's question. "I didn't tell Ivo because there was no point," she said. "We'd get in trouble, and more important, what good would it do?"

Kana looked at her as if she were especially dim-witted. "Has it occurred to you that maybe Line went *back*?"

Marin stared at him, equally astonished. "Back to the pond—why?"

Kana pointed a finger at her neck.

"My necklace?" she replied. She paused to consider this possibility, and the wheelbarrow clattered to a stop. *The necklace.* She'd lost it at the edge of the pond. It had happened in the haste and confusion after Kana had fallen into the canyon.

Might Line have gone back for it? The thought had never even occurred to her. It was ridiculous. Line wouldn't do that. Not just before the boats came. "No," said Marin, shaking her head and pushing the wheelbarrow back into motion. "Absolutely not. He wouldn't do something that stupid."

Yet, at the very moment she said this, doubt entered her mind. "Kana—*would* Line go back for my necklace?"

Kana thought carefully. "Probably not," he concluded. "At least, not anymore. Not with Francis depending on him."

Marin nodded, relieved. "The okrana will find him."

Just then, they turned a bend in the path and Deep Well came into view.

CHAPTER 12

DEEP WELL WAS BUILT ON A HILL AND SURROUNDED BY
an array of impressive trees. There was a northern ash, a
ginkgo, and several enormous firs. The centerpiece was a
gnarled, ancient-looking wick tree whose vines were used to
make torches. Wick lit easily and lasted for several hours—the
okrana swore by it. Now the tree was picked clean, like everything else around Bliss.

The house itself was a sprawling structure with inset circular windows and a moss-covered slate roof that had a thick
tower rising from its center. At the top of the tower was a widow's walk encased in glass and a powerful signal lamp. For the
last several years, with the sun low in the sky, this lamp had remained lit so the town's fishermen could find their way home.
Once the furriers arrived, the light had been extinguished, another sign that the hour of departure was near.

The house shimmered in the dying sunlight because the
stones used to build it were speckled with minerals. The front
door, which was covered by a thin layer of cork, served as the
town's message board. It had been loaded with notes related

to the upcoming move: requests for help in moving and cleaning, as well as for supplies, such as extra suitcases and trunks. Now the board was empty—as was most of the house. In truth, the building was more of a banquet hall than a home. The main floor was devoted to the town's only indoor meeting area, complete with several fireplaces and four enormous wooden tables. The house's sole inhabitant was Bliss's aging mayor, who lived in an apartment on the second floor.

"Come in, come in," beckoned the mayor, a small bald man wrapped in several layers of pale blue silks. "I almost gave up on you. It wouldn't do to be late for our departure!"

Marin and Kana set down the wheelbarrow, picked up the crate, and set it down in the large main room. The woodwork here was astounding. Artisans had carved thousands of designs across the walls, including trees, vines, mountains, clouds, and rivers. At the very top of the room, built into the ceiling, was a cupola with four large windows that—in sunnier times—allowed light into the room. The surfaces of the wooden tables had recently been waxed, and they shone in the light of the flickering candles. On the nearest table stood a dozen bottles made of greenish glass, sealed with corks and melted wax, and filled with dark liquid.

The mayor followed their gaze.

"Those bottles are all that remain of the Noon wine," he said. "The rest go to the furriers to pay for our passage. When you were smaller, the whole town harvested these grapes in the Noon vineyards. What a wonderful time that was. . . " His voice trailed off and he smiled.

"Are you leaving the bottles behind?" asked Marin as she ran her fingers across the cool, dusty glass on the neck of a bottle.

"Of course not," said the mayor. He reached out for one and cradled it possessively. "They're coming with us. We'll open some on special occasions, but I mean to save at least two for the best day of all—the day we come back home."

Marin thought briefly about returning to the island in fourteen years' time. It seemed impossibly far away. She had more pressing things to worry about. The mayor could see it in her face and he cocked his head sideways, like a bird.

"Yes, what is it?" he asked.

"Where does the phrase *the houses must be without stain* come from?"

The mayor looked at her with an air of infinite patience. "My dear, it's just a saying we tend to use when the hour of departure draws near. It's nothing to concern yourself about."

"Yes," said Marin with determination. "But why was it carved into the statue of the hag—down by the sea?" She saw Kana's confusion and quickly explained to him what she and Line had seen.

"Ah, of course. That old statue," said the mayor slowly. He rubbed a hand across his bald head, then crinkled his nose. "I haven't seen that since I was a boy."

"Who made it?" asked Marin, eyeing the mayor carefully, studying his face.

"You are a curious girl," replied the mayor, as if that answered the question. He thought for a few seconds more. "Well, there's not much to tell. The statue came with the island. All of it was a divine gift—a perfect home, ready to be inhabited. And for this we are eternally . . ."

"Grateful," said Marin, finishing the sentence for him.

"Yes, quite right," said the mayor as he gave Marin a smile. "But enough of this—you've come here to do a job, and we're all in a hurry, aren't we? Open the crate, will you?"

Kana edged his way past his sister to get a better look, and asked the mayor what was inside. The light from the candles obscured his vision.

"You shall soon see," said the mayor. Then he frowned. "Silly me, you're blind, aren't you? But now everything is better. Is that right? How fortunate. Be a good lad and lend me a hand."

Kana dropped to one knee, unfastened the latch on the front of the box, and pried its lid open. Inside was a set of a dozen knives. They looked like steak knives, only much, much larger. The handles were huge slabs of beautifully carved wood—four fists in height—and the blades were gleaming shanks of silver, each the length of a grown man's arm.

"Whose knives are these?" asked Kana.

"They belong to the house," explained the mayor. "I don't like to keep them on display because, well, they are a bit unwelcoming. And since there is no easy place to store them here, I kept them in the nearest available house—yours. Help me put them back in their proper places, will you? Be careful, though. They are exceptionally sharp."

The mayor took two knives from the box and walked over to the largest of the room's fireplaces. Just above the hearth sat a long piece of polished wood that served as the mantelpiece. Built into the mantelpiece, at regular intervals, were a dozen narrow slots made of copper. The mayor took a knife and slid its blade into one of the slots until the hilt on the handle rested snugly against the mantelpiece. This action created a terrible screeching, grinding noise that made Kana and Marin recoil.

"Those are sharpeners built into the mantelpiece," explained the mayor. "Whenever you pull out a knife, or return a knife to its proper place, the slot hones the blade. Ingenious, isn't it?"

"I see why you keep them in storage," said Marin.

The mayor shuffled his feet and then drummed his fingers impatiently on the wooden table. "Hurry, now," he said. "I need to close this place up and get down to the loading area. We're shorthanded now that the okrana have gone looking for that boy."

Marin and Kana helped the mayor put the remaining knives into their slots. At one point, the mayor glanced at Kana and remarked, "That's a nasty cut you have on your face. How did you do that to yourself?"

"It was an accident," said Kana quietly. "My own fault."

"Pity," muttered the mayor.

Marin looked away.

When they were done with the knives, the mayor extinguished the remaining candles, casting the room into darkness. "Drat," said the mayor. "Now I can't see a blasted thing."

"Let me help you," said Kana, taking the mayor by the arm and guiding him to the doorway.

"Well, thank you for everything," the mayor said as they reached the front door. He fumbled for something in his pocket, then laughed. "Silly me," said the mayor. "I took the lock off this door last week." He closed the door but took special care not to close it entirely, leaving it open just a crack. Marin, Kana, and the mayor stood at the entryway for a moment.

"Mr. Mayor," said Marin hesitantly.

He raised his eyebrows. "Another question?"

Marin nodded.

"Quickly, then," said the mayor.

"I heard that, once, the furriers didn't bring enough boats and people were fighting—" began Marin.

"That was a long time ago," interrupted the mayor. "Rest assured, it won't happen again."

"What happened to the people who were left behind?" asked Marin.

"They perished," said the mayor quietly. "Though not right away."

"What do you mean?" asked Kana.

"This happened before my time," said the mayor. "Those who were left supposedly found a citadel on the Dwarf Oak Islands, and stocked it with supplies to last them through the Night. I sailed to those islands as a boy. Pleasant area for an outing, but certainly no place to live." He shook his head. "No one can last through the years of darkness. You'd freeze, starve, or go mad—probably all three."

He glanced at Marin's worried face and smiled reassuringly.

"Not to worry," he said. "Everyone is nervous the first time they leave the island. It's a long voyage to the Desert Lands, but once we're there, everything will be fine."

"But what if—" began Marin.

"What?" snapped the mayor, face strained.

"What if we don't find Line by the time we need to leave?"

"In such an event, there is a plan," said the mayor.

"What kind of plan?" pressed Marin. Kana, who had turned to leave, glanced back, suddenly interested in what the mayor had to say.

"Along the Coil River, there is . . ." But the mayor never finished. "I'm sorry, child, but this is not the time to explain. The okrana know, and that's most important." With that, the mayor nodded curtly and began hobbling down the path that led to the cliffs and the sea beyond.

Kana and Marin walked back toward their house, with Kana pushing the wheelbarrow by himself now that it was empty. Light was draining from the western sky rapidly, and darkness seemed to be spilling out of the woods unchallenged. In several places, the road drew so close to the woods that it almost felt as if they had stepped inside and were trespassing amid a tangled web of roots, branches, and twisting trunks.

At one point, Kana stopped next to a large, slightly concave rock, known locally as Table Rock. In past years, when the sun was higher in the sky and daylight illuminated this area, families used to come here for picnics.

"It'll be good to be here again in the Morning light," said Marin.

"Maybe for you," replied Kana.

Marin winced. He was right. In such light, Kana would be blind. This was, of course, the very point that she had been making to Line—months earlier, back at the pond—but there was no value in bringing that up now. "I'm sorry," she said. And that was all.

They resumed walking. The only sound was their wheelbarrow creaking as it rolled along the path.

"You really think Line went back to the pond?" asked Marin after a while. "I can't see him doing it."

"I haven't talked to Line much in the last couple of weeks," said Kana. "Your hunch is probably as good as mine."

"I wasn't trying to ruin your friendship," said Marin quietly.

"I know," said Kana, leaning into the wheelbarrow and pushing it over a large tree root. "Look, if he doesn't turn up in the next hour or so, we'll find Ivo and tell him about the pond."

"Yes," said Marin. "I'll tell him."

They continued walking. Minutes later, voices shouted in the distance. Several hundred yards ahead, they saw the flicker of a wick torch. Soon, more torches appeared.

"It's the okrana," said Marin.

"That was fast," said Kana, squinting into the distance.

They quickly closed the distance between them and the okrana. Ivo stood in the middle of the group, stony-faced, and it was impossible to tell whether he brought good news or bad. Marin strained her eyes, searching frantically for Line.

"Did you find him?" she called. "Ivo?"

Ivo shook his head but didn't stop walking. Apparently he was too pressed for time to talk.

"No signs of him at all?" Kana called out.

Ivo ignored the question.

Toward the end of the procession, Marin spotted one of the youngest members of the okrana—a gangly, pimple-faced teenager named Asher—who happened to be their second cousin.

"Asher!" shouted Marin. "What happened?"

Asher pretended not to hear, but slowed to let the other okrana pass. He waited a few seconds until they were out of earshot, then whispered to Marin and Kana.

"We know where he is," Asher said.

"You do?" Marin breathed a sigh of relief. "Is he all right?"

"He went to the Upper Meadows to pick mushrooms, then headed toward the bog," said Asher. "Someone saw him there earlier. He must have got stuck is all. We're going back to town to get some sticks and boards."

Marin nodded. The best mushrooms were in the bog. Pickers often got stuck there, in the quick mud. It wasn't especially dangerous in itself, but it was nearly impossible to escape without help. That's why you were never supposed to pick there alone.

"It shouldn't take long," said Asher. He turned and looked back at the other okrana. "We'll bring him down to the loading area as soon as we get him out. I'll give him a good kick in the pants for you."

"Thanks," said Marin. She turned to her brother and, for the first time in a long while, they smiled at each other.

"But you should hurry," added Asher. He leaned in conspiratorially. "They say there might not be enough boats—some people may have to leave their luggage behind."

CHAPTER 13

BACK AT SHADOW HOUSE, KANA AND MARIN FOUND their mother in the foyer, studying a scroll of yellowed paper. The scroll was the floor plan for the house, which showed every room, closet, nook, and stairway. Scribbled in the margins were notes written in faded ink.

"What are you doing?" asked Marin.

"Oh, you're back," replied Tarae with a start. "Good—your father has returned as well." She now wore a long, coarse robe with a thick travel cloak on top. Marin couldn't help but feel a surge of relief to see her mother in her old clothing. She wanted things to be more, well . . . normal—even if just for a few more hours.

"The candles are burning down," said Tarae. "Don't you think it's much colder? I *cannot* get warm."

"We saw the okrana," said Kana, who was blinking in the dim candlelight. "Seems like they found Line."

Tarae smiled fondly at Kana. "Yes, that's what your father heard, too. Thank the southerly winds. Now go help your father in the parlor. We need to be down at the loading area in an hour. There are rumors of too few boats."

When Kana and Marin entered the parlor, they discovered a large wooden crate that their father had hauled up from the basement. He was using the claw on the back end of a hammer to pry it open. The box opened in a flurry of dust, and Anton pulled out an oversize cast-iron plate. It was twice the size of a dinner plate and looked quite heavy. "These go on the dining room table," he said. "There are ten of them—so space them out evenly."

"We're *setting the table*?" asked Marin. She looked at her father, astonished.

"Yes," said Anton flatly.

"Father—this is too much!" said Marin.

She looked at Kana for support. Kana arched an eyebrow but said nothing.

Anton put up a hand. "Please—not now."

Marin knew that this was not the time or place to make a fuss, but she couldn't help herself.

"But it's ridiculous!" said Marin. Her voice had turned querulous.

"Here we go again," mumbled Kana. Marin glared at her brother.

"I know you find this strange," said Anton. "I'll explain in just a bit. All right?"

Marin forced herself to calm down. Ever since Line's disappearance, she'd been wound altogether too tight. It would do no good to get her father upset. "All right."

Kana grabbed two plates from his father's hands and walked

toward the dining room table. Marin followed his lead and took two plates herself. They were enormously heavy, and she had to strain not to drop them. Within a few minutes they had set the table and returned the crate to the basement. When everything was done, their father turned to Marin and Kana.

"You want to know the truth?" he asked. "Fine."

He paused and leaned on his broom.

"Let me ask both of you a question. When I sneeze, what do you say?"

Kana raised an eyebrow.

"What do you say when I sneeze?" Anton repeated.

"Bless you," Kana replied.

"Right, but *why* do you say it?"

Kana shrugged.

"Sometimes in life, we do things simply because we've always done them," explained Anton. "Perhaps there were once reasons, but we have forgotten them. A very long time ago, people believed that whenever a person sneezed, their soul exploded out through their mouths and into the air. They also believed that the devil was always lurking about and might snatch up that soul. So they said *bless you,* to stall the devil until the soul could shoot back down into the person's body."

"That's nonsense," said Marin, throwing her hands in the air.

"You're probably right," said Anton. "But you still say *bless you.* And until a moment ago, you didn't even know why."

"But that's just a saying," said Kana thoughtfully. "That's different from all of this business with the locks, and the furniture, and setting tables."

Marin nodded, happy to have her brother as a temporary ally.

"Is it that different?" asked Anton. He folded his thick arms together. "The truth is that we don't know why we do a lot of things. We kiss talismans and break bottles of Noon wine over the bows of new fishing ships believing, rightly or wrongly, that it'll keep us safe. If it works, we keep doing it. Everything that we've been doing, we do for one simple reason. For generations, *it has kept us safe*. Every household in Bliss follows *these* directions, and upon return to our homes fourteen years later, everything is in perfect order. Nothing is damaged—nothing is broken."

"But, Dad, do you really believe these superstitions keep us safe?" asked Kana.

Anton shrugged. "I can't tell you for certain. What I do know is that we do these things—and we have remained safe—so we keep doing them."

"That's it?" said Marin. "You just follow these made-up rules, like children playing a game, and you don't even know why?"

"Why are you so upset?" asked Anton. He frowned in confusion.

Why? These were the rules governing their lives—and they made no sense. Again she looked at Kana: *Why are you so calm about this?*

Anton smiled. "Marin, don't you see? Only children entertain the fantasy that adults know how and why everything works. Being an adult is accepting the not knowing."

After a moment's pause, Kana stepped forward and took a

plate off the table. He held it in his hands, trying to estimate how much it weighed. He looked at his father quizzically. "It feels like you're preparing this house for somebody else."

"That's right!" said Marin.

"Who would stay here?" asked Anton. "Who could possibly survive the Night? Don't tell me *you two* believe the children's tales about the spirits."

"Of course not," said Kana calmly. "But what's the point of all this?"

"I've already told you," replied Anton, raising his voice just enough to show his waning patience. "And besides, I'm your father, and expectations that above should be enough."

Marin stood up in irritation. "This is crazy—all of it," she muttered. She glanced back at the dining room table, with the heavy plates sitting there rather ominously. "Is there nobody in this town who thinks for themselves?"

Tears welled up in her eyes. It was as if all the stress in her life—the fighting with Kana, the imminent move to the Desert Lands, and the disappearance of Line—had suddenly overwhelmed her. Sensing her distress, Anton reached out to his daughter and took her arm. But Marin pushed him away and retreated to the other side of the room.

Anton sighed heavily, and Tarae walked in. "We leave in ten minutes," she announced, oblivious to what had just happened. "Why don't you go upstairs and take a last look around?"

Marin nodded, grateful for an excuse to leave, and ran up to her room. She had only a few minutes left in this house and she wanted to spend them alone. Marin exhaled heavily and lay down on her bed.

She felt something sharp hit her head. When she sat up, she discovered it was the copper box her mother had given her. She still hadn't opened it. Of course, Marin knew what was inside the box, but she was suddenly curious to see it up close.

There was very little light in the room—just a lone candle—and Marin held the box close to the candle to see it better. The exterior was plain, though well polished. Four tiny clasps, one on each side, held it together. They were stiff, but Marin soon had them open. She lifted off the top and peered inside. Lying in a row were six hollow rods, each four inches long. They were made of a smooth, gray-blue stone; at the end of each rod was an evil-looking scalpel. They glittered sharply. Marin picked one up and lightly touched a blade with her thumb. A drop of blood welled out.

Marin cursed and returned the rod to the box. The drawer containing the scalpels lifted out, revealing six squat bottles of liquid underneath. Their metal tops were threaded. Marin lifted them out individually and held them to the light. Five of them were dyes—white, blue, green, gold, and black—the colors of her mother's skin markings. The sixth looked clear.

She stared at that particular bottle for several seconds, then tried screwing the top onto the end of its hollow rod. It fit. She held the rod as if it were a fountain pen, then ran the scalpel across the rough exterior of the mattress. The sharp blade cut the fabric immediately. Marin blew out the candle. The room fell into absolute darkness, except for a thin glowing line on the bed and a glowing bottle stuck to the end of the rod.

Marin stared at the scalpels, imagining herself cooped up in some dingy cellar in the Cloister, marking herself with these tools for a whole year. She'd have nothing in common with the other desert girls. They wouldn't even speak the same tongue. And throughout that time, she wouldn't see Anton or Kana or Line. Only her mother would be allowed to visit.

"Never," whispered Marin to herself. She was filled with rock-solid certainty. "I won't do it."

CHAPTER 14

A FEW MINUTES LATER, MARIN RETURNED TO THE parlor, standing alongside her mother and Kana, waiting for Anton to finish up. They were all dressed in their seafaring clothing: wool caps, cloaks, waxed canvas pants, and knee-high boots. Finally, they heard Anton's voice coming from the foyer. "The okrana just ordered us to the loading area." There was a long pause. "I've been told to say that anybody who re-fuses will be dragged out."

"Is that a joke?" asked Kana.

"No," said their father as he appeared in the parlor. "Every-one is getting cranky. But don't worry. This happens every time we leave the island." Anton grabbed a candle from the window-sill and handed it to Marin. They exchanged glances, and a hint of irritation lingered in his eyes. "No confirmation on Line yet," he said. "I'm guessing he's down at the staging area."

Marin nodded.

Together they walked outside and stood in front of the darkened house. Two members of the okrana were waiting solemnly for them. They were both old—not as old as Palan, but from his generation. They each held high a blazing wick torch. Rivulets of sweat rolled down their faces, and they were trembling slightly.

"This is a new beginning for us," said Tarae as she put her arms around Marin and Kana, drawing them tightly to her. "The Desert Lands are waiting." The happiness in her voice was unmistakable. Neither Marin nor Kana replied.

"Remember the front door," said one of the okrana.

"Of course," said Anton. And very carefully, he closed the door so that it remained open just a crack.

The okrana helped them pile their luggage onto a small, rickety handcart. And then, together, with Anton pushing the handcart, they walked through the shadows—westward, toward the cliffs. Kana and Tarae brought up the rear. Tarae was walking slowly—she had a nagging fear of tripping in the dark—and Kana guided her gently, draping an arm across her back.

"You know, the Night is beautiful in the desert," said Tarae. "The sky is clearer there and the stars are more numerous." She smiled at Kana and ran a hand through his hair.

Kana said nothing. Three days of sunlight and three days of darkness. For Kana, this meant three days of vision and three of blindness. His mother had been fretting about this lately, as if she were personally responsible for the habits of the sun.

"Don't worry, Mother—it'll be fine," Kana said. "It'll be easier than the years of daylight that I had here."

"I know you'll miss all this," said Tarae, gesturing vaguely toward the darkness around them. "But I think a change of scenery might be good for you . . . you'll sleep better once we're off the island," said Tarae with an air of certainty.

"Really? Why is that?" He sounded unconvinced. His mother was trying her best to tiptoe around his feelings, but somehow this extreme tactfulness made it worse.

She glanced at him sideways. "Just call it a mother's intuition."

Several minutes later, they arrived at the cliffs. The area was always busy with people coming to and from boats, but today it was crowded with people, boxes, suitcases, sacks of flour, rolls of fishing nets, caged chickens, and other supplies of all kinds and quantities. Children ran wildly, caught up in the excitement of the moment, and dogs chased them. The noises—shouting, crying, talking, barking—were overwhelming.

Only the faintest pinprick of orange remained in the western sky. Marin walked over to the edge of the cliff and looked down. Several men were descending to the pier via a spiderweb of ropes secured to the cliff face. Nearby, a series of makeshift wooden cranes had begun lowering loads of crates. Down below, several dozen ships with bright yellow sails were moored along Bliss's docks.

"LOOK FOR YOUR FLAGS!" yelled a burly, gray-haired okrana. He wore a leather vest and the dark green clothing of a woodcutter. He spoke through a large, cone-shaped speaking trumpet. "CALMLY WALK TO YOUR FLAGS!"

"Which way is Glimmer Glen?" a woman called out, her long white hair escaping in strings from her shawl. She was cradling a suitcase to her chest.

"ALL THE WAY AT THE END," boomed the man through his speaking trumpet.

Cloth banners were tied to the end of slender flagpoles, which were stuck in the ground at regular intervals throughout the staging area. Next to each pole stood an okrana with a bound codex in hand.

"Where's our flag?" asked Kana.

"Night Fire is down this way," replied their father, pointing to a distant blue flag with two red swirling lines. "They always put it down there."

Where is Line? Marin looked around anxiously for any sign of him, or of the okrana who had been searching for him. "Excuse me," said Marin, tapping a gray-haired okrana on the shoulder. "Have they found Line—the boy who went missing?" The man just stared at her as if she were speaking a foreign tongue. It was maddening. If Line's parents were alive, they would be raising hell.

She grabbed her father's arm. "I don't see Line—I'm going to go look around."

"No," replied Anton firmly. "Wait until we get to the flag, and then we'll make inquiries."

It took several more minutes before Marin and her family arrived at the grassy knoll where their flag was fluttering. Standing rigidly next to the flagpole was one of the okrana's youngest members, a thin teenage boy with kinky black hair and crooked teeth. The boy nodded at Marin's parents solemnly, then opened up his codex and began flipping through pages of vellum until he found what he was looking for.

"Four of you?" asked the boy. He frowned. "It says here there are three."

"No—it's four," their mother quickly replied. She glared at the young okrana boy.

"Shadow House?"

"Of course," she replied, glancing at Anton. They exchanged a look that Marin found hard to decipher. Fear, anger, annoyance, fatigue, sixteen years of marriage—perhaps all of it at once.

"That's your luggage?" asked the boy. He frowned again.

"Yes."

The boy paused. "You may have to leave some behind."

"Why?"

"I have no further information—these are my instructions. Please be patient," he replied. The words coming from his mouth sounded dutifully rehearsed.

Their neighbors, young parents with a sleeping baby, approached the knoll, and the young okrana turned to them. Marin's mother moved several feet away and collapsed to the ground with an exhausted sigh. She called to Marin and Kana but was interrupted by the sound of shouting.

"They're coming!" someone yelled. "The furriers have climbed up from the cliffs."

Similar shouts rang out along the cliffs.

"Stand up!" hollered the teenage okrana who stood by their flag. "On your feet now!"

CHAPTER 15

ALL AROUND THEM, TOWNSPEOPLE WERE RISING TO their feet and shouldering their bags. A group of furriers had arrived and were stalking through the crowd. They were fierce-looking men, with sunburned faces, chiseled jaws, and eyes the color of shallow water. Several of them brandished rifles with gleaming bayonets. It was odd to see the furriers so well armed. Nobody in Bliss had guns except for a few of the okrana, and theirs were ancient muskets.

As the furriers walked past, one of them—a small, wiry man with blond hair—stopped to stare at Marin and Kana, then walked toward them. Anton frowned and stepped forward, blocking the furrier. The surrounding area grew quiet and all eyes were drawn to this sudden face-off. Anton said nothing. His face was a mask, showing neither bravado nor weakness.

"Your boy," said the furrier, pointing to Kana. "He has our eyes." And it was true. Kana's pale blue eyes were a rare trait among the people of Bliss.

Anton seemed unsure how to respond. The furriers rarely talked with townspeople.

"The boy," repeated the furrier. "He is yours?"

"Yes, of course," Anton replied. He stepped forward, took his hands out from under his traveling cloak, and looked the furrier square in the eyes.

The furrier raised his eyebrows. "Are you sure about that, old man? His eyes mark him as one of us." He laughed hoarsely. Tarae walked over to Anton and placed a hand on his shoulder.

The furrier leered at Tarae, then winked. Anton's hands balled into fists. Marin studied her father closely, wondering what he would do. But he did nothing. The unanswered insult was too much for Marin. "His eyes are different because he's blind," she called out. "Does that mean you're blind, too?"

The furrier stared at Marin with open interest. "You have a wild spirit," he said. "I will watch for you on the boats."

Marin forced herself to glare back at him—she refused to give him the satisfaction of appearing scared.

Anton turned around and shot her an unmistakable warning with his eyes: *Keep out of this.* Meanwhile, the furrier laughed and walked away.

Tarae yanked Marin to her side.

"What's wrong with you, child?" she hissed. "Don't even *look* at those men." Everyone in their area was staring at them. Thankfully for Marin, it only lasted a few seconds, and the nervous energy of the departure returned.

Marin continued to watch the furriers as they walked away. She felt her father's presence next to her and, rather suddenly, she felt ashamed of herself. Marin had been so concerned about the loss of her own independence that she'd missed the larger truth. They were *all* at the mercy of the furriers.

In the distance, she could see the furriers speaking with the mayor. The conversation didn't seem friendly. The mayor's face grew red and pinched, and his hands curled into fists. He rocked back and forth and shook his head vehemently while the furriers stood there, impassive. Marin couldn't make out the words, but she registered the mayor's change in tone. It shifted from annoyance to pleading. And then it was over. The furriers walked away toward the cliffs, their guns glinting in the last dregs of sunlight. The mayor and the townspeople watched them go.

Not long after this, the teenaged okrana with the kinky hair pushed his way back into the center of their gathering and, once again, stood ceremoniously by the flagpole.

"Attention, Night Fire!" he yelled. "The furriers collected more furs than they expected. There will not be room for all of your provisions."

"What about *people*?" one of their neighbors shouted. "Is there room for all of the people?"

"I think so," replied the boy. He paused for a moment to consult his codex, as if the answer might be hidden away in its pages. Then he looked back up. "Truth is," he said, "I don't really know."

Suddenly, everyone was talking at once, asking questions, shouting accusations, and demanding answers. The same thing was happening at the other flagpoles. The wind came up suddenly and added to the general cacophony. In the distance, the man with the speaking trumpet was trying to reestablish order. "EVERYBODY SIT DOWN!" he called. "ONLY THE EL-DERLY AND INFIRM ARE BOARDING NOW. THE REST OF

US WON'T BOARD FOR FOUR MORE HOURS. AT LEAST FOUR MORE HOURS!" But his voice only seemed to raise the overall volume of the crowd. It was amid this pandemonium that Marin caught a glimpse of a little boy collapsed on the ground.

Without a doubt, it was Francis. And he was alone.

Marin shook free of her mother's grip and pushed her way through the crowd. Francis lay on the dusty ground, curled up on one side, his eyes half open and brimming with tears.

"Francis!" said Marin, kneeling down and placing a hand on his back. "Where's Line?"

He just whimpered and kept crying.

She forced herself to sound calm. "Francis, just a few hours ago, someone saw Line down at the bog. Where is he?"

Francis shook his head. "It was a mistake. Some other kid— he wasn't even stuck."

"Who said it was a mistake?" demanded Marin. "Ivo?"

"The mayor," said Francis. Tears streamed down his dirty face. "I knew it wasn't Line at the bog," he said, still proud despite everything. "Line never gets stuck."

"Francis—you have to think hard," implored Marin. "Was there *anything else* he wanted to do before he left? Something he hadn't done?" Marin was conscious that her voice had begun to sound harsh, but the panic in her stomach was coursing through her body.

Francis shook his head no, but then stopped suddenly. He grabbed her hand and squeezed it hard. "A few days ago, he told me that he wanted to do something for you but probably wouldn't have time. He had lost something of yours in the woods."

Marin's heart began to race. *Damn it.*

She turned back to Line's little brother. "Francis, listen to me," she said. "Do you see your neighbors over there?" She pointed to a nearby group of children clutching at a woman's skirt.

He nodded.

"Stay with them," she said, rising to her feet. All around them, people were still shouting heatedly. "I'm going to find Line, but you need to help me. When my parents ask about Kana and me, you tell them you saw us helping the old people board the boats. It's just a little lie, and it will help us find Line. We won't be gone long. Understand?"

Francis nodded.

"Promise me."

"I promise," he replied, his eyes round and scared.

"We'll find him," said Marin. She patted his forehead, stood up, and weaved her way through the crowd until she found Kana. He was standing a few feet away from their parents, who didn't notice that she'd come back.

"You were right about Line," she said in a low voice.

Kana turned, his mouth opening in disbelief. "You've got to be kidding me."

"We have four hours to find him," she said. "Francis is going to tell Mom and Dad that we're helping board the boats. We'll be quick. There and back shouldn't take us more than two hours."

Kana stared at her. "It'll be dark," he said. "Much darker than before."

"I know," replied Marin. She leaned even closer, until she could feel his breath. "That's why you have to come with me."

They stared at each other. Finally, Kana nodded. "Let's go."

CHAPTER 16

KANA AND MARIN SPRINTED THROUGH THE EMPTY town, hugging buildings and avoiding open spaces where they might be spotted by the okrana. The only living creature they saw was a mangy old dog that someone had tied to the front post of a one-room house. The dog was barking mournfully, as if he understood that he had been left for dead.

"I can't leave him like this," Kana said, stopping for a moment to undo the knot on the dog's leash. As soon as he was free, the dog scurried through the front door and back inside the one-room house where he lived.

They ran through Bliss, past their old home, Shadow House—now silent and empty—and followed a faint path only Kana could see. In this direction, there was just one dwelling closer to the woods than Shadow House, and it was often forgotten. It was a ramshackle cottage whose flimsy walls and roof were supported by the gnarled, twisting limbs of several willow trees.

"You think the hermit is still there?" asked Marin.

"Why would he be?" asked Kana, shaking his head. "I doubt anyone else is as stupid as we are."

Stupid or not, Kana felt better running along the path than sitting with the rest of the town by the cliffs. If anything, he appreciated these last, stolen few moments on the island—the cold air, the scent of evergreens, the glimmer of dew trapped in pinecones. *This is almost worth the risk,* thought Kana. *Almost.* He didn't even mind his sister being here with him because, for once, she seemed contrite and agreeable. *She needs me now.* That was the crux of it—so she was simply following his lead, silently. This was something to be savored.

The path faded even more as they passed the hermit's cottage, and at the edge of the forest the path simply disappeared. Kana picked a stick off the ground and used it to poke around the thick underbrush until he found the opening he was looking for. It was hidden by a tangle of dead branches and covered with a thick, gauzy curtain of spiderwebs, which he tore through with his stick. It was strange how spiders were now everywhere, in these months before departure. Some of the largest ones, with legs that were colored a bizarre motley of green and gray, turned up in pillows and blankets. In the school yard, many kids claimed that during Night, every square inch of the island was crawling with spiders. But Kana knew this was just speculation. *Everyone is an expert on the Night,* thought Kana. *Even though no one's seen it.*

He pushed through the torn webs and carefully climbed through a tangle of low-hanging branches. After a few seconds, they emerged onto a narrow trail that cut through a jumble of young trees. While Kana waited for Marin to struggle through, his mind echoed with the warning from his dream.

Stay away from the woods, child—don't let them see you.

Kana looked around at the unfolding of the heavy forest—the thick tapestry of leaves, needles, damp earth, and moss. A chill ran up his spine. *Don't let them see you.* Who were they? And *why* shouldn't they see him? He ran his hand across his forehead. He was being childish. It was just a dream. And yet it tugged at him—as if he had tied a string around his wrist to help him remember something, but now he could not recall what it was he was supposed to remember.

Kana led the way deeper into the forest. He walked along the trail at a brisk speed. On their last trip into the woods, they had marked their path with white paint. Though faded, it was still there, and absorbed enough ambient light to help them find their way. *Would these markings be bright enough for Line to see? Maybe. If he had the sense to bring torches.* The ground underfoot was shrouded in darkness, and Marin tripped repeatedly over roots that crossed the trail.

"Here," said Kana, offering up his hand. Marin clasped it in hers and they continued down the path. After a hundred yards or so, it opened into a small clearing. Old-growth trees bordered the area, their leaves and branches filling the open space overhead. The space looked like a grand vaulted room with tree trunks for walls and branches for a ceiling hundreds of feet above them. Kana remembered the giddiness he felt at discovering this space months before.

Together they ducked through an opening between two

trees and headed down a very narrow path, following the dabs of white paint. The trees and branches were so tightly pressed here that they resembled walls of woven wicker. It had been this way when they found it. In places, the forest walls hemmed in so tightly that they had to step sideways along the path to keep going.

Kana maintained a fast pace, pausing only once, when he felt a pinprick on his arm. It was a drop of ice-cold water. Another landed on his neck, then again on his arm. He looked up. It was impossible to get a decent view of the sky, but the air smelled moist, and he guessed it was raining far above.

"Are we taking too long?" asked Marin, breathing heavily. "I can't tell."

Kana studied his sister's face for a moment. She was deeply distraught. He was scared, too. His pulse was racing. Neither of them should be in the woods. They—and Line—should be waiting patiently to board the furrier boats. *And we're taking this risk for what? A necklace? Line, how could you be so stupid?* He had completely lost his head for Marin.

"Will we make it?" asked Marin.

"Yes," replied Kana. "But we have to move faster—just in case." He took her hand again and they began to run.

CHAPTER 17

"STUPID, STUPID, STUPID," MUTTERED LINE THROUGH gritted teeth. He had been repeating these words for hours. As he chanted his mantra, he looked up from the bottom of the rocky pit and stared at the darkened sky. The walls of the pit, which rose upward for twenty feet, were made of small stones embedded in dry earth. Line was an exceptional climber, but those walls had proved impossible to scale. He simply couldn't get a decent hold. Every time he grabbed a rock or a piece of earth, it broke away or crumbled in his hand. On one occasion, he'd made it almost two-thirds of the way up, then fallen backward. He hit the ground hard and slashed open his left forearm on a sharp-edged rock in the ground. The cut was long and deep, and really hurt. *What is wrong with me?* He had already hurt his ankle when he first fell into the pit. Now he had his arm to worry about, too.

It was hard to remember how long he'd been stuck there. Twenty-four hours? Could it be even longer? He felt his stomach churn—from lack of food or worry. Probably both. It was supposed to have taken an hour—thirty minutes there and back. He had been careful. He'd followed the markers. He had taken no chances along the way. But despite his caution, despite knowing the way, he still tripped, stumbled, and fell into this hole—and now he couldn't get out. It must have been an old trap to hunt animals, and it had caught him.

Line studied his left arm in the dim light. He brushed away the dirt and saw blood welling from a wound that stretched almost from his wrist to his elbow. The ribbed sweater he was wearing—already frayed at the arms—had torn even farther. He flexed his fingers several times and rotated his wrist. He could still climb.

Line glanced upward at a strange-looking tree branch that jutted out over the edge of the pit. The branch was thick, round, and bulbous; in the dim light it almost looked like a human head. In fact, when Line had first laid eyes upon it— hours ago—he'd thought it *was* a person. He had even called out to it. But after the thing didn't reply, or move so much as an inch, Line supposed that it was just a branch. And yet the branch looked so weirdly human in its form that Line continued to glance up at it, half hoping and half fearing that it would move.

And then it *did* move. Well, more accurately, it disappeared. One moment it was there, and the next time he looked up, it was gone. Not long after this, Line began to hear rustling in the grassy plain above him, just beyond the perimeter of the pit.

"Hey!" he yelled. "Hey, I'm stuck down here!"

He shouted for another few minutes, then gave up and sat

in the pit. Soon, however, the noise returned, and this time, instead of shouting, he listened. There was something deliberate and calculating about the rustling. A dark silhouette appeared for a second at the edge of the pit, then vanished.

Line couldn't get a good look, but he swore the silhouette resembled a woman. Still, he'd been down in the pit so long that he no longer fully trusted his eyes. He trusted his instincts, though—and they told him there was a person up there. Why this person wouldn't help him—or even respond to him—he couldn't guess.

Line limped around the pit, looking in vain for something he'd missed. He clenched his fists and pounded them against the crumbling wall, then sank to the ground and whispered, "What am I doing here?"

But he knew the answer to that question. Despite his best efforts to act the part of the responsible parent, Line was—by his very nature—an impulsive person. It was impulse that lured him into the woods with Kana and Marin several months ago. He still recalled his elation at finding the pond in the middle of the forest—its surface as gleaming and still as a piece of darkened sea glass. He remembered the entire scene with startling clarity. Before swimming, Marin had taken off her necklace: a simple piece of jewelry consisting of a silver chain and an oval pendant. The pendant was a sunstone, a milky crystal mined from the rocky, ice-strewn isles of the Polar North.

Sunstones weren't especially pretty, but they were exceedingly rare. Sailors prized them for the way they polarized sunlight. Even on a cloudy day, you could hold a sunstone up to the sky and use it to determine the precise location of the sun. Marin's sunstone had belonged to her paternal grandfather, who had been a storied sailor. Marin's father had given it to her on her tenth birthday, when she was first allowed to sail small skiffs on her own. Even at ten, Marin was a better sailor than many of the adults.

Before swimming in the pond, Marin unclasped the necklace, and Line inspected it before shoving her unceremoniously into the water.

Later, when Kana fell and cut his cheek, neither Marin nor Line gave another thought to the sunstone. It wasn't until Marin returned home that she realized the sunstone wasn't in her satchel. Line must have forgotten to return the necklace after looking at it.

She confronted him the next day. "I can't believe you lost my grandfather's necklace!"

Line shook his head vehemently. "No! I swear to you—I put it back in your bag."

"Well, it's not there," she replied, her eyes blazing.

"This isn't about your necklace," he said. "You're upset about Kana."

"It's not my fault," she said as her eyes welled up with tears. "I can't stay with him every single minute."

But they both knew that they shared blame for Kana's fall. Of course, Line had apologized, but it wasn't enough. There was no undoing it. In the ensuing weeks and months, Line began to believe that retrieving the sunstone might begin to make things right—if not with Kana, then perhaps with Marin. When they left the island, their lives would change dramatically. Soon they would be in the Desert Lands and Marin would be in the Cloister. Alone. Line wanted her to have that stone, to feel its weight and to think of the island. Maybe even of him. And that impulse had led him back into the woods and, ultimately, right into this pit.

Line sat up.

He thrummed his fingers nervously against the dirt, and that's when he felt *it*—a short, sturdy piece of wood. Line groped around and discovered several other shards like this one. An idea came to him. He lifted a piece and tried to bend or break it. It did not—perhaps it was sturdy enough to take his weight.

Gripping two pieces of wood tightly, he began to climb by stabbing them into the soft walls of the pit and hoisting himself upward. It was arduous work and very slow going. He moved about a foot at a time, sweating and grunting as he went. Line wielded the sharp pieces of wood expertly—like daggers. He had always been good handling knives. Finally, after ten minutes or so, he was within several feet of the surface. He was almost there, but his situation was precarious. The earthen wall near the top of the pit was very loose. Bits of soil and rock began breaking away and hitting him in the face.

Line glanced down at the bottom of the pit and struggled to drive the sticks further into the wall. He grunted with the effort and looked back up. When he did, he saw it again: The silhouette of a woman peering over the edge. Her face was shrouded in shadow and appeared weirdly elongated, as if warped by a concave mirror. Moments later, the sticks began to loosen, and Line began to slide. Suddenly, he noticed a sturdy vine dangling over the edge. *Why haven't I seen this before?* But the question was lost in a surge of adrenaline as he grabbed the vine. When he finally hauled himself up over the lip of the pit, he saw only the silent forest. The woman—if she'd even existed—was gone.

CHAPTER 18

THE PATH TO THE POND ROSE STEEPLY, ZIGZAGGING across a series of boulders. Kana knew they were getting close. Marin leapt onto the nearest boulder and started to climb, but slipped and fell hard.

"Marin!"

Kana ran to her side. She waved him off and scrambled to her feet. Her chest heaved from the exertion of running, and sweat ran freely down her face. They paused for a minute, suddenly aware of a strangely glowing light above them. It was a perfect circle, hanging low in the Evening sky, pale white and lumpy, as if newly born.

"What is it?" asked Marin.

"*The moon*," whispered Kana. "It's beautiful." He was breathing rapidly but wasn't spent. He stared up at the sky, entranced. His face was awash in a ghostly silver light. Both of them had heard of the moon, a celestial body which was said to cause madness, and only appeared during the years of darkness. Its light seemed magical. It was not nearly as strong as the sun, but it was far more powerful than any torch or lantern. And unlike sunlight, it did not glare or blind Kana in the least.

They kept climbing, quickly, but with a sense of caution. When they made it past the boulders, they pushed through a swath of smaller trees and emerged into a large clearing of rock dotted with clumps of tall grass. Somewhere in the middle was the pond. Trees surrounded the clearing—except on the western side, where it dropped off into the steep canyon. The chalky white rock reflected moonlight, making it possible for Marin to see. She yelled for Line but heard nothing.

Marin started toward the canyon, squinting and craning her neck.

"He's not down there," said Kana. He was right behind her. "This is nowhere near where you left your necklace."

Marin glanced back at Kana's voice. "You're right. He has to be near the pond. If he got this far."

The wind suddenly picked up. It was bitingly cold.

"LINE!" shouted Marin, as loudly as she could. "LIIIIINE!"

They held their breath, hoping for a response.

Kana raised his arm. "I heard something. Did you?"

"No."

He pointed toward the northern end of the clearing. "There."

They walked that way for a minute, until they both heard a muffled shouting.

"LINE!" Kana shouted back. They ran toward the sound. Seconds later, Line appeared. His face was pale. He was leaning on a branch, half running, half limping, like an animal just released from a trap.

They raced toward him. When they were only feet away,

Line tripped and fell heavily. Kana sped forward and caught him before he hit the ground. He struggled for a second to keep Line upright, but kept his balance.

"Th-th-thanks," Line stammered. He voice was almost imperceptible.

Marin wrapped her arms around both of them. "Line, are you okay? Did you . . . what did you . . ." She was babbling, barely aware of what she was saying.

"My brother . . . Francis. Is my brother all right?" asked Line. His cheeks were taut and his eyes were red. Specks of dirt and pine needles dotted his reddish-brown hair.

"Francis," Line repeated. *"Is he safe?"*

Marin stared at him for several seconds, until his words finally sank in.

"Yes, he's fine," she replied. "Scared, but fine."

"Did the boats come?"

Marin nodded.

"Who's with Francis?" asked Line.

"He's with your neighbors," said Marin. "Soon he'll be with you."

"Let's go, then." Line started to run, but tripped and struggled just to stand. Kana helped steady him and noticed the rip in his sweater and the gash on his forearm. It looked bad. He asked Line about it, but Line shook it off.

"It's just a scrape," he said.

"That's more than a scrape," said Kana. "You'll need to—"

BRRRRRRRRRM! BRRRRRRRRRM!

Two thunderous sounds echoed through the forest. They all looked at each other. Without another word, Kana began running toward the path home, followed by Marin and then Line.

At the edge of the clearing, near the canyon, Kana stopped and looked back. Marin and Line were far behind. She was helping him limp along, but it was clear that Line couldn't run. Kana uttered a soft curse. His insides crawled with impatience as Marin and Line approached. Line was breathing heavily and sweat poured off his body. Up close, his mouth was set in a tight line and his eyes blinked wildly. Locks of his hair stuck wetly to his forehead.

"Kana," said Marin. "Run ahead and tell them to wait. Just in case. Going back is always easier—we won't get lost."

As if in response, a faint cry came from deep within the canyon. Kana looked up sharply. *Was that an animal or the wind whistling?* Kana walked over to the edge of the canyon. It was at least several hundred feet deep, and the walls were quite steep. His eyes fell upon a perfectly rectangular slab of rock, roughly thirty feet high, located midway down the opposite side of the canyon. Someone had either carved the slab out of the cliff face or placed it there. There were dozens more like this one, jutting out of the canyon walls. Farther down, he caught a glimpse of movement.

He turned back. Marin and Line were staring into the canyon.

"Are those *boxes* carved into the rock over there?" Marin said.

"I don't know," said Kana. " But I'm not leaving you here."

"Why not?" she asked.

His eyes flicked back to the canyon. "I'm just not."

CHAPTER 19

SECONDS LATER. THEY WERE ON THE PATH TO TOWN. moving as quickly as they dared. Words were kept to the bare minimum. *Step to the left. Take my hand.* At one point, the path narrowed so much that they had to walk single file. Marin was last, with Kana leading and Line in the middle. At times, she had to stop herself from pushing them forward. *Come on, come on, come on.* And then Line would trip, or let out a pained grunt, and she was reminded that they were going as fast as they could. Unfamiliar squawks and rustling came from both sides. At times they were very close by, and Marin found herself glancing backward, half expecting to see someone or something on the trail behind them.

Kana knew they were moving slowly. Far too slowly. He didn't have a timepiece, but he, too, sensed the minutes ticking away. *How long have we been gone? An hour and a half? Two hours?* Impossible to say. But it was taking too long. That much was certain.

Eventually they came to a small break in the woods—a glade speckled with waist-high zebra grass. Line muttered something and threw the branch he'd been leaning on to the ground. He collapsed and clutched his ankle. Marin sat down next to him and placed her hand on his heaving chest.

"Just a minute," gasped Line. "Got to catch my breath."

"You all right?" asked Kana. He was circling the glade, looking at the ground.

Line gritted his teeth. "I'm fine."

"You need a decent crutch," said Kana. "It'll help you move faster."

"I was thinking the same thing, but I haven't seen anything." Line let out a long, drawn-out sigh.

Kana stepped away from the glade and began foraging among the trees. They heard a sharp snap. Moments later, Kana returned to the trail with a long, sturdy stick that had a naturally curved handle at the top. Kana held it up for Line to see.

"Good?" asked Kana.

"Yeah—just knock off another few inches," said Line, pulling himself up to a sitting position.

"Got it," said Kana.

Kana used his foot to apply pressure to the bottom of the stick. There was another snap, then Kana handed the stick to Line. Marin helped him stand, and the curved handle fit perfectly under his armpit. Line would have been hard-pressed to carve a better crutch.

"Don't suppose you saw any lekar while you were out there?" Line asked as he struggled to his feet.

"Don't press your luck," said Kana with the thinnest of smiles.

"Too late for that." Line shrugged. "Thanks, though—this'll help."

They continued on, at a faster and more controlled pace. Line's crutch helped immensely, and they made such good time that Kana began to hope that the furriers wouldn't have started the general boarding yet. They took a wrong turn only once, and retraced their steps quickly. But in time, they came across familiar markings and areas they had been before, and at last exited the woods not far from the hermit's house.

Marin turned to Kana.

"Go!" she said. "We're through the woods, safe and sound. Run down to the boats. Tell them we're here. Hurry!"

Kana nodded and took off at a sprint. Marin and Line followed behind as quickly as they could. *They'll be there,* Marin told herself. She bit her lip until she felt the sting. *There is no way they could have left so quickly. They'll be there. They've got to be there.* Marin forced Line to move fast, at times nearly dragging him along. They passed through the main street of Bliss and paid little attention to the darkened houses. *They'll be there,* she told herself with every step. *They've got to be there.*

When they emerged from town, they saw the ocean for the first time. And in the distance, the last wisp of sun had disappeared. *Nightfall.* Marin's heart was in her throat. The air seemed colder already, but what she noticed most of all was the dark. She looked at her hands, and already the details—knuckles, fingernails, old scars—were hard to see. They had been told of how quickly the darkness would fall when the sun finally disappeared. It took years and years for the sun to make its way across the sky, but only minutes for Night to arrive.

Far ahead, at the cliffs, flags still fluttered at the loading area. Marin saw boxes and suitcases—hundreds of them. The okrana said that *some* of the luggage might be left behind, but this looked like all of it. Clearly, they were still boarding.

"Where is everyone?" Line asked. He was jerking his head left and right almost spastically.

Marin looked again. Everything was there . . . except for the people. What's more, the luggage seemed to be in terrible disarray. Possessions were strewn about as if a tornado had plowed through the area. Some of the flags were still standing, but others leaned to one side, and a few were snapped in half.

"I'll check," said Marin, breaking into a run. She couldn't stay at Line's pace any longer. Kana was in the distance, by the cliffs. He was surrounded by a wasteland of debris—shirts, pants, coats, books, shoes, cracked jars, combs, brushes, shovels, blankets, pots, and plates. She yelled for him as she drew nearer. Kana's attention, however, was on the ocean.

"Where are they?" she gasped as she reached his side.

Kana pointed at the horizon. The sun was gone but they could see the distant image of the ships in the glow of the rising moon. The furrier vessels were miles away, sailing in tight formation, heading due west.

"No," Marin whispered. "They wouldn't . . ."

She jumped up and down and waved her arms. Surely they were close enough for someone to see them.

"MOMMA! DAD! We're here! *Come back!*"

Kana started yelling, too, and for several minutes they screamed themselves hoarse. Line picked up a discarded flagpole, its cloth banner torn in two, and waved it over his head. The ships continued on their course.

"It's not possible," Marin whispered. And yet she knew it was. Of course it was. *How many times had they told us?* They had no choice. The furriers set the rules. And then there was the unstoppable force of the tides. They had left precisely on schedule. Any thoughts to the contrary were simply the wishful delusions of a child.

Gradually, Marin became aware of her surroundings again. A mud-smeared doll lay facedown in the thistle. A cracked clay pot sat next to it, with its contents—a thick bean stew—soaking into the ground. Next to it lay a scrap of cloth—torn from a shirt, or pants, or a jacket. It was smeared in blood. These scenes were repeated all over the loading area. The town's well-practiced departure had been brutally swept aside. Whatever the reason, the loading process had broken down so completely that treasured possessions had been cast away like table scraps.

"It must have been a disaster," said Kana. "No one would notice if three kids weren't where they were supposed to be—not at first, anyhow."

Marin looked down at the pier. The tide was as fast—and as strong—as predicted. Already the sea had retreated about two hundred feet, exposing the rock and pebble-strewn seabed. Her legs buckled and she fell to the thistle, staring at the distant image of the ships with ferocious concentration, as if she could will them back. *They will realize what happened and change course.*

The ships grew smaller and smaller until they were the

tiniest of specks on the horizon. And then Marin couldn't see them at all because her eyes were awash with tears. The truth of the situation was rising up within her like a bubble. She tried to press it back down, to pretend it wasn't there, but slowly it crept back up. There was no ignoring it, so she tried to accept it gradually. *The boats are gone.* That was a fact she could see with her own eyes. *My parents are on the boats.* Okay. *Me, my brother, and Line are still here.* She could feel the panic rising again as she built to the final truth. *Night has fallen. And it will last for a very long time.* And then Marin was sobbing. Kana tried to comfort her, but she shrugged him off and hugged her knees.

"It's getting cold," said Kana. "We can't stay here."

CHAPTER 20

LINE BOLTED AWAY FROM THE CLIFF'S EDGE AND BACK toward town. He sprinted, then hobbled, then sprinted again. Kana and Marin called after him, but he kept moving as if he didn't hear.

"Where is he going?" asked Kana. Even from far away, Line looked crazed.

Suddenly, Marin knew.

"Back to his house," she replied. "He's looking for Francis."

As Line ran, he imagined his brother huddled in his bedroom and—in the intensity of the moment—Line wasn't certain whether he hoped to find Francis there or not. He started yelling Francis's name when he was several hundred feet away, and continued until he burst through the front door. He stood there and listened. The house was silent, everything arranged where it should be; RAT, SNOUT, and TEETH hung from the walls, staring at him through the darkness.

"FRANCIS! *I'm here!* FRANCIS!"

Line paused, not even daring to breathe. Silence. He ran upstairs to Francis's room and opened the door. The room was empty. He moved on to his room, since in recent months Francis preferred to sleep there. It was empty as well. The only indication that someone had been there was a small, child-size depression on the bedcovers. Line's hands shook. He walked to the bed, kneeled, and pressed his face against it. He could smell his brother's scent, sweet like tree sap. *This is where he was sleeping when I left him.* Wild, paranoid visions ran through his head—of Francis running back home at the last minute before boarding, screaming for him.

Line collapsed onto his bed and began to sob. It was a terrible sound, like a death rattle. Horrible, scalding guilt tore at Line. *Francis is completely alone—parentless, and now without even a brother. And it's my own stupid, bloody, damned fault.* Line lay there, motionless, eyes closed, overwhelmed.

Several minutes later, he became aware of another presence in the room. He opened his eyes and saw Marin.

"Leave me alone," said Line.

"I promise you, Francis will be fine," said Marin. She placed a hand on his back. At one point, Marin tugged on his shoulder, trying to rouse him off the bed, but he refused to be budged.

"Leave me be," he repeated.

Marin leaned in close.

"The neighbors were looking after him and so were my parents," she said. "I promise you—Francis is on one of those boats."

Line said nothing at first, just pressed his face harder into the bedcovers. "I left him," he whispered. "I left him alone in this house and I never came back."

Marin's hand was firm on his shoulder. "Line, listen to me: you're going to see him again—soon."

He looked at her questioningly, but with a sudden emergence of hope. "How?"

"Kana went down to the base of the cliffs. He saw some small boats there. One of them looks light enough to push out to the water. If we hurry, maybe we can catch the furriers. But we need your help."

Line considered this. Then he nodded, wiped his eyes, and stood up. He walked over to the corner of the room and grabbed an old wool sweater that was hanging on a peg. He had neglected to pack it, and suddenly it seemed like a godsend. He was already wearing one sweater, but it was ripped and rather thin. He put on the second one, too, relishing the added warmth. Marin took his hand and they walked down the stairs.

Down by the pier, at the base of the cliffs, they found Kana standing next to a boat. It lay on its side in a mat of shoreline weeds and mud. It was a small, two-sailed sloop that the villagers used to teach children how to sail. Line had used it often as a younger boy. The nearby fishing boats would be much better, but they were too heavy to drag across the exposed seabed to the ocean.

"It's just a sloop," said Kana, "but I figured it's worth a try."

They began pushing. At first, the boat wouldn't budge, despite their straining. They slipped in the wet ground and fell, over and over. Then they tried to flip it, but it was too heavy to keep upright.

Finally, Line called a stop.

"Gather some logs," he said.

"Rollers?" asked Kana.

"Yes," said Line. "We can roll the boat on top of them—just like the time we got your uncle's boat stuck."

"Good," said Kana.

They spent an hour gathering logs, then pushing the boat onto the rollers. Although it moved, it was still slow going. Another hour passed, and they had only moved the boat about twenty feet. The seashore looked even farther away now. At their current pace, there was no way they could catch up with the receding tide. Line knew this, but he kept pushing, as did Marin and Kana. The boat inched forward. Line put too much weight on his ankle. He stumbled awkwardly, narrowly escaping being pinned by the boat.

"Line!" yelled Kana.

"I'm okay," replied Line, though he knew he was exhausted. He hadn't eaten in a long time. Marin's arms trembled with fatigue as she put every ounce of strength into pushing the boat another inch. Kana was the only one who still seemed to have any stamina. He felt surprisingly strong, but he knew better than to waste energy trying to move the boat alone.

"Stop," said Kana. "We need to rest."

Marin and Line stopped. They understood what Kana meant. This wasn't going to work. They would have to find another way. Kana turned away from the boat and began walking up the cliffs.

"Where are you going?" called Marin.

"Back to town."

Kana walked up the sloping, grassy hill, acutely aware of how dark everything had become. It was just like people said: nothing came swifter than Night. Of course, Kana could see well, but Marin and Line could not. The rising moon would help; that was something. He glanced back at them. They were following close behind, clutching each other and stumbling frequently. No one spoke. The physical and emotional toll of their ordeal had finally caught up with them. The sense of panic that had consumed them for so many hours gave way to a feverish sense of unreality, as if none of this were really happening to them—as if by merely collapsing to the ground and closing their eyes, they might wake up safe on the boats.

"We need to rest somewhere," said Marin. Her voice was slow and wearied.

Kana plodded ahead and kept his eyes focused on the town, which appeared as a mishmash of overlapping shadows. He couldn't see perfectly, but he could distinguish between the various shades of blackness to make out the contours of the roofs, the fences, and the gateways of Bliss.

"We should go to the mayor's house first," said Kana. "There might be a note on the message board."

Kana took both of their hands, and together they walked into the growing darkness. No one spoke after that, nor were they tempted to. They walked past the giant hourglass that served as Bliss's official clock. The hourglass, which was mounted on a great stone pedestal, was flipped when the luminescent sand ran out—about every twelve hours. Because the position of the sun changed so little from day to day, this hourglass was the town's way to mark time, and they used it to set all of their windup clocks and watches. Currently, almost all of the sand had fallen into the lower chamber.

They continued walking through town. According to custom, all the doors to the houses had been left open, and whenever the wind blew, a chorus of old, creaking hinges groaned as the doors swayed back and forth. Then, quite suddenly, there was a violent gust of wind and several dozen doors slammed shut all at once. Marin jumped.

Their pace quickened as they approached Deep Well House.

"Can you see anything on the door?" Line asked Kana.

"Yes," replied Kana. You could hear the excitement in his voice. "There's a note."

"Thank God," said Marin.

Kana pulled them along faster. They soon reached the flagstone path leading to Deep Well House. They could see the white paper hanging from the front door, but it was only when they were a foot away that they could read what had been written. It was a single word scrawled in a childlike script:

HIDE

CHAPTER 21

"HIDE?" SAID MARIN. SHE WAS INCREDULOUS. "HIDE WHERE?"

Line stepped closer and removed the note from the door. He turned it over in his hands. Apart from the one scrawled word, it was blank. "Hide from what?"

Marin snatched the note from Line and crumpled it, then let it fall to the ground. "Where can we possibly hide?" she said, looking at Line and Kana. "This is a joke—it has to be."

Kana picked up the note and smoothed it out. After examining it for several seconds, he shook his head. "It's not a joke," he said. "We're stuck here, and that's a fact. Maybe there's a place to hide in town, but I don't know where that is."

On the boats, Marin thought bitterly. *That would be an excellent place to hide.* She grimaced. *What we really need now— what we have to have—is rest.* "We're tired," she said slowly, feeling the fatigue on her tongue. "Let's stay here—in the mayor's house—at least for a bit."

Line shook his head firmly. "No—the tide is going to keep rolling out." His forehead bristled with sweat, and to Kana, he looked disturbingly pale. "And it's only going to get darker—and colder. We need to make a plan—*right now.*"

"I know," Marin replied. "But there's no quick fix. We already tried pushing the boat, and I can't think of anything else we can do. We can come up with a plan while we rest."

Line nodded.

Kana opened the door, and they ventured into Deep Well House. The cavernous main hall was pitch-black but for a murky shaft of moonlight that filtered from the glass-enclosed cupola overhead. As the various shades of black began to take on subtle hues, Kana discerned a narrow set of stairs at the far end of the room. These led to the mayor's quarters.

"This way," said Kana.

Kana led the way up the stairs until he came to a closed door. He jiggled the doorknob. It was unlocked—of course. He pushed it open and entered an opulent room with wood paneling, velvet curtains, leather couches, and fur rugs—all illuminated in the dim glow of the rising moon, which cascaded in through several bay windows. *Did the mayor live this lavishly—or was this just how the house was supposed to be arranged after the envelopes arrived?* In the center of the room sat the biggest bathtub that Kana had ever seen. It resembled an indoor pool, only it was shallow, no more than four feet deep. Steam rose from the water.

Marin shook her head. "He left it this way?"

"I always thought he was strange," said Kana, as if this explained everything. He moved to the shadows of the room and began looking through cupboards.

Marin turned to Line. "I can't believe the mayor has a heated pool."

"I can," said Line, leaning over to get a better look. "It was probably a rule he had to follow for this house." In a quivering old-man voice, he said, *"You shall leave the pool heated."*

Marin chortled and dipped a hand experimentally into the water. It was warm—bordering on hot. She placed her hand against her cold cheeks and neck. Seconds later, Marin realized that Line was disrobing—first his shirt, and then his pants. Embarrassed, she turned away.

"I'm going in," said Line. "I'm freezing; this island has become an icebox. And after being stuck in the bottom of that pit . . ." His voice trailed off as he began to climb in. Marin couldn't help but stare as Line slowly entered the pool.

"This water isn't boiled," he said. "You can smell the minerals. It must come from a hot spring that someone managed to divert." He sat down and groaned with satisfaction.

"You should wash your arm," said Marin. "That cut doesn't look so good."

Line nodded slightly, but his eyes were closed and he looked half asleep as he lay in the pool with his head resting against the edge.

"I found some matches and candles," Kana called out. From across the room, a lone flame sparked to life. "I don't need them, but you two might."

Marin turned away from the pool as Kana approached. His nearby presence set her mind churning again. "What about the signal lamp?"

Kana frowned. "What about it?"

"I think we should light it before we get too comfortable."

"Really?" he said. He looked around, then sank into a leather couch. "Why should we do that?"

"Because," said Marin. "If the signal lamp is on, they'll see it and know to come back for us."

"Marin—be serious," said Line, his voice rising from the darkness of the bathtub. "You really think that's a possibility?"

"Probably not," admitted Marin. "But we should keep it lit even if there's the *tiniest* possibility that someone could see it."

"No one's coming back for us," groaned Line, who was now almost fully submerged in the water.

"What about the note?" asked Kana. "It said to *hide*. Lighting the signal lamp isn't exactly hiding."

"Look," said Marin. She was getting impatient now. "There's probably a very narrow window for them to notice that we're missing and turn around. Maybe just a few hours. It would be stupid not to send a distress signal."

"We're not getting rescued," muttered Line.

Tired from the back-and-forth, Kana sank deeper into the couch and closed his eyes. He needed to shut all of this out for a moment.

Meanwhile, Marin approached the pool and sat down on the floor next to Line's head. She raised her knees to her chest and wrapped her arms around them. "Why do you keep saying that they're not coming back for us?"

Line raised a hand slightly, then let it splash back into the water. "My guess is that they don't even know we're missing," he replied. "You saw how the luggage was left—people proba- bly got separated, shoved onto different boats." Line opened his eyes and shifted position to look at her. His wet arms glis- tened in the candlelight. "Eventually they'll realize, but by then, the tide will be too far out for them to come back—even if they wanted to."

"Maybe," said Marin. "But they might realize sooner, so I'm lighting the signal lamp anyway." She got up and walked over to Kana. "Come on," she said, poking his shoulder. "I need your help."

"Maaaarin," Kana moaned, pushing his head deeper into the pillows.

She poked him again.

Arguing with her was fruitless. "We'll light the lamp," he agreed, peeling himself from the couch. "And look for a ham- mer and nails. If we're staying here, even for a little while, we need to lock the door."

Marin nodded somberly. She grabbed a candle and followed her brother. As they walked downstairs, she placed a hand on Kana's shoulder. The way she looked—so serious and sad— softened Kana's edginess.

She closed her eyes for a moment, then sighed. "I feel terri- ble about all this."

Kana shook his head. "It's not your fault," he said as they headed down the stairs. "It just happened—that's all."

CHAPTER 22

MARIN AND KANA SEARCHED THE MAIN HALL FOR A staircase that led to the tower. Neither of them had ever actually been in the tower or seen the signal lamp up close, so they had to try every door. They hoped to find tools along the way, but nothing turned up. Eventually they entered the kitchen, a large room with a vaulted ceiling stained from years of cooking oil and smoke. There were several wood-burning stoves here, a large granite washing basin, and countless wooden cabinets— empty except for a few candles, matches in a waterproof box, and an oilskin jacket. They took everything.

Between the kitchen and the main hall, they passed through a narrow pantry lined with closets whose shelves were usually filled with linens. The linens had been replaced with dozens of giant cast-iron bowls. The metal rims were intricately carved, but the basic form was brutally simple and very, very heavy. They were a lot like the dinner plates they'd set their table with before leaving for the boats.

Kana continued searching the closets, then stopped in front of the middle one, which was big enough to walk into.

The interior smelled oddly pungent, like rotting plants. Kana stuck his head inside and then, not entirely satisfied, stepped into the closet.

"What's in there?" asked Marin.

"More bowls."

"Just what we need," said Marin with a half smile. "Right?"

There was no response. Several seconds later, Marin tried again.

"Kana? Hey—Kana?"

Marin peered inside the closet. It was as if Kana had disappeared. Then she heard wood creaking above her. Marin stuck her hand deep inside the closet and felt nothing but empty space. Finally, her hand closed on the handle to an open door. She called out to Kana. When he didn't answer, Marin stepped into the closet and through the door. It was a tight fit, and she had to bend over to avoid hitting her head. The light from the candle illuminated a tight spiral staircase that continued up into the darkness. Marin began to climb.

She stopped counting the steps at thirty and continued on. A minute or so later, she arrived at an open area, like the attic in her house. It was dusty and so dark that the candlelight didn't reach very far. Marin pictured the mayor's house from the outside and tried to guess where they were.

"Kana?"

"Right here." Kana's voice sounded as if it was only inches away.

Marin gasped. "You scared me. Do you see anything?"

"At this level, just a lot of boxes," said Kana. "But the signal lamp is at the top."

Moonlight coming through the glass dome high above them illuminated a brass-plated receptacle with an oil lamp and several large glass lenses. Marin raised the candle high and began to take in her immediate surroundings. The room itself was narrow and cylindrical, its walls lined with deep wooden shelves that spiraled to the ceiling. The lower shelves were stacked with wooden boxes that appeared to be placed haphazardly, but the shelves above were more organized. Boxes and cloth sacks sat neatly on well-polished shelves, which were sealed off by screen doors. Nothing looked familiar.

The shelves themselves were beautiful works of carpentry, carved to resemble the branches and trunks of trees in the forest. An inset ladder to access the storage rows ran all the way up.

"Can you light the lamp?" Kana asked Marin. "If I'm too close when it lights, I won't be able to see for hours."

Marin nodded and ascended the ladder quickly. When she reached the top, she examined the lamp. "We're in luck," she called down. "There's oil in the reservoir. It looks like it just drips down into the burner, so it should stay lit for a while. Turn away—I'm lighting it now."

Seconds later, there was a flash. The signal lamp shone a powerful beam out toward the sea. It gave Marin a burst of hope; anyone who looked back would know immediately that someone was still in town. The signal lamp also lit up a narrow portion of Bliss—starting with the path leading away from Deep Well and continuing on past the carved gables and cornices of houses closer to the town center. The light dimmed farther away, and Marin could see only a hint of the fishmonger's stall on the edge of town. She looked on silently until the acrid smell of vaporized oil became too much, then she started down.

Near the bottom of the ladder, Marin paused to examine a forest scene carved into one of the screen doors. The trees in this forest were imposingly tall, with gnarled limbs that extended out like fingers. To Marin, the trees appeared solemn, mutely witnessing what no living being should see. She lifted the door, dislodging a thin spray of dust, and revealing the large wooden box emblazoned with brass filigree that sat inside.

"What did you find?" Kana asked.

Marin's voice was muffled. She held the ladder and the candle in the same hand, freeing up her other hand to pull the box forward. It was clearly built to contain something heavy; every few inches, the wooden slats were reinforced with metal strips.

"What is it?" called Kana.

"It looks like a toolbox," Marin shouted. "Father has a similar one."

Seconds later, Marin paused her efforts and glanced back down at Kana.

"Help me with this—I can't open it up here, and it's too heavy to lower by myself."

The box weighed at least ten stones, probably more, and took several difficult minutes to bring down. Its metal clasps were stiff with age, and Kana had to hold it in place while Marin worked at the clasps. At last, the lid sprang open.

Kana frowned. The box held an ax, one unlike any he'd seen before. The cutting edge was razor thin and two feet long, and its wooden shaft was thick and well-worn. The head had a vicious-looking spike on the end, so it could also be used as a pike. It was so heavy that Kana could barely lift it out of its carrying case.

"This does *not* belong to the mayor," he said, picturing the slight old man.

Marin felt uneasy just looking at it. It wasn't just the spike or the cutting edge; it was the wooden handle, too, with its deeply grooved whorls and gouges. The wood was perfectly smooth, proof that it had been used often. She looked at Kana. "Maybe it's just a lumberjack's tool," she ventured hopefully.

Kana laid the ax back inside its carrying case and closed the lid. "No—this is for killing. And the person who can wield this ax . . ." His voice tapered off. "We should get back to Line."

CHAPTER 23

THEY DIDN'T BOTHER RETURNING THE BOX TO ITS original place. It was too heavy to lift, and neither of them wanted to linger in the attic. They made their way to the mayor's quarters and found Line lying on a couch near the edge of the pool. He was wrapped in a heavy wool blanket. At first, Marin thought he'd passed out, but then he looked up when they entered.

"How are you?" she asked.

Line pulled down the blanket and held his injured arm out in front of him. "It still hurts, but at least I soaked it for a while."

Marin walked to the couch and held the candle over Line's body. "Can I see?"

Line raised his arm to the light. His forearm was red and swollen, even though the wound itself looked unchanged.

"It's not getting better," said Marin.

"I have some lekar for you," added Kana. He motioned Marin away, then bent down to look at the arm himself.

"Hmm," said Kana, grimacing theatrically. "I'm afraid we'll have to cut it off. Just in case."

"Away with it, then," replied Line with a smile.

Kana may have been joking, but he'd also voiced what they all were thinking. A condition like Line's, left untreated, could quickly turn into gangrene. Everyone on the island knew about gangrene. There was a time, several sun cycles before, when woodfern had simply disappeared. This meant there was no reliable remedy against infections, leading to numerous amputations. You could still see these old-timers—elderly men and women with missing fingers, toes, even hands. Palan, the old man they'd met on the cliffs, was one of them. His left hand had been taken after a minor cut had stubbornly refused to heal.

Kana went to the pool and scrubbed his hands with the warm water. Then he walked back to Line, reached into his pocket, and pulled out a small wooden container with a metal screw top. Inside were a few ounces of the bright yellow ointment. Line nodded appreciatively as Kana applied the ointment to his wound.

"Thanks," said Line with a sigh. He leaned back in the couch and looked up at Kana. "So—did you find anything downstairs? Any treasures?"

"No," Kana said, a little too quickly. Line raised his eyebrows but said nothing.

"I still want to barricade the door," said Kana. "It shouldn't be too hard. Marin, could you help me move this furniture?"

"A barricade?" said Line. He yawned loudly. "Against what? The dark? Let's just sleep for a while."

"I'd feel better if the door was locked," said Kana. He couldn't help but shake his head at the irony. He'd been horrified when Anton had bolted the windows, dreading the thought of being locked inside his bedroom. *And now, here I am, wanting to lock myself up. Perfect.*

Line yawned again and looked at his friend. It was as if the hot water had sapped all sense of urgency from him. "Kana, come on," said Line. "You need to take a dip. You, too, Marin. And then, if you still want, we'll do the barricade."

"No, thanks," said Marin. "I just want to sleep."

Kana eyed the bathtub. It did look rather inviting. "Fine," he said finally. He walked over to the pool, stripped to his undergarments, slipped into the warm water, and closed his eyes. Line was right—it felt amazing. After a few more minutes, he climbed out and took a towel from a neatly folded stack. He wiped his face, noticing how thick and luxurious the towel felt. *And the mayor decided not to take these? Go figure.*

Kana looked around. Line and Marin were lying on adjacent couches and seemed to be sleeping already. For a moment, he considered waking them up to barricade the door, but now the idea seemed paranoid and a little silly. After all, they weren't in the forest. He dressed and sank into a plush couch. In a matter of seconds, Kana was fast asleep.

Several hours later, Kana awoke to his sister whispering in his ear. Marin's terrified face was about six inches from his. She was holding a too-bright candle that trembled wildly in her hand.

"Someone's downstairs," she whispered.

Kana sat up. "Are you sure?"

"Yes," said Marin. "Listen."

Neither of them spoke for almost a full minute. There was only silence. Kana was about to tell his sister to go back to sleep when they both heard the unmistakable sound of footsteps below—heavy, slow, and deliberate. Then came the grinding screech that meant someone had pulled a knife from the mantel. Moments later, the stairs began to creak.

"BLOCK THE DOOR!" shouted Kana. "LINE—WAKE UP!"

In a flash, Kana and Marin sprang to their feet, stumbled across the room, and grabbed hold of a wooden dresser that sat near the apartment door. Line joined them seconds later.

"What's going on?" he said.

"Footsteps," Marin replied. "We need to move this dresser. Now."

The dresser was heavy, but it moved. Marin, Kana, and Line all gave a final push and the dresser slid into place, blocking the doorway. The footsteps grew closer, steadily moving up the stairs. A few seconds later, the footsteps stopped and the doorknob turned. Marin, Kana, and Line pushed against the dresser with their backs against it, feet out in front of them for traction. Still, the door opened a crack, perhaps a quarter of an inch, before they were able to push the dresser back into place.

"Who is it?" yelled Line. "What do you want?"

Kana could sense his and Marin's fear. He never realized that the emotion had such a distinctive scent.

Seconds later, the door rattled in its hinges and the dresser began to slide. Whoever was on the other side of this door was tremendously strong. Kana, Line, and Marin all braced themselves against the dresser, using their legs, backs, and arms to keep it in place. It wasn't enough. The door continued to slide open and a wet, throaty grunt came from the other side.

"Come on!" screamed Line. "Harder!"

They rallied and pushed back. A moment later, the door abruptly clicked shut, as if whoever or whatever was on the other side had given up. There was a full minute of calm. They heard their adversary breathing in deep, baritone grunts. Soon, the sound of breathing was subsumed by the scrape of a sharp blade slicing into the wood on the other side of the door. The sound continued for another moment, then stopped.

The same heavy footsteps retreated down the stairs. The house fell silent.

Kana, Marin, and Line slumped to the floor, muscles twitching with exertion. None of them stirred. They just sat there in a prolonged state of shock. Finally Marin spoke.

"What just happened?" she asked the dark room.

The two boys were silent.

"Who was that?" asked Marin.

"More like *what* was that," said Line. "Did you hear that breathing?"

"It knew we were here," said Marin. "It came right for us."

"Well," said Kana, "we weren't hiding—with the signal lamp being lit and all."

Marin scoffed. "You think this is happening because we lit the signal lamp?"

"Stop," said Line. "It doesn't matter. We have a problem, because they clearly know we're here." Despite the warm pool, the room felt even colder now.

"They?" asked Marin. "What makes you think there's more than one?"

Line stood up, exhaled, and shook the tension out of his arms.

"Just a guess," he replied. "If there's *one* of those things living out there, it seems logical there'd be more. Question is—what do we do now?"

Kana pulled himself up as well. He looked at the dresser. "I guess we start by opening the door."

Marin shook her head. "Why would we do that?"

Kana turned to Line for support. "We can't stay in here forever. Besides, I want to see the other side. You heard that carving, right?"

"Right," said Line. "Let's have a look."

"Fine," said Marin with a slight nod of her head. "Just be quick about it."

CHAPTER 24

TOGETHER, LINE AND KANA PUSHED THE DRESSER AWAY from the doorway. Kana grabbed the knob and, ever so slowly, opened the door. They entered the darkened hall. Three grooves were carved onto the door:

| | |

"What are you looking at?" asked Line. "I can't see a thing."

"Hash marks on the door," said Kana. "Give me your hand." Kana took Line's fingers and guided them along the grooves.

"Three hash marks. That's it?"

Kana stepped back to see the entire door, then looked up and down the hallway.

"That's it," he concluded. He patted the door. "I never realized how thick this is—any other door . . ."

Marin came into the hallway. "The hash marks must represent the three of us."

"How could it know there's three of us?" asked Kana. "Whatever it was—it was on the *other* side of the door. It couldn't see us."

Marin walked down the hallway to the top of the staircase. She listened intently but heard nothing. The creature had vanished—or else it was just being very quiet. That last thought gave her a shiver, and she hurried back to Kana and Line.

"Let's go back inside," she said. "We won't figure anything out standing here in the hallway."

Upon entering the room, they immediately pushed the barricade back into place. Marin lit a few more candles, and they sat together on the couches. Going back to sleep was impossible. A clock on the wall read six thirty, not that it mattered. Still, Marin took the clock off the wall and wound it. Time was just an abstract concept, not a description of anything real. But it was Marin's habit to wind clocks and she saw no reason to stop now.

They sat on the couches, speaking softly but mainly listening, for a full hour. Nothing stirred. Finally, Marin stood up, stretched, and began pacing from one end of the room to the other. After a few minutes, she spoke. "We need to eat—even if that means going outside."

"I agree," said Line. He reached over to an end table and lit a candle. The room shimmered in a murky half-light. "Now that you mention it, I'm starving."

"We also should talk about a plan to get off the island," continued Marin. "You guys were right about—"

Kana sat up abruptly. "I don't believe my ears," he said.

"She said it," confirmed Line, laughing.

"If you're finished gloating . . . ," Marin said. "The point is—we can't count on getting rescued. Our problem is the tide. Right? The tide is supposed to roll out for a long time, and *far*—maybe hundreds of miles. So walking to the ocean doesn't make sense, because once we get there, what do we do? To have any chance of getting to the Desert Lands, we need two things. One: a boat. Two . . ."

"A way to the sea," finished Line.

Marin turned toward Line and nodded. "Right. So what about the Coil River? Doesn't it start east of here, somewhere in the forest?"

Line sat up and leaned his elbows on his knees. "Yes," he replied. "It's fed by an aquifer and dumps into Southerly Bay." After a pause, he continued. "I've sailed up the Coil before. There's a little fishing depot about a mile or two upriver. The freshwater fishermen keep it stocked."

"Exactly," said Marin, her eyes locking first with Line's, then Kana's. "Dad used to go nearby that depot to fish. There's a hut there—right? He got to it by sailing around Shiprock Point, and then into the bay."

Line stood up and walked to the pool. He leaned over and felt the water—it was still hot. He turned back to Marin. "That's how people usually go," he said. "And the depot always had an emergency boat, just in case there was trouble." He thought about this awhile longer. "But how does that get us off the island? The water's gone. Southerly Bay must be a desert right now—filled with dead fish."

"Think about it," insisted Marin. "If there's a river flowing from the island, it won't just stop now that the ocean has receded. It'll keep flowing across the old seabed, until it reaches the sea."

Kana couldn't help but grin. Marin was right.

133

Marin turned to him, her eyes flashing with excitement. "If we can get to the fishing depot, we can take the spare boat all the way to the sea. From there, we head southwest. This may have been the emergency plan the mayor was talking about. He mentioned the Coil, remember?"

Kana looked up at Line. "It sounds promising. Line, what do you think? You're the best sailor here—could we actually cross the sea in that fishing depot boat?"

Line raised his wounded arm above his head and let it drop. He grimaced. "That boat is small, but at least it has a sail. It's only meant to get around Shiprock Point, but if we manage to avoid storms, we'd get pretty far." He glanced at Marin. "But what we really need is . . ."

"A sunstone," finished Marin.

The two of them locked eyes, remembering yet again that day by the pond, deep in the forest. Line nodded. "To get to the Desert Lands, the furriers sail just shy of southwest, at two hundred twenty-one degrees. With a sunstone, it'd be easy to follow them."

"If it's so easy, why do we go with the furriers instead of building our own boats?" asked Kana. "It seems crazy to depend on them."

"I didn't say it was *easy*," replied Line. "Just easy to follow them—for a while. Storms come to the North Seas around Nightfall. And the furriers have the right kind of boats for storms. We'd have to be unbelievably lucky with the weather, and with getting enough water and supplies—"

"You may be right," interrupted Marin. She put a hand on Line's shoulder as she spoke. "But there's no point in talking about that now. I'd love to be worrying about ocean storms—it would mean we're off the island. What we need now is a destination. Let's scrounge up all the supplies we can and head for the fishing outpost."

Line had a faraway look in his eyes. "I wish we had a map of the island. It might help us get to the depot quicker."

"I have one hanging in my room back at Shadow House," replied Kana. "I can get it."

"I'll go with you," said Marin. "I want to check the grocer's stand next to the hourglass to see if any food was left behind."

"What about the visitor—the creature or whatever it was?" asked Line. "Maybe we should all go."

Marin glanced at Line's arm. "You need to rest," she said. "Kana can take me there on his way to Shadow House. I'll go to the grocer's stand and head straight back."

Kana looked unconvinced. "On your own?"

"I'll bring a candle," she replied. "Besides, the signal lamp is still on. And the moon is out."

"Speaking of the signal lamp," said Line. "What do we do now—just leave it on?" His voice sounded reedy and distant.

"Why not?" said Marin. She walked to a nearby chair and picked up the oilskin jacket she'd found downstairs. "They could still come back for us." With an air of finality—*discussion over*—Marin looked at Kana. "Ready?"

Instead of answering, Kana watched Line walk to the nearest sofa and lie down. Kana's eyesight was so sharp that he could see the sweat gathering along his friend's hairline, even though the room was quite cold. "Line—are you all right?" he asked.

Line didn't hear him. He was lost in thought. His mind turned over the sequence of events leading up to this moment: losing the sunstone, leaving Francis alone in the house, going into the woods *after* the tide turned, falling into the pit, missing the boats. He could call it bad luck, but that would be dishonest. It was mistake after mistake. *All his.*

"Line?" said Kana again.

Line picked up the corners of his sweater and used them to wipe his cheeks. After several long seconds, he turned to look at Marin and Kana. His eyes glimmered wetly in the candlelight.

"I'm sorry," said Line at last. "It's my brother . . . I just can't stop thinking about him."

Marin walked over and sat on the edge of the sofa. "Francis is safe," she whispered. She put a hand on top of his head and ran her fingers through his thick brown hair.

Line nodded slightly. *Of course that's what you would say. But that doesn't mean it's true.*

Kana sat down next to Marin and shook his head. "I feel bad for Mom and Dad, too," said Kana. "I'm sure everyone will think it's their fault. Because they couldn't keep track of us."

"Maybe they can take care of Francis," whispered Line. He sighed heavily.

"Everyone will take care of Francis," insisted Marin. She tried to sound confident—as if this were a certainty. "We'll get to the Desert Lands. We just have to stay focused." She patted Kana on the arm. "Let's go."

CHAPTER 25

AS THEY LEFT DEEP WELL HOUSE, KANA DREW MARIN'S attention to its ornate cupola, which was built into the ceiling of the banquet hall. One of its four windows had come unlocked, and the wind pushed it back and forth on its hinges.

After noticing the open window, they walked to the wall closest to the cupola. Kana examined the ornate carvings on the wood paneling, which—in this particular spot—was a rendering of a flowing river. There were also a great many small divots—deep and perfectly circular, uniformly distributed across the wall.

A tingle ran up Marin's spine. She had seen these divots before—beneath the carpets in her parents' house. *Somehow, this is important—it means something—but what?*

Together they left Deep Well House and headed down the narrow path to town. The last time Marin and Kana had walked this way, they'd been rolling an empty wheelbarrow home. Although the path was the same, everything else was different: the moon rising in the darkness, the thin layer of frost that had appeared on the grass, and a faint smell of dust and cold mud.

To keep from tripping as they walked, Marin held Kana's arm. They paused frequently to listen. There was only the sound of their own feet as they moved quickly along the path.

Marin shivered. "When you go home, see if there are any blankets," she whispered. "It's so cold—and I'm guessing it's going to get worse."

"Okay," Kana whispered back. He stopped a minute later when they reached a fork in the road. He listened and looked but sensed nothing unusual.

"You really want to go by yourself?" he asked. "It's so dark, and—speaking from experience—it can be terrifying to be blind."

Marin nodded and squeezed his hands. She smiled. "Thank you, but I'll be fine. I have the candle—and the signal lamp."

Kana turned and eyed Deep Well House. The signal lamp was shining bright as a beacon. He turned back to Marin. "Okay, then," said Kana. "Take the fork on the right. You should reach the grocer's stand in less than five minutes. Watch where you're going." As he watched her walk away, Kana fought the temptation to chase after her. *She'll be okay. Marin is always okay.*

He turned to the task at hand. It was simple enough. *Get the map,* he told himself. *Get the map and get back to the mayor's house.* As he pressed on, the path skirted close to the woods, and his thoughts drifted to the woman from his dream. It was as if she hid in the darkened corners of his brain, appearing only when he was alone. He repeated all his usual mantras. *It's just a dream. Don't obsess. Stay focused. Dreams aren't real.*

In truth, it wasn't just the dream that bothered him.

In the last few months, as the sky had grown darker, he had sometimes felt as if he was being shadowed. When he ran by the woods, he swore he could hear the faintest sound of footsteps running alongside him. Whenever this happened, he thought of his great-aunt Malony. But he also considered the alternative: *What if he wasn't going mad?*

Kana crested a small hill that offered a panoramic view of the distant sea. The tide had rolled out a mile or so—maybe more. Moonlight glinted off the exposed sand. He was shocked to see how quickly it had happened. Indeed, it felt as if everything was happening faster than expected—the sun setting, the tide going out, the dark falling, and Bliss being abandoned.

He began to run, which helped focus his thoughts. Soon his house came into view. It lay vacant, still, and cold—like a corpse. As he drew nearer, he saw that it was just as his family had left it. Lights were out, curtains were drawn, the front door was open just a crack. For a moment, he was seized by the desire to turn and retreat. *This is ridiculous,* he thought. He pushed open the front door, which issued a long creak that echoed through the house.

"Hello!" The moment he spoke, he felt stupid. *Who am I expecting?* Still, he couldn't help calling out again, "Hello!" His voice bounced harshly off the walls. It sounded different in the empty house. Kana walked through the entryway and down the main hallway into the parlor. There were no carpets to muffle the sound of his footsteps. It was very dark. He entered the parlor and was walking across the room when dimly—as if via a sixth sense—he perceived that something was off about the room.

He craned his neck upward. Splayed across the ceiling in blue, faintly glowing ink were thousands of symbols. The writing covered the ceiling and the rafters. In the middle of it all was a circular object resting on clouds—the moon.

Just then, a floorboard groaned overhead. Kana suppressed a childlike impulse to yell for his parents. Then he heard a slightly different sound. It was the strain of old wood torquing under pressure, creaking rhythmically—as if someone was in his room, rocking back and forth on the old chair. Then a barely audible whispering started—just like in his dream.

"*Hello?*" he said in a near whisper.

The only reply was the steady creak of the rocking chair.

Kana barely contained the urge to run. He needed the map of the island and the map was in his room. *I'm imagining those sounds,* he told himself. He needed the map. He needed to go upstairs. So he walked to the main stairs and began climbing. The floorboards groaned under the weight of each step that he took.

When he reached the top of the stairs, he could still hear the creaking of the old rocking chair. Down the long, darkened hallway, the door to Kana's room was cracked open slightly, just as he'd left it. He walked deliberately toward it. When he reached the door itself, the whispering stopped. He had just moved his hand toward the doorknob when a soft whisper of a voice scratched its way through the darkness.

"You shouldn't be here." It was a woman's voice. The woman from his dream.

Kana froze. For a second it felt like his knees were too weak to hold him up.

"Who are you?" asked Kana, voice trembling.

"I'm all you have."

Kana placed his hand upon the doorknob and opened the door. He scanned the room. It was empty, but the window that had been bolted shut was open and the rocking chair was still moving, ever so slightly. *Or am I just imagining this?*

He raced to the far wall and pulled down the wooden frame that was hanging there. He extracted the map, rolled it up, and put the empty frame back on the wall. As he turned to go, he saw the dim image of his own reflection in a mirror that was affixed to his closet door. He didn't recognize himself. His shoulders were enlarged, as if he had suddenly put on several pounds of muscle. He touched his cheekbones and chin, trying to remember whether they had always been this prominent. Seconds later, he realized he was trembling violently. It seemed to confirm his worst fears.

It's happening. It's happening to me—just like Great-Aunt Malony.

"I have to get out of here," Kana whispered aloud.

"*Yes*," said the voice.

Kana spun around. Nothing. An instant later, he was pounding down the stairs and out the door. If he ran hard enough, the sound of his breathing would drown out all the other sounds, effectively muting the world around him and making him feel as if he were in a dream.

He was halfway back to the mayor's house when the outside world intruded. Something was about to happen. A rich and fetid smell rose from the woods, accompanied by rustling noises that quickly grew louder. Soon the entire woods seemed to be alive with movement. Branches snapped and the ground shook.

Kana glanced around—the woods were on one side and a grassy field was on the other. Running into the field seemed colossally stupid. It was wide open with nowhere to hide. Going into the forest was unthinkable. Suddenly, he knew what he had to do. Kana tucked the map into his pants. He darted to the nearest tree, right at the edge of the woods, grabbed a low-hanging limb, and pulled himself up. He moved quickly, shimmying upward, going as high as he could. Kana marveled at his own speed and strength. Never before had he been so agile.

Moments later, a group of wild boars stampeded out of the woods and into the open grass of the field. They charged forward, pushing and gouging each other madly with their curling tusks. Several headed straight for the tree where Kana hid, then swerved around it at the last second.

Kana was entranced. He had never seen a boar. Most people believed them to be extinct. After their charge, the boars milled around, confused and snapping at each other. One of them lay motionless in the grass, blood spilling from a gouge in its shoulder. Soon the herd disappeared into an area of thick bushes, and Kana breathed again. His body was rigid as he stared at the dead boar on the ground. Why had the boars done this? Only one explanation made sense: something had panicked them enough to drive them from the woods.

CHAPTER 26

MARIN WALKED QUICKLY BUT DELIBERATELY. ALTHOUGH she told herself she was in complete control, the candle betrayed her fear, because her arms refused to stop shaking. Beyond the small circle of light around her, it was too dark to see clearly, so Marin kept her eyes on the ground. Out of nowhere, her mind conjured the image of Line entering the water at the mayor's house. She saw the curves of his shoulders and the way the candlelight both obscured and framed the tendons in his neck.

Marin sped up. *Food,* she thought. *I just need to focus on getting food right now. Carrots would be nice.* She tried to visualize bright orange knobby carrots, and as she did, she felt calmer. Food. That was the main reason for leaving the relative safety of the mayor's house.

First, she would get the food. Then she would get the other thing—if she could find it. In truth, this is why she had insisted on getting the food by herself. *I have to go back to the cliffs,* she told herself. *It will be there—it has to be.*

As she entered town and walked past houses that she knew

so well, Marin felt herself growing angry. It was a slow but steadily rising feeling. There was no doubt she had been lied to. Her father, the okrana, the mayor. Especially the mayor. *What a farce.* She and Kana had found a vicious battle-ax in the mayor's house on the way to light the signal lamp. The mayor had obviously seen what was on those shelves—they were in *his* house. *He knew far more than he had let on.*

Most of all, Marin was angry at herself. She should have demanded that her father, or the mayor, tell what they knew about the years of Night, even if they didn't know a lot. Instead, she had backed down and accepted some half-witted explanation about what people say when they sneeze. Marin thought back to the mayor's condescension—he obviously considered her to be a child. It may have proved difficult to get more information from him, but still . . . She smiled to herself, imagining a reenactment in which she'd grabbed the mayor by his sweater and shook him until he told her the truth.

Marin looked at the houses as she went through town. She had played in them, eaten dinner in them, and gone to them on her mother's behest, to borrow sugar or a pot. Soon she came upon a modest one-room house with a low-slung roof. This was the house where she and Kana had found—and untied—the old dog on the previous day. What really caught Marin's eye, however, was the house's front door. The moon illuminated a single hash mark carved into the wood, identical to the ones that the creature had carved at the mayor's house. This one had a line across the middle. Marin walked onto the front porch, listened at the door, and then pushed inside.

She lifted the candle, revealing a cramped room with a table and several rickety chairs. Marin looked down and saw a dark puddle of liquid at her feet. She squatted, candle in hand, to get a better look. She gasped and turned away. Her feet brushed something heavy. It was the lifeless body of the dog they'd freed, its brown fur matted with sticky, dark blood.

Marin recoiled. And then it clicked. *The hash marks.* On this particular door, they meant that there was something inside the house—in this case, a dog—and the cross through the mark meant that it had been taken care of. *Killed.*

Marin spun around, bolted from the house, and dashed back into the street. She moved so quickly that her candle went out. Not that she cared. There was enough moonlight in the sky to see, and she was too scared to fumble for matches. Marin looked around frantically. *Am I being watched?* Nothing stirred. The abandoned town of Bliss was silent. Marin shook her head. Focus. She had to focus.

Carrots. Just get the stupid carrots.

She ran to the grocer's stand two blocks away and, with trembling fingers, relit her candle. The stand itself was just an open-air shed with discarded food lying on the ground nearby. A frayed cloth sack with a broken handle was ground into the mud next to the shed.

Marin knelt to look at the food. Most of what she found was brown and half rotten. It had been drizzling, so everything was wet. As she filled the sack, the wind gusted, and Marin felt grateful to be wearing the oilskin. The sack was almost full when she noticed a series of holes scattered across the soft, muddy earth. The holes were small, round, and fairly deep— just like the ones on the walls of the mayor's house and the floors of her own house. The holes appeared in clusters of five. Roughly ten inches behind each cluster was a large indentation the size of a man's fist.

She realized with a start that these markings were *footprints*. The large oval indentation was the mark of a heel and the five holes were from toes—only they must have been more like talons than toes.

Marin grabbed the sack of food and hurried away from the grocer's shed. She still had one more thing to do before she could return to Deep Well House. She walked quickly—toward the cliffs. *Almost there,* she told herself. *Get it and run back.*

Soon she was at the cliffs, at the loading area. The wind was fierce and bitterly cold. Suitcases were everywhere, many of them half opened and hemorrhaging wisps of clothing. In the dark they looked like slabs of rock. Marin stepped gingerly through this wasteland, afraid of what she might come across. She thought of looking through the suitcases for more food, but the image of the blood-covered dog overpowered this idea. She shouldn't be here, anyway—she had come for just one thing.

Where is Night Fire? I need to find Night Fire—the blue flag with the two swirling red lines.

She passed half a dozen flags, none of them hers. Then, just as she was about to turn around, she saw it. The flag was drooping off its pole, but the pattern was unmistakable. She went to it and began searching the ground. She saw her mother's bag first (the crimson cloth was a giveaway) and then her own—an old leather-bound trunk—which lay next to it. She fidgeted with the clasp. Her heart pounded in her ears, making it hard to think.

Marin knelt beside the trunk and buried her free hand in the mess of clothes, papers, and keepsakes that she had carefully chosen for the trip to the desert. She came across a long muslin scarf and a thick sweater. She took off the oilskin, put on the sweater and scarf, then slipped the jacket back on. It was a tight fit, but it felt wonderful to be warm.

Marin kept looking and soon found her mother's copper box peeking out from under a pair of sandals. The marking scalpels. Marin remembered her mother's pained face and thought of that lost moment—she'd hoped to make up for it on the boats. She grabbed the copper box and shoved it into her pants pocket. *I'll see my mother again,* Marin vowed. *And when I do, I'll be damned if I don't show up with her family heirloom.*

At last, she discovered what she was looking for—the thing she had truly come to find. It was a tiny bag made of black velvet. She sat back on her heels and sighed in relief. As she traced her finger across the bag, she wondered how to tell Line and Kana. She'd have to reveal the contents to them sometime, and she understood—implicitly—that they might never forgive her.

CHAPTER 27

"WHAT TOOK YOU SO LONG?" ASKED KANA. "WE WERE getting worried." He and Line were sitting comfortably on the couch in the mayor's quarters. After Marin's cold, wind-blown walk to town and the cliffs, the closed quarters of the candlelit room were a shock.

"How about *thank you*?" Marin replied, dumping the sodden carrots and apples onto the floor.

"What happened?" asked Line, pulling himself upright on the couch. He was staring at her damp, blood-smeared pants. "Is that blood on your pants?"

Marin followed his gaze. Her pants looked horrific, a mix of mud and blood. "Don't worry—it's not my blood."

"Then whose?" asked Line. He stared at Marin, mouth half open.

Marin glanced at Kana. "It came from a dog that Kana untied yesterday," she explained. Marin quickly recounted what she had seen at the one-room house, including the crossed-out hash mark on the door.

"So whatever marked our door was trying to kill us—just like the dog," said Kana. "Is that what you're saying?"

"Maybe," she replied. "Can you think of another explanation?"

"No," said Kana with a furrowed brow. "Not really." He was about to say something else, but stopped and looked curiously at Marin's clothes. "Where did you get that scarf? And the sweater?" He paused, and his eyes widened with surprise. "You went all the way to the loading area? For clothes?"

"I was freezing," said Marin in a low voice. She was conscious of Line staring at her as well. "I was cold, okay?"

Kana didn't immediately respond, and Marin tried to divert the conversation. "You're only wearing a shirt and pants. Aren't you cold?"

He looked down at his clothes, as if considering them for the first time. "No . . . I mean, I don't know . . . I guess not."

Marin looked at Line. "And you?"

"I'm fine," he said. "I grabbed another sweater—it'll be enough for now. Unless it gets much colder."

Marin nodded and sat down next to the food on the floor. She grabbed the slimy end of a carrot, wiped it on her pants, and bit in. It was disgusting, but she forced herself to chew. When she looked up, she realized that Line and Kana hadn't moved.

"Join me," she said. "It's edible, I think."

Kana declined, saying his stomach was upset. Line sat down next to her, wincing as he did so. She asked about his arm.

"Not bad," came Line's response. "It hurts, but I think it's because the swelling has gone down—that ointment really works."

"Do you think—"

Line interrupted her. "I'll be ready to go," he said. "I'll be fine, just let me eat for a second." Soon, he had a mouthful of carrots.

Marin decided to stop talking—Kana and Line were not in the mood and it was probably better to focus on the tasks at hand. She began sorting through the apples while Kana slid the dresser and a bureau firmly against the door. Kana then returned to the couch and watched Line and Marin eat in silence.

Eventually, Line looked up at Kana. "You didn't tell her the good news yet."

"You're right," replied Kana. "I smelled wood smoke on my way back from the mayor's house."

Marin considered this. "What do you think it means?"

"Well, it could mean that someone's using one of the town's fireplaces," Kana replied. "Which means someone else was left behind—just like us. It sounds crazy, but—"

"Tell her where you think the smoke was coming from," said Line.

"The hermit's shack," said Kana.

Marin thought back to when they passed the hermit's shack on the way to find Line. She hadn't smelled anything, and the shack seemed empty.

"Strange," she said. "But if the hermit is around, that *is* good news. I mean, it's not good for the hermit—obviously—but it's good for us. It would mean I'm wrong about the hash marks and, you know, about the houses being systematically cleared out. We should take a look at his place on our way out of town."

"Did you see anything else in town?" Line said, smiling at her. "Besides the dead dog, I mean."

Marin frowned. "You don't have to be so callous about it."

"I'm not being callous," Line replied. He looked down at the half-eaten apple in his hand. "I'm just stating a fact—the dog was dead, wasn't it?"

Kana leaned forward from his perch on the couch. "Marin—what else did you see?"

Marin told them everything, including her theory about the small divots being claw marks.

"I've seen those divots before," said Line. "They're all over the place. I figured it was just a stylistic thing—you know, like all the curlicues and squiggly lines carved into wood panels and trusses on all the houses."

"Those would have to be very sharp claws," Kana remarked.

Line stood up with a sudden burst of energy and addressed Kana. "I'll say this much—if any of those creatures come after us, we've got sharp claws, too." He reached under the couch and picked up a long knife, its blade gleaming in the flickering light of the candles. Marin recognized it as one of the knives from the mantelpiece downstairs. "I took one for each of us," said Line. "They're very pirate-like—wouldn't you agree?"

Marin smiled uneasily as Line brandished the knife.

"Don't I look rather dashing?" he asked. He posed dramatically, using his good arm to swish the knife through the air like a storybook pirate.

"Yes, you are terrifying," said Marin. "Now put that down. It's too sharp to play with."

"Aye, me lovely, I fancy some leg of beast for dinner!" said Line in a pirate's brogue. "I'll eat the meat off the bone with the claws I cut from the Night demons!"

Line pranced around the room with the knife, carrying on with his brogue. He ran to Kana and fake-attacked him.

"Line!" called Marin. "Put the knife down, before you impale my brother."

Line paused and lowered the knife. He nodded, then sank down next to Kana as if suddenly exhausted. He turned to face him. "Here," he said, "this can be yours."

Kana took the knife Line had given him and turned it, watching it glint in the light of a weak candle. "No, thanks," he said. "I've never been good with knives. I'd probably just cut myself."

Marin rolled her eyes and smiled.

"As you wish," said Line. He slid the knife back under the couch, then looked around uncertainly. Marin tried to change the subject. She went to the map that Kana had retrieved from Shadow House. Kana had set it down on a small desk near the couches where they'd slept. Marin bent over and studied it.

"Isn't there a path through the woods that leads to the Coil?" she called out.

Line walked over to join her. "Let me see."

Marin beckoned to Kana as well. "Come have a look with us."

The three of them studied the map. Kana pointed to the shoreline. "The tide has already rolled out at least a mile," he said. "So we could just walk out along the seabed, past the

Dwarf Oak Islands, around Shiprock Point, into Southerly Bay, and then up the river."

"But Marin is right," said Line. "There's also a path across the woods."

Kana was confused. "Where?"

"Here," said Line. He picked up a candle and used the hot red wax dripping from it to mark a line on the map that cut across a narrow swath of forest. "I'm not exactly sure where it goes, but I know where it starts. The okrana use it when they travel into the mountains for their solstice hunt. It starts by the cemetery. Just past that is the stone arch. The trail goes under the arch, cuts through the woods, and should go right down to the river—just upstream from the fishing depot. It's about a tenth of the distance." He looked at Marin and Kana. "But honestly, I'd rather *not* go back in the woods. I'd prefer walking along the seabed, even with my sore ankle."

Kana nodded in vigorous agreement. "You're right," he said. "We should avoid the woods."

The three of them studied the map again. Marin traced a line from Bliss to Shiprock Point, and then along the coast to the mouth of the Coil. "All right," she said. "So we walk across the seabed to the fishing depot." She stood up straight and glanced around the room. They had a plan. She put her hand on Kana's shoulder. "Are we agreed?"

Kana kept staring at the map. "I think so—it seems like the best option."

"When should we leave?" asked Line. "I'm ready whenever. Now?"

"Soon," replied Marin. "We need to make something to help support your ankle, and maybe Kana can look around for more food." She paused. "Line—are you sure you don't want more clothes?"

Line shook his head. "I'm fine with what I have, but I'll see if I can find a hat." He exhaled with relief and rubbed his hands through his hair. It was good to have a plan. Of course, so much could go wrong, but to know what would happen next, to regain some measure of control over their fate . . . It provided hope for the first time since they were left behind.

CHAPTER 28

IT ENDED UP TAKING SEVERAL HOURS FOR MARIN AND
Kana to find the materials necessary to fashion a proper brace,
build it, and then affix it to Line's ankle. They used wooden
slats from a chair, wire from a whisk that Marin found in the
kitchen, and padding from several of the mayor's pillows.
But once completed, the project appeared well worth it. Line
was much more comfortable now. While he was looking for
materials, Kana ransacked the mayor's house but was unable
to find a single additional morsel of food.

"We should go," said Line. "There's no point in sticking
around here. And I'm sick of waiting."

Marin looked at the clock on the wall, which she had
wound several hours ago. It was a few minutes past eight—
nearly dinnertime. More important, it was a reminder that
they'd been awake for ages.

She looked at Line. "How much have you slept here?"

He thought about this for a moment. "I don't know—a few
hours."

"And before that?"

"Before that . . . I don't know . . ."

"And you were up for at least twenty-four hours in that hole," said Marin with a shake of her head. "Kana and I haven't slept much, either. It's freezing outside and we probably won't be able to stop until we reach the fishing depot. It's going to be a nasty, cold slog. And then we'll be in a small boat on the open sea." She paused for a moment to let it all sink in. "I want to leave, too, but I think it's smarter to rest here for a few more hours."

"What about the thing?" asked Kana. "We're just going to wait here for it to come back? Maybe we should go to another house. Maybe our house, or Line's." However, as soon as he said this, he realized he had no interest in going back to his house.

Marin looked at Line. "What do you think?"

Line nodded at the door. "That's the heaviest door I've seen in town," he said. "I don't think going somewhere else would give us *more* protection."

"And the signal lamp?" asked Kana.

"I'll turn it off," said Marin with a heavy sigh. "It's only going to attract attention."

"You understand what this means, right?" asked Kana. "If we turn it off, we have to be clear about what we're saying. *No one will rescue us. We do it ourselves. Together.*"

For a moment, Marin was slightly short of breath. She felt as if she were standing at the edge of an endless chasm, teetering, about to fall.

"We can do it," she whispered.

The room was silent. She stared at Kana, then at Line. They nodded.

"All right," she said, more to herself than to anybody else.

Marin turned and left the room, knowing that both of them were staring after her. She walked through the darkened house, entered the closet in the pantry, ascended the stairs, climbed the long inset ladder past the mysterious, heavy boxes, and emerged onto the widow's walk. She placed her hand on the top of the signal light. It was warm. She looked out at the narrow, triangular swath of light that the lamp was casting over Bliss. Somehow turning the light off felt like an act of surrender. She took several deep breaths. *It makes sense,* she told herself. *You're doing this to protect the last three people on this island. Do it.* Marin stretched out her arm and turned the knob. The town fell into darkness.

By the time she returned to the mayor's quarters, Line and Kana had moved the two main couches so that they faced each other, creating a space large enough for the three of them to sleep. There was a nest of sheets, a few blankets, and some towels to cover themselves with. They were already lying down, but when she crept into the room, they stood up without a word and all three pushed a massive armoire in front of the door, along with the dresser and bureau.

Marin was the last of the three to get back under the blanket. The open space was next to Line. She blew out the one candle that was still lit, huddled against the length of Line's body, and tried to relax. Line turned on his back and slowly took her hand in his. He turned to look at her. They were very close, so close that Marin could feel his breath on her cheeks.

"Thank you for rescuing me," he whispered.

"I haven't yet," she whispered back.

Marin slid her free hand into her coat pocket, feeling for the velvet bag that she'd retrieved from her luggage. She then wiggled her fingers into the bag itself, feeling the long silver chain and the clunky sunstone. Merely touching the necklace filled her with guilt and no small amount of self-loathing. This was the reason that they'd been left behind. And she'd had it all along.

Months ago, when she'd returned from the woods—after her failed adventure with Line and Kana—she'd looked inside the leather satchel and hadn't found it. Marin had been furious with Line for leaving it by the edge of the pond. Then, a few days later, she picked up the satchel again and realized it was too heavy to be empty. The necklace was hidden within a tear on the inside seam of the bag.

Marin was both relieved and horrified. She'd intended to tell Line right away, she really had, but the right moment had never come. And after a while, it became too awkward to admit what happened. Then Line had gone looking for it, which was incredibly stupid, but the truth was that it was all *her* fault. She had been too embarrassed to tell Line that she'd found the necklace. It was her own stubborn pride that brought them here, and now their lives were in jeopardy.

Marin would have to tell them at some point, that much was clear, but perhaps it made the most sense to wait until they'd found the spare boat at the fishing depot and were making their escape along the river. At such a time, they'd be so glad to have the sunstone that they might forgive her. That was her hope. In any case, it would do no good to tell them now. Everybody was tense enough as it was. Marin kept rubbing the sunstone with her fingers, as if this would wipe the problem away. Finally a heavy drowsiness came over her and she fell into a deep sleep.

Sometime much later, Marin woke to a piercing sound. She thought then of the knives below, and of the sharpeners. Marin cursed. *The knives. We should have taken all of them out of the mantel.*

Slow, heavy footsteps came up the stairs. They sounded much louder than last time.

"It's back!" she shouted. She didn't dare voice her other thought—it sounded like there were more than just one.

In a heartbeat, Marin, Line, and Kana were on their feet. Together they braced themselves against the armoire and dressers that barricaded the entranceway. Then the pounding began—huge, powerful blows. WHAM! WHAM! WHAM! There was no doubt about it. There were several bodies trying to force their way in. If it weren't for the barricade, the door would have blown open. Still, the furniture shuddered ominously. The ferocity of the blows was unmistakable—the *things* on the other side of the door were determined to get in this time.

"Hold!" screamed Line, who was pushing madly against the armoire. "HOLD!"

They all focused their efforts on the massive armoire. If it slid away, the dressers behind it wouldn't be strong enough to keep the door closed. They lined up against the armoire, dug their heels into the ground, and pushed with all the ferocity of those whose lives hung in the balance. The armoire slid forward an inch, and then backward an inch, again and again.

The hinge that fastened the top of the door to the wall

started coming loose. The screws were being yanked out—it wouldn't be long before the top of the door separated from the wall entirely. But there was nothing they could do about it.

The battering at the door continued for several minutes until, suddenly, Kana slipped at the same time that the door bulged inward from a series of ferocious blows. The force of this new attack jettisoned Kana backward. He sprawled across the floor and the armoire slid forward several inches. The door creaked open. Marin screamed. Grunting erupted from the hallway, and the door was under such pressure that it seemed to bend. Kana threw himself against the armoire with tremendous force. His effort seemed almost superhuman and, amazingly, the armoire slid forward by a half a foot and—once again—the door to the room closed.

Shortly after this, the battering stopped. One of the creatures bellowed and they heard a splintering, cracking sound. Marin's heart sank. It was over. The door was breaking.

"It's just a knife—the door is holding," gasped Kana, seemingly reading her thoughts. Then came the sound of squeaking floorboards as the *things* made their way back down the stairs. Then silence. A long, eerie silence. A minute passed. Then another. Kana, Line, and Marin slumped to the floor, out of breath. More time passed. Finally, they rose to their feet and began to clear the barricade. When the furniture was moved away, they stood at the door and listened.

Silence.

Line tensed and put his hand on the doorknob. "Ready?" he whispered.

"Do it," replied Marin.

Line opened the door in a fluid motion. Kana, out first, confirmed that the hallway was empty. He looked at the door. It was cracked in several places. Directly above each of the three hash marks was a knife stuck into the wood. Line reached up and tried to extract one of the daggers. It wouldn't budge.

Marin stood at the top of the stairs and listened. Kana joined her.

"They're gone," Kana said. "Or at least they're not in the house anymore."

"They'll be back," said Marin. She looked around, taking in the pervasive gloom, polished banisters, walls, floors, and ceiling. A feeling of clarity descended upon her. "Don't you see? They built this house." Then she extended both arms and gestured all around. "They built *all* of this."

"She's right," said Kana softly.

"Do you think the mayor knew?" asked Line, eyes trained on the floor.

"Doesn't matter at this point," said Marin. She reached down and began to tighten the laces on her boots. "What matters is, this town is *theirs*—and they want it back."

CHAPTER 29

THEY GATHERED UP THEIR POSSESSIONS AND PUT THEM in the sack Marin had found. It wasn't much: their remaining handful of candles, several lengths of rope, a nearly empty box of matches, a well-used flint, and the leftover food she'd gathered. Marin and Line each carried a knife from the mantelpiece, and Marin had the copper box with the marking scalpels. They walked quickly through the darkness, heading for the hermit's cottage. It was raining steadily and within minutes they were soaked. The rain was piercingly cold, and Marin was grateful again for the oilskin and the extra clothes.

Overhead, the air was alive with the frenzied chirping and fluttering of bats—tens of thousands of them. They had arrived within the last twelve months, following the Night, and their numbers had been increasing steadily by the week. The bats seemed to live in the forest, yet every few days or so, they suddenly appeared near the coast to feed. The rain in particular seemed to enrage them, and now they dove aggressively toward the ground, swooping so close that the three of them had to hunch down to protect their faces.

And then, as suddenly as they appeared, the bats vanished. Tiny pellets of ice began falling from the sky. The hail lasted for just over a minute, but it was enough to sting their faces and hands before it shifted back to rain. The weather finally cleared and, in relief, they slowed their pace. They were nearing the hermit's house.

Since leaving Deep Well House, Marin had thought only of the dark path in front of her. She fully expected something to jump out at them, and she gripped the knife so hard that her hand began to ache. When she eased her grip on the knife, other thoughts began to reenter her mind. She thought of her parents. *Where are they now?*

"I suppose it was stupid to think that he would come back for us," said Marin finally.

"Who?" asked Kana.

"Father."

Kana slowed as he considered what Marin said. "I'm sure he would have come if he could," he said at last.

"I want to believe you," she replied. "I really, really do, but—"

"You're not giving him enough credit," said Kana. "I know you're talking about what happened with that furrier, but what was he going to do? Yell? Hit him?" He shook his head. "No. His concern was getting us onto the boats—even if it meant being insulted."

"You're right," said Marin with a sigh. "I guess . . . I just hated seeing Dad that way—I never thought he would let anyone treat him like that. He just seemed so . . . powerless."

Line was walking next to them, listening to the conversation. He hadn't seen the furriers, but what he heard from

Marin made him think again of Francis. *Who's watching over him—now—at this very minute?*

"If there was any way, Father would have come back," said Kana. "I'm sure of it."

"Right," said Marin. *"If there was any way."*

For his part, Line was glad to hear Marin talk this way. He didn't blame the adults, but he didn't expect anything from them, either. When his mother died, Line had assumed that the town would simply take care of them. And it had—for about three days. After that, they were slowly forgotten. He wasn't bitter about this. Not anymore. But he understood: *At some point, when things go wrong, you have to fix them yourself.*

They continued on in silence. Minutes later, they smelled smoke.

"What do you think?" asked Line.

Marin looked around and sniffed the air. "His is the only house in this area. If he's still here, that would be a *very* lucky break."

"It seems pretty crazy for him to have stayed, unless he *really* hated the Desert Lands." Line laughed darkly. "Do you think he's just hanging around, sipping dandelion wine, making popcorn, and waiting for us to show up?"

Marin glanced wryly at Line. "Dandelion wine? Popcorn?"

"Dandelion wine and popcorn would taste good about now," said Line with a smile. "He's not as strange as people in town think. I talked to him a few times."

Marin was about to respond but noticed Kana's gait was off, as if he had a pebble in his boot.

"Are you okay?" she asked her brother.

Kana stopped and looked at her. "I'm fine," he replied. "Why?"

"It looked like you were limping a little," said Marin.

Kana shook his head. They continued walking as the scent of smoke grew stronger and stronger. Finally they rounded a bend in the trail and came upon the hermit's ramshackle cottage. Smoke billowed from its chimney. This wasn't the smoke of a dying fire. This was the smoke of a blaze that had just been stoked with fresh wood. One of the windows flickered with a faint light.

Kana looked at Line. "Should we knock?"

"No," said Line. "There's another door around back."

The three of them circled the house, walking slowly but deliberately. The place was in terrible disrepair. Several of the windows were cracked, the walls were tilting, most of the gutters were already on the ground, and the roof was so buckled, it looked in danger of caving in. When they finally found the back door, Marin took a step forward and listened for any sounds of movement inside. There were none.

"I don't hear anything," whispered Marin. "Uh, what's that smell?" Suddenly, she was aware of being alone.

"Line? Kana?"

Kana's voice floated in from the darkness. "We're behind you—knock."

Marin stepped forward and rapped her fist against the door's wooden frame. There was no reply. She knocked again, but after a second or two she just grabbed the old brass doorknob and pushed the door open. She stepped into the cottage and was immediately struck by a putrid odor. The first floor of the house was one large room, the dim space partially illuminated by the blaze of the fire that crackled in the stone hearth.

"Hello?" called Marin.

Silence.

"Hello?"

Still nothing. Kana and Line joined her inside.

"I don't think he's here," she said.

"So who built the fire?" asked Kana. He found himself hungry all of a sudden, as if his appetite had awakened with a start.

"Probably the hermit," said Line. "But he spent a lot of time in the forest. Look at this place. Would you want to spend your days hanging out *here*?"

"What could he be cooking?" asked Marin. "It smells disgusting."

The three of them all sniffed the air at once.

"It's not so bad," said Kana. "And I've got the weakest stomach of anyone I know."

Together, the three of them looked around the room. It was a labyrinth of clutter. Wooden crates were strewn about, some empty, some filled with scraps of wood. Fishing gear of all sorts—nets, lines, hooks, and buoys—were scattered across a rickety kitchen table. Overhead, hanging from the rafters were strands of dried herbs, musty pelts, fishing rods, rusting animal traps, empty bottles, and coils of fraying rope.

In the far corner of the room was a small area that looked like the kitchen. The wood-plank walls were stained with soot. There was a water basin, a stack of tin pans, some well-worn utensils, and a few jars of spices. Line did a quick scan of the area in the hopes of finding some food. There was none. He did, however, find a small trapdoor in the floor, but when he opened it, he saw that it was merely a garbage chute that emptied into a foul-smelling pit.

A steaming cast-iron pot hung from a hook over the hearth. Marin walked over to the fireplace to take a closer look at what, exactly, was cooking. At first glance, she thought it was just an ordinary brown stew—with some sizable chunks of meat—until she realized that the chunks of meat were, in fact, the sinew and muscle tissue of bats.

She blanched and took a step back. "No wonder he was a hermit," she said under her breath.

"What is it?" asked Line as he walked over to have a look. Kana was on the other side of the room, looking at the front door.

"Bats," said Marin.

"Marin! Line! Come over here," said Kana. They ran to the front door—the one they had opted not to use when entering the house. Kana had opened it and was staring at something.

"What is it?" asked Line.

Kana stepped outside, walked forward several feet, and then abruptly stopped. He turned back toward the front door, looking grim. "You need to see this."

Marin and Line walked over. Carved into the wood of the door was a hash mark that had been crossed out.

Kana pointed into the darkness beyond the house. "It gets worse."

Marin had absolutely no desire to go out and see for herself, but she lit a candle and took Line's hand and, together, they ventured into the darkness. They didn't see anything at first. In fact, Line almost stepped on it accidentally—then he glanced down and saw the brown grubby fingers, the long bent arm, and the prone body of the hermit. He was lying on his stomach, face pressed into the earth. Line knelt down, grabbed hold of the shoulder, and, with some effort, began to flip him.

"Line!" said Kana. "I wouldn't do that . . ."

But it was too late. The body flopped over, revealing the hermit's front side.

Line recoiled instantly. The man's torso was soaked with the blood that now covered Line's hands. A trickle of blood still oozed from the hermit's head and neck, which were marred with a number of small, perfectly round puncture wounds. There was no point in taking the man's pulse. He was clearly dead.

CHAPTER 30

THEY RAN BACK TO THE HOUSE. KANA IMMEDIATELY locked both the front and the back doors, sealing them shut with sturdy iron bolts. Apparently, no one told the hermit to remove his locks—or perhaps he just didn't care. Line walked to the washing basin in the little kitchen and began rinsing his hands, then scrubbing them with a small piece of soapstone. The blood came off fairly easily, but Line continued to scrub for several minutes.

As he ran the stone over his skin, Line tried to force the image of the dead hermit out of his mind. He couldn't dwell on this. It was not useful information. It would not help him get off the island. *That's it. That's the key. Every piece of information, every fact, every thought—it all needs to be sorted into two simple categories. I should've realized this before, in the pit. There are thoughts that will help us escape and thoughts that will not. And all thoughts about dead dogs, dead hermits, dead relatives, and missing brothers have to be placed squarely in the unhelpful category. Those unhelpful thoughts have to be blocked out. They don't exist.*

Marin walked over to Line and put a hand on his shoulder. He was hunched over, concentrating fiercely on his hands. "Are you all right?"

"Of course," said Line, still scrubbing.

"I'm serious," said Marin. "Are you all right?"

"I'm fine," said Line flatly.

"You don't sound fine," said Marin. She glanced worriedly at Kana, who was beside her.

"How would you like me to sound?" asked Line without looking up. "The dead hermit has *holes* in his body. That dead dog in town probably had *holes* as well."

Marin looked grim. Line was right—being confronted with this was horrific. But there was no time to think about it. Whoever, whatever had done this was likely nearby. She needed Line to see the urgency. Finally, several minutes later, Line finished washing his hands, dried them, and then stood quietly, staring into the fire.

"We should go," said Marin.

"Yes," said Line. "That's a good—"

"Shh—what was that?" asked Kana.

This time they all heard it—a faint rattling—metal jiggling against metal. They glanced around the house quickly. It was the doorknob to the back door, twisting back and forth. Moments later, the front door started rattling, too.

"What do we do?" whispered Marin.

Line was one step ahead of her. And a thought had formed in his mind. A good thought. A useful one. *The trapdoor. The garbage chute.* Line put his finger to his lips, walked back to the kitchen, and gestured for the others to follow. He knelt next to the chute, pulled it open, and slid inside. Marin hesitated; now the rattling on the doors had become a pounding.

"Come on!" hissed Kana.

Marin dropped to the floor, dangled her legs through the trapdoor, and followed Line into the pit. Moments later, Kana came through, then lowered the door, plunging them into complete darkness. They tried to remain as still as possible, which was difficult because they were crouching in piles of rotting fish heads and prickly fish skeletons. There was also a steady flow of something beneath them—water, ooze, sludge, it was impossible to tell.

Overhead, they could hear the telltale sounds of wood splintering. Line began pawing through the trash. *What we need is a way out. Everything else is a distraction. Ignore the things smashing down the doors overhead. That's irrelevant. In fact, it isn't happening. There's only one good fact. Water on the ground is going somewhere.*

"Help me!" whispered Line. "There's water trickling here. It means there's an opening."

There was an explosion of noise above them. Two heavy thuds, one after another, like rifle shots. The front and back doors landed heavily on the floor. A mist of dirt and soot fell from the floorboards, and Kana had to stifle a coughing attack. Line was still digging, faster now, as if he'd found something. Moments later, they heard the sound of footsteps above them— heavy, plodding footsteps. Marin squeezed Line's leg to stop him from digging. The footsteps passed directly above. They could hear the floorboards groaning under the weight. For a moment, the footsteps stopped. Marin, Kana, and Line all held their breath. Then the footsteps resumed again and began ascending the steps to the second floor of the house.

"The water goes into a tunnel," whispered Line. "It's narrow, but I think we can squeeze through. I'll go first—follow quickly."

Marin grabbed his sweater. "Wait—where does it lead?"

"I don't know, but I can feel fresh air coming out." Line slithered his way into the tunnel. The entrance *was* narrow, and the rock scraped him at the knees and along his back, but he got through. Kana went next. Finally it was Marin's turn. As she crawled toward the opening, the sound of the footsteps overhead grew louder. Whoever it was had returned to the first floor. She crawled quickly, and in her haste she felt something slice into her leg. She cried out. Above, the reaction was immediate. Footsteps thundered and the entire house seemed to shake.

"Marin!" called Kana, poking his head back into the garbage pit from the tunnel. "Hurry!"

Marin moved toward Kana's voice. Kana reached out, grabbed his sister's hand, and pulled her toward him. There was a loud creak overhead, the trapdoor opened, and a shaft of murky light illuminated the garbage pit. Marin lunged into the tunnel entrance and pushed herself forward. After several feet, she emerged in a cave barely large enough to sit upright. There was a faint glow at the opening, though, and she could smell the brine of the sea and hear the distant chirping of bats.

She and Line crawled toward the opening, but Kana remained in place. Despite his impulse to flee, he wanted a glimpse of what was behind them. The thing, whatever it was,

was thrashing around—trying to pass through the trapdoor and enter the garbage pit below. But it was too big to get in.

For a split second, Kana thought he saw a foot, although that wasn't the right word at all, because it wasn't really a foot. It was a gnarled, greenish claw with five hooked talons—and just a glimpse was enough to send him chasing after Marin and Line.

CHAPTER 31

"GO—GO—GO!" KANA YELLED. HE BOLTED OUT OF THE tunnel and crawled to Line and Marin, who were perched at the edge of the cave entrance and looking down.

"Is it behind you?" gasped Marin.

"I don't think so," he said, looking back into the darkened cave. "It's probably too big to fit, but I can't be sure."

"Let's not find out," said Line. "Kana—can you see a way down the cliff wall?"

Kana inched his way to the edge and looked down a steep cliff that dropped nearly a hundred feet down to a rocky beach below. The rain had stopped and the sky was lighter than before. The moon peeked through the clouds. He glanced out toward the horizon. The sea had withdrawn a long ways and in its wake was a vast expanse of rocks, strewn with kelp and seaweed. It was a spectacular, otherworldly landscape. There were great rock formations, canyons, clusters of coral, and the carcasses of thousands of fish.

The most pressing matter was getting down the cliff. He examined the edge and saw a chicken head—a bulbous knob of rock sticking out of the cliff face. Lithe as a cat, Kana swung his legs over, grabbed the chicken head, and disappeared over the edge. He hung there for a few seconds as he looked for his next move. Despite the direness of their circumstances, he was pleased by how easily he could maneuver along the wall. He had never climbed as well as Marin, but now he felt supremely confident.

Just to his right, about five feet away, was a dark seam in the rock that ran straight down to the shoreline. It was a natural feature sometimes found in the cliffs, and for those with climbing experience, it made an ascent or descent doable—even easy. This particular seam gradually widened into a chimney—a crack wide enough to fit an entire body. Descending this particular chimney would be easy for Marin, even in the dark. Line would have a harder time because of his ankle, but the brace would help. On an island like theirs, with its perimeter of high cliffs, most people could free-climb all but the steepest of headwalls. The only complication now was that it had been raining and the rock face was wet.

"There's a way down!" yelled Kana as he continued his descent. "Just over the precipice, there's a nice chicken head—hang from it and then crab-walk to the seam on your right. Farther down, it'll open into a chimney. Take it slow—the rock is wet and icy in a few places." They heard Kana continue down the wall.

Line nodded at Marin to go next.

"No, you go ahead," said Marin, pushing him gently toward the precipice. "You have to be careful of your ankle—and your arm."

"Go on," he said. "Please. If I'm in front, I'll slow you down." There was a solid resoluteness in his voice. "There's nothing coming . . . If it was, it'd be here by now."

Marin hesitated, then walked up to him and hugged him close. "Be careful," she whispered. Then she walked to the edge of the cliff and slipped over with practiced ease.

Line glanced back at the empty mouth of the cave. He wanted to follow Marin immediately, but knew he had to wait. He was injured. He wasn't entirely certain how well he could climb; if he fell or slipped, he didn't want to be right on top of her. Line counted out a full minute to give himself maneuvering room. By the time he'd counted to thirty, he was sorely tempted to fling himself over the edge. He kept glancing back, dreading what he might see or hear, but the cave behind him remained silent.

Fifty-eight, fifty-nine, sixty.

Just as Line began descending, Kana's feet touched the rocky shore at the base of the cliff. Kana had gone incredibly fast, much faster than was prudent. His arms and fingers burned with exertion. He moved several feet away and watched Marin and Line pick their way down the cliff. Marin would be down in no time. Line was slower and the jerky way in which he moved made Kana anxious.

"Come on," he muttered. "Come on, Line."

Then suddenly, way above—at the top of the cliff—a flicker of a shadow caught Kana's attention. *Did I really see it? Is my mind playing tricks on me?* No. There it was again. Something was moving across the cliff, toward Line, and quickly.

Kana screamed at the top of his voice, "LINE! LINE! ABOVE YOU!"

Startled, Line bobbled his grip on the cliff and hugged it even tighter. At first, he couldn't understand why Kana was screaming. But then he caught a glimpse of it. Something was moving down the cliff. He was at the top of the seam, before it opened up into the chimney. He froze against the wall. He needed to find a better defensive position, but where? The chimney, of course. However, the seam that he was climbing angled downward and did not open into the chimney for another eight feet. The noise from overhead was getting louder. He didn't have time to inch his way along.

Instincts kicked in. *I have to move. Now.* Line leapt, free-falling for a fraction of a second, and then using all the strength in his good arm—he caught a rock outcropping. Seconds later, he'd pulled himself flush against the chimney.

His heart was pounding, all his senses were activated, and for the first time in what seemed like ages, he felt totally and utterly alive. Other thoughts and fears vanished. Francis, the mayor, the boats, the sunstone, the fishing depot—all of it was replaced by complete presence in the moment. The thing was coming fast.

It was almost there.

Line reached behind him to grab the vegetable sack tied to his back. He withdrew his long knife and felt its weight in his hand. His breathing slowed and he felt distant from himself, as if he were a mere observer. *Wait for it,* Line told himself. *Patience is the key. Wait for it.*

As it drew closer, Line went completely still. A clawed foot appeared on a rock a yard or so above his head. Line fought the urge to slash at it. *Wait for it. Wait for it.* Soon, he was rewarded by the appearance of two legs edging their way into the chimney. They were a foot or two away.

Now. Line hurled himself up and thrust the blade deep into the creature's thigh.

The creature screamed and tried to pull away, but Line was quicker. Still gripping the handle of the knife, he yanked it downward so that the blade ripped through leg muscle and ligaments. Hot blood sprayed Line, but he held on and plunged the knife deeper into the creature's leg.

Its scream turned high-pitched. The creature pulled itself up and away from the chimney. Line lost his grip on the knife and it fell away. He clung to the chimney, aware that his arms and legs were trembling uncontrollably. *Easy,* he told himself. Line forced himself to peel individual fingers away from the rock. They throbbed. He dimly heard Marin and Kana shouting. All of this happened in a feverish blur. Line descended as quickly as he dared, aware of a terrible thirst gathering in the bottom of his throat. Then, suddenly, he was off the cliff. Exhaustion enveloped him, and he crumpled to the ground.

Marin knelt at his feet, concern etched across her face. "Line?"

"Did I kill it?" he asked.

"Kill it?" said Marin. "I don't know."

"Then I probably didn't," said Line. "Or it would have fallen."

Line glanced down at his hands, which were covered in blood. Again. He knelt over a nearby pool of stranded seawater and rubbed the blood off his hands, all too aware that he had done the same thing in the hermit's house. The water was bracingly cold. Once his hands were clean, he splashed water on his face. For a moment, he began to replay what just happened in his mind, but then he shook his head and forced himself to stop. *Not useful.*

He looked up at the cliff, then at Kana. "Are there more?"

Before responding, Kana stood for a full minute, studying the cliff face. "I don't see anything," he said at last.

Line nodded in relief. "Did you see what happened to my knife?"

"No," Kana replied, shaking his head. "I didn't see it drop—I was looking at you." He glanced at Marin. "Did you see it?"

Marin sighed. "No," she said. "Here, take mine."

Line examined the blade. "Keep it," he said finally. "My arm hurts too much for me to use it well." It was hard for him to admit this, but it was a fact. *Only facts will help you escape—not hopes, fears, or wishes.*

Kana turned away from the conversation; something on the exposed seabed drew his attention. He walked forward several paces across the slippery, seaweed-covered rocks, then stopped.

"What is it?" Marin called.

"A statue of a woman. And there's another one just like it farther out."

Marin looked at Line. "Palan's statue. The hag."

"Does it have writing on it?" she called out.

"Yes," Kana called back. He had to shout louder to be heard. "It looks like more rules."

CHAPTER 32

KANA, LINE, AND MARIN WALKED ACROSS THE OLD seabed until they arrived at the statue of the hag. The statue itself was nearly eight feet tall, and it stood atop a ten-foot pedestal. It was an old woman, with long hair and a hollowed-out face. Two similar statues stood a few hundred yards away in either direction. All three statues had their backs to the island.

Kana walked right up to the pedestal to examine the algae-encrusted writing on the hag's long shield. He read it out loud:

THE HOUSES MUST BE WITHOUT STAIN.
LEAVE THEM AS THEY WERE.
COVER YOUR SCENT.
FLEE THE NIGHT OR WE WILL COME FOR YOU.

Kana looked back at Marin and Line. "Warnings," he said. "Probably for anyone who comes to the island riding the Morning Tide."

"*Leave them as they were,*" repeated Marin. "I guess that

accounts for all the crazy rituals—closing this door, not closing that door, SNOUT here, TEETH there . . ."

"The last line is clear enough," said Line. "And we're breaking that rule right now."

All three stood there, shoulder to shoulder, staring at the stone hag and the words carved on her shield. Line thought about the last sentence: *Flee the Night or we will come for you.* His mind felt feverish. *We will come for you.* Was this a useful fact, or was it something he should ignore? He felt troubled, and the trembling in his stomach spread to his arms and fingers.

"We should go," said Line. "It's a long way to the mouth of the Coil, and I'm guessing those things will keep hunting us."

They walked on, heading southeast along the coast, toward Shiprock Point. The only sound was the scraping of their boots against the mud and sand of the seabed. Kana led, and was so agile that he forgot to slow down for Marin and Line. At one point, Line slipped and then fell on a seaweed-covered rock. Marin grabbed his arm to help pull him up. Just then, Kana called out. His voice sounded distant. They couldn't see him, but he reappeared only a minute later.

"You won't believe this," he began, but stopped when he saw the drawn faces in front of him. "What happened?"

"We're fine," said Marin. She dug her hands into her oilskin. It seemed to be getting colder by the hour. "What did you see?"

"The tide rolling back uncovered something incredible. Come—I'll show you." Kana looked excited in a childlike way. His reaction made Marin even more curious.

Kana led them for another twenty minutes, until they

arrived at a rock outcropping that offered a better view. In the distance—perhaps two or three miles away—two stone towers rose from the sea floor. Halfway up, the towers were connected by a bridge. At the base of the towers was a stone structure that looked like a sturdy fortress. The towers were slender and round, but their tops were the most intriguing feature of all. Instead of ending in a spike or turret, as castle towers often did in storybooks, each tower ended in a garden, complete with rocks, trees, and grass. Because the seabed descended quickly as it fell away from the island, at this distance, the tops of the towers were actually at eye level.

Line rubbed his face with his hands, partly to wipe away the strain of walking fast, partly because he couldn't believe what he saw. He grabbed onto Kana's shoulder. "I never would have guessed—*never*."

Kana nodded in agreement.

"This is crazy," said Line. "But I think . . ." He shook his head. "No—can't be."

"What?"

Line stared some more. He looked at the towers, then back to the island, as if trying to solve a puzzle. "Are those the Dwarf Oak Islands? The tops of the towers, I mean. I think I *recognize* those trees. I've sailed around them before."

"The Dwarf Oak Islands," said Marin slowly, as recognition dawned on her. "That's where the mayor said the citadel was supposed to be. In a way, he was right. The citadel is *underneath* the islands."

Line looked at the towers with a frown. "You think *our* people built that?"

Marin studied the towers again, taking in their sheer size. "No way," she said. "How could they? Those towers are huge—it must have taken years to build them. And they'd be underwater during Day. The creatures must have built them. It's the only explanation."

"Then maybe we shouldn't be going toward it," said Line. "*They* don't seem to like us in their buildings."

"But we have to go in that direction," said Kana. He pointed to the forested shoreline beyond the towers. "It's the only way to get around Shiprock Point and make it to the mouth of the Coil."

"I guess . . . ," said Line, but he didn't sound convinced.

Suddenly, Kana spun around and looked behind them—back toward the cliffs.

"*What?*" Line asked, turning around and seeing nothing but seabed.

Kana paused and stood absolutely still. His posture reminded Marin of a feral cat hunting birds. When he finally relaxed, he shook his head. "Nothing—just keeping an eye out."

It didn't matter what he said. The mere fact of him turning and looking back was enough to rekindle the panic they'd felt climbing down the cliff. Kana took off at a brisk pace, while Marin and Line struggled to keep up with him. An hour passed, and Line began to slow. He and Marin paused while Kana scouted ahead.

"I wish Kana hadn't run off," Marin said, pushing the hair out of her eyes and gazing into the distance. "I don't care what he's doing. We should be sticking together."

"Funny—isn't that what Kana said when you wanted to go to

the vegetable stand on your own?" observed Line with a smile.

Marin stood several inches deep in a swirl of rocks, mud, and seaweed. "I guess." She lifted her head to look up at Line. "Do you think he's all right? I haven't seen him *eat* in . . . well . . . a long time."

Line stepped toward Marin and drew her close. Her cheek pressed against the softness between his collarbone and neck. "He's fine," Line said. "He's in better shape than either of us. Did you see him when we were trying to hold that door shut, back at the mayor's house? It started to swing open and he pushed it back. Practically by himself."

"I hope you're right," said Marin. She didn't sound convinced.

They continued to pick their way across a treacherous assortment of slippery, seaweed-covered rocks. In the distance, thunder rumbled every few minutes. It was odd to walk here. It smelled and felt like the sea, but—other than a few pools of stagnant water where starfish lingered—there was no seawater to be found. An hour passed, then another, and Kana still did not return.

At one point, Marin noticed that Line had started cradling his injured arm. He noticed her glance and rolled his eyes. "I'm fine," he said. "Stop worrying."

"But what about your arm?"

Line moved it gingerly. "Better, I think. Or, at the very least, not worse."

She looked at him, trying to decide whether to believe what he said. "Good," she said at last. "Still, we should get more lekar when we catch up with Kana." She looked around, half expecting to see Kana right next to them.

"He's just scouting ahead," said Line. "He'll circle back. This is what he does—just like when we hunted for mushrooms." Then he chuckled darkly. "And if he's gone—well, can you really blame him for leaving us?"

"Not funny," said Marin.

"Sorry," said Line. "I'm just saying, he'd be on the boats right now if you hadn't tried to rescue me."

"You're right," said Marin dryly. "We should have left you."

They continued through puddles of vanished ocean. Soon they could smell brine. They were close to the retreating shoreline.

"Sometimes I think you've been too good to me," said Line. He sounded distant, contemplative. He was looking away, as if he were talking to himself.

"Please don't say that," she said, grabbing his hand.

"Why *shouldn't* I say that?" asked Line.

She quickened her pace, putting several feet between them. "Just don't."

Line sped up, stepping quickly over the slippery rocks, trying to catch her. "All I had to do was get on the boat with my brother," he continued. "That was it. And I messed it up. And if you hadn't come back for me . . ."

"Don't," said Marin, looking down at her feet. She didn't dare make eye contact with him. "Maybe . . . maybe I'm not as good a person as you think." As she said this, she slipped her hand into her coat pocket and clasped the necklace with her cold, numb fingers.

Line raised his hands, palms toward the sky. "What does that mean?"

"Well, it's just that . . . ," she started, and then stopped, as if simply grasping for the right words.

Line took a step toward her. "I don't understand."

"Lower your expectations," she said finally. "That's all."

CHAPTER 33

AS THEY NEARED THE CITADEL, THEY SAW KANA AT LAST.
He was on a mound of rock, sitting so still that, initially, Marin
didn't realize he was there. When he moved, Marin let out a
little yelp.

"Kana!" She hurried over to him. "There you are."

"I was just waiting for you," he said. He jumped from his
perch and looked back at the citadel. "I think I found a way in."

"In there?" asked Line, following his gaze.

"Where else?" asked Kana. He motioned casually toward
the citadel. "It shouldn't be hard. Don't you want to go?"

For a moment, they all stood quietly, eyeing the citadel.
There was an undeniable allure to the idea of having a roof
over their heads. It was just a few hundred yards away. Water
surrounded it like a moat, but in several places it looked quite
shallow.

The citadel itself was an imposing structure, rising from
the water and up toward the sky. At the very top, they could

see the trees that formed the towers' roofs. Never in a million years would they have guessed that the Dwarf Oak Islands were, in fact, the peaks of two stone towers. The sides of the towers were covered with a thick coating of barnacles and sea kelp. In many places, large clusters of coral had actually begun to grow on the outer walls. They saw no windows, and it seemed possible—though highly unlikely—that parts of the interior had stayed dry during high tide.

"Doesn't makes sense," said Line with a shake of his head. "Our plan was to find the fishing depot and leave. How does going inside help?"

"We might find something we can use," said Kana, glancing backward at the massive citadel. "Plus, I'd like to climb one of those towers and look out, get a sense of our route to the fishing depot."

Line narrowed his eyes but said nothing.

"Just stay here," said Kana quickly, gesturing for them to sit. "I'll go in, look around, and come right back."

Marin's teeth chattered. A roof was more appealing than the open air. As if on cue, ice-flecked rain returned suddenly, and in force.

Marin raised the oilskin above her head for protection. "We can't wait here," she shouted to Line over the noise of the rain. She turned to Kana. "You know a way in?"

Kana pointed to a shallow pool of water near the citadel. "Over there—I found some stones to walk across. We should stay mostly dry."

The rain turned to sleet, which stung their faces as it fell.

Marin glanced at Line, who had pulled his sweater above his head just like Marin had with her jacket. He nodded: *Let's go.*

They followed Kana as he stepped carefully across a series of rocks poking out of the water. Up close, the citadel did not look like the kind of structure that could be scaled—the stone was slick and smooth. But scaling it wasn't Kana's plan. Instead, he crept around the base of the tower until he found a small lip of stone that protruded from the wall. Directly above this was a narrow opening. It looked like an arrow slit that had begun to crumble and expand during its years underwater.

Kana jumped up and thrust his right arm into the opening, searching for a hold. The interior wall was less polished than the exterior, and he was able to grab onto a chunk of rock. He flung his left arm to join the right, hung there for a second, and then pulled himself inside. It wasn't easy to squeeze through the crumbling opening, especially at shoulder level. Perhaps he had misjudged how big he was. It took another few seconds before he'd wriggled inside and fallen heavily onto the wet stone floor. His arms ached and he gasped for breath, but he was safe. The opening was narrow—even narrower than the tunnel in the garbage pit beneath the hermit's house. This gave Kana a measure of confidence. Nothing large would be able to get in.

Soon afterward, Marin emerged through the same crumbling arrow slit, followed by Line, who carried their meager sack of possessions. Line reached into the sack, took out a candle, and lit it. It cast a weak but wide light. The floor was strewn with bits of coral and smashed shells and the rocks glistened with a slimy film of seawater.

"Maybe we'll find something upstairs," said Kana. He pointed up, but they couldn't see anything in that direction.

"What do you think the chances are that we'll find a tin of biscuits and a barrel of cider?" asked Marin. Her voice echoed faintly.

"I wish," said Line. "Lots of dead fish are more likely."

"How do we get upstairs?" asked Marin.

"This way," said Kana. He led them to a narrow spiral staircase that wound up into the darkness. The stone stairs were in terrible disrepair. Some were solid, but others were loose from the years of being submerged. Near the top of the stairs, there was a flutter of movement as something swooped down, brushing Marin's face and hair. Startled, Marin stumbled backward. Line caught her, but dropped the candle. It hit the floor and all went dark.

"What happened?" asked Kana.

"Just bats," said Line. He sounded more disgusted than annoyed. "But we dropped the candle."

"We can pick it up later when we leave—just take my hand," said Kana, extending his arm to Marin. "We're almost there."

Moments later, they emerged onto more solid ground. Marin took out another candle and lit it. The staircase continued farther up into one of the towers, but they stopped and entered a large room with a vaulted ceiling, about the size of the mayor's dining hall. The room looked as if it had once been used as a chapel. There were two fireplaces on either end, several rows of stone pews, a stage, and a pulpit. The rock walls were engraved with ornate carvings—swirls, curlicues, and divots—that bore a striking resemblance to the wooden scrollwork on the houses in town.

The floor was strewn with debris—waterlogged wooden timbers, smashed pieces of pottery, shards of glass, and a stack of three iron gates that had rusted together. A pile of bones were scattered in one corner. Some looked human. Kana investigated the dark room while Marin and Line stood close together in the candlelight.

Line bounced on the balls of his feet, trying to warm up. Although they had shelter from the rain, the citadel was an oppressively cold place. *"Flee the Night or we will come for you,"* said Line as he eyed the bones in the corner.

"You think those were our people?" asked Marin.

Line rubbed his cold hands together. "Probably."

"And what—they tried to hide here, thinking they'd be safe?"

Line frowned, trying to imagine this. He took a step closer to the bones to get a better look. "Maybe," he said. "I guess their plan didn't work."

Kana emerged from the darkness, using a hand to shield his eyes from the glare of Marin's candle. He held up a rusted plate and showed it to Marin. Her eyes widened in recognition. Just like the plates at home.

That settles it, thought Marin. *They use this place—or at least they have in the past.*

"Kana, there's nothing here," said Marin. "Line's right—we need to leave for the fishing outpost."

Kana put the plate on a nearby stone pew. "Give me a few minutes," he replied. "I just want to look around. I'll run right back."

"All right," she said, still staring at the rusted plate. "But be quick. I'm ready to go."

CHAPTER 34

KANA CLIMBED THE SPIRAL STAIRCASE. IT NARROWED substantially and became claustrophobic, the only respite being small windows that allowed moonlight to enter. Cold rivulets of water streamed down the wall like tears. He continued upward until the staircase ended in a roughly cut stone ceiling. An inset trapdoor that was rusted shut and covered in barnacles was the only exit. Next to the door was an iron lever. Kana pulled down, but it didn't move. He placed his foot on the lever and used all of his body weight to press it down. There was a prolonged groan, and slowly, the metal doorway overhead lifted open. The stairway filled with the scent of the sea.

As he emerged from the stairway, he saw that the exterior of the door had the appearance of a glacier-scrubbed rock. It was cleverly done. A visitor to the Dwarf Oak Islands sitting on the rock would never guess that there was a stairway below.

Kana walked slowly around the island. There wasn't much to it—grass, boulders, the remains of an old campfire, a rock ledge that used to be a pebble beach, and a few small oak trees with their scraggly limbs swaying in the breeze. Kana remembered camping here with his family when he was about six. He and Marin had caught fish and cooked them on sticks over the fire. Their parents laughed and joked, and a refreshing wind masked the sun's heat. They certainly didn't imagine that they were sitting on the very top of a citadel.

The memory seemed to be from another life.

Kana walked to the southwest side of the island and looked out toward the ocean. He scanned the horizon but saw nothing. The furrier boats were, in all likelihood, hundreds of miles away by now. He had assumed this to be the case, but seeing the empty water made it more real.

Kana crossed over to the other side—the side facing north, where they once lived. He stared over the expanse of the old seabed they had crossed to reach the citadel. For several minutes, he watched for movement but saw none. Then he looked up at the cliffs. For a moment, he thought he saw a flicker of motion, but it was too far away to be certain. The seabed itself was vacant and still.

Finally, he walked to the southeast corner of the island. From here he could see Shiprock Point and the mouth of the Coil. This was the route they intended to take to the fishing depot. Immediately, he saw that the way would be difficult, if not impossible. The seabed here was uneven—plunging downward into steep canyons and rising into jagged peaks. It would be better to travel overland . . . but that meant returning to the island. *How will I break the news to Line? Because I'm sure he's going to love hearing this.*

Kana returned to the glacier-scrubbed rock that disguised

the spiral staircase. However, instead of descending, he sat down. Kana stared at his boots. For a second, he imagined Line and Marin watching him, witnessing what he was about to do. He shuddered at the thought, and forced it from his mind.

Slowly and methodically, he undid his laces. He paused for a moment, as if afraid to remove the boots. Part of him wanted to pretend it wasn't happening, but he'd been doing that for months now. All the clues had been there: his vision returning, the nightmares, the headaches, the nausea, even his newfound strength and endurance. He had been in denial. No more.

Gritting his teeth, Kana pulled his pants up to his knees and yanked off the boots. His feet, if you could even call them that anymore, were a bloody mess. Five long, curling, pointy talons had replaced his toenails. He'd also grown a sixth talon, which protruded from the back of his ankle, just above the top of his boot. Wearing boots had constricted his feet, forcing his talons into his own flesh. The skin covering his feet had turned reptilian—dark green and covered with scales—except for those places where wounds oozed dark red blood.

Kana stared blankly at his feet, trying to grasp the ugly reality of the situation. These talons had appeared and grown in a matter of hours. They hadn't been there when he bathed in the mayor's pool. As soon as the sun disappeared beneath the horizon, his metamorphosis had accelerated sharply. Kana ran his hands along the calf of each leg. The muscles bulged. They seemed about twice as big as normal—and the skin here was tightening, shifting into moist scales.

He wouldn't be able to hide this from Marin and Line much longer. A tingling sensation was spreading across his face and ears. He touched this area gingerly with his fingers; it seemed no different. Still, it was probably only a matter of time before the rest of his body began to transform.

Transform into what?

Very carefully, he stepped to the edge of the island and stared at the rocks below. It was a long way down, several hundred feet, and if he fell he would certainly break his back on the rocks. Normally, he would be afraid even to stand this close to the edge, but now he felt no sense of vertigo. The fear was gone, replaced by something totally different, almost primal— an animal instinct. He stared down the sheer vertical wall of the citadel and *knew* that he could walk on it. Kana suppressed a momentary doubt, stepped off the edge, and used his talons to grip the outside wall. He took a tentative step down, bobbled, lost his footing, and began to slip. He steadied himself by grabbing the wall with his hands, then climbed back onto the island.

Once he regained his composure, he tried again, but this time he went more slowly. He swung his legs over the precipice and tested the grip of his talons against the stone. Carefully, he began to climb down the sheer wall. He relied mainly on his feet—both to bear his weight and to maintain his grip— but he also used his fingers to keep himself flush. It was easier than he thought—and it was certainly easier than the climbing he had done before.

Kana climbed back to the top of the citadel and stared at his island home. He caught a scent wafting up from the forest—and knew instantly that it was the fetid, musky smell of a warm-blooded animal. He craved this nourishment so powerfully that it frightened him. It felt like a force pushing up from his stomach and muscling into his throat. Kana wanted to feel disgusted with himself. He wanted to cringe in horror at what he was becoming because, as unnerving as that would be, it would still mean that all of these changes—the talons, the scales, and his new appetites—were part of some foreign bug that had somehow infected him. But that wasn't how he felt at all. This thing that had taken hold of him was emerging from within—as if it had been there all along.

It felt *right*.

The idea that he was Kana, a shy, weak boy from Bliss, seemed like a distant memory, even an illusion. He was becoming someone else, or *something* else. And as he grappled with this, he understood what he had to do in the coming days—and what this meant for Marin and Line.

Kana gritted his teeth and forced his boots back on. He could feel new wounds opening, but he ignored the pain. Marin and Line couldn't know about this. Not yet, anyhow. His priority was to make it to the Coil and to get them on a boat and away from Bliss. It didn't matter that he hadn't seen movement on the seabed. The creatures would be here soon.

Of this, he was certain.

CHAPTER 35

MARIN HAD NEVER BEEN GOOD AT WAITING. AS SHE paced to the far end of the chapel, she came upon a narrow doorway that she hadn't noticed before. It opened into a stairwell that spiraled into the darkened depths below.

"There's a set of back stairs here," announced Marin. She looked up at Line, who was sitting on a bed of crumbling stone. "Maybe I should check them out."

Line shook his head. "Bad idea."

"I won't go far," said Marin.

He stood up and joined her at the doorway. They stared into the darkness below. "It doesn't look promising," he said. "Just wait here—Kana will be back soon."

"Maybe there's a supply room down there."

Line raised an eyebrow. "Doubtful. But if you have to go, we should do it together."

Marin peered into the stairwell, then turned back to Line. "I want to go," she said. "I can't just sit here."

Line placed his hand on her shoulder. "Wouldn't you rather stay? We can play spin the skull and take turns doing dares and telling embarrassing stories."

Marin smiled and brushed the curls away from his eyes.

"You're right," said Line, nodding. "We don't have any whole skulls—maybe a nice femur?"

"You're a sick boy," said Marin. She put a hand to his forehead. He didn't feel feverish, which was a relief. "I guess you haven't lost your sense of humor."

"Soon," said Line. "That'll happen when the hypothermia sets in."

Marin gave Line the candle. "I'm going to have a quick look at those stairs, okay?" She pushed away from him gently.

"You should take the candle," he replied, grabbing her arm as if he didn't want to let her go.

Marin shook her head.

"It's our only one," she said. "At least until we find the one I dropped. Don't worry—I'll be within shouting distance."

"Wait a second," he replied.

Line picked up a piece of sodden wood. He wrapped several strands of dried seaweed around it, and thrust the makeshift torch toward the candle. It smoked terribly, but it kept a tiny flame going.

He handed it to Marin.

"Be quick," he said. "I don't think this torch will last long."

Marin walked back to the doorway and proceeded down the stairs. She descended slowly, testing each step to make sure it would hold. Loose pebbles and sand shifted under her feet.

Water dripped steadily from somewhere nearby, and the walls were cold and slick.

After twenty feet or so, Marin stopped. She could see very little, even with the faint torch. Her heart was beating so quickly that she felt her ears throb. The sound of dripping water had grown louder, although its location had shifted. Now it sounded like it was below her.

"Marin? Everything all right?" Line's voice sounded distant.

"I'm here," she shouted back. "I'll be back soon."

In the silence that followed, the dripping water sounded louder and closer, as if it were moving toward her. Marin extended her hand in the direction of the noise and felt the hard, cold surface of a wall that abruptly ended in a corner. She moved closer to investigate and realized she had come upon another staircase. It was smaller and more narrow. *Does it go all the way down to the sea?* Maybe it led to a storage room with supplies. Doubtful, but worth checking.

Marin turned to descend the smaller staircase. Droplets of water began to fall on her. The torch fizzled and went out. The darkness was total, but it didn't matter. She knew how to get back, even in the dark. She dropped the torch and tiptoed down several steps, pausing frequently to feel the walls. They were wet but not crumbly.

Marin forced herself to keep going. She placed her hand only inches from her face—but she couldn't even see that. The dripping water grew louder. Now it sounded almost like a stream. The air turned pungent and moldy. Her throat tickled. And then the staircase ended. Feeling with her hands, she discovered an iron gate that spanned the entire passageway. In the middle of the gate was a half-open door, which screeched terribly as she swung it open.

Marin stepped through the gate and stood on the other side. She knew she should return to Line. It was useless to be down here in the absolute darkness. And yet she lingered, trying to imagine what this space could be. A vast storehouse, or a passageway, or a basement, or . . . It was tantalizing.

She took a step forward and realized that the sound of water had stopped. *When had it stopped?* She couldn't remember. A sudden unease crawled up her spine, and she retreated back through the gate.

"Yes—you should leave now."

Marin whirled around. The voice—soft, a little raspy, and strangely accented—drifted toward her from somewhere in that space. It was a woman's voice, but unrecognizable to Marin. She felt rooted in place, as if heavy weights were strapped to her legs.

"In the forest, many things are waking—and they want you gone. Do you understand?"

It took Marin several seconds to comprehend these words. She felt as if she were underwater.

"Go back and follow the stream through a gully. Take the trail past the old walls. Then the forest trail beyond the white stone arch. Do you know it?"

Marin nodded.

"You will find the river—and a cave. Inside is a sea vessel. Take it and leave."

"Who are you?" Marin asked. She was finding it hard to speak. "Do you mean the fishing depot?" Her voice wavered, despite her conscious effort to control it.

"Quiet."

Water began to drip again, but there was something else—another noise, a shuffling of rocks and gravel on a nearby surface.

"*Go*," said the voice. "They have your scent—and they are coming for you."

CHAPTER 36

UP ABOVE IN THE CHAPEL, LINE SAT QUIETLY. HE RUBBED his temples in short, staccato movements. The pressure felt good. At the same time, he closed his eyes so tightly that he could feel his facial muscles ache from the effort. When he finally relaxed, he thought—for the briefest of moments—that he heard Francis's voice, thin and faint in the distance.

"Francis?" he called out. It was crazy to think that his brother might be here, but he couldn't help himself. "Francis?"

Line pictured his brother huddled in a ball, whimpering himself to sleep—just like he'd done after their mother died.

Stop. This is not useful. Line stood up and shook his head violently. Then he wiggled his legs, trying to loosen his calves and quads. *Pull yourself together.*

It was the pain in his arm that brought him back. His ankle was feeling better, but his arm was worse. It was really hurting now—both throbbing *and* itching. He needed more lekar. The throbbing seemed to extend beyond the arm, radiating up into his shoulder. He felt the pulse in his neck. It was fast. *Too fast?* He wasn't sure.

Line looked up suddenly.

He thought he'd heard something far above. Line walked into the stairwell that led to the roof and called for Kana. No reply. He climbed the stairs for a minute or two, shouting Kana's name, but there was still no answer. He turned back. Kana was often like this—running off on his own for long stretches. He used to do it all the time when they foraged together. *Damn, Kana was good at finding mushrooms. Those eyes of his—they could spot anything in the darkness.* And lately, it was more than just his eyes that were remarkable. Line thought back to when Kana had pushed that door closed at the mayor's house. *Who knew he had that kind of strength?*

Line moved his hurt arm and yelped. Tentacles of pain ran up into his shoulder and neck. He looked down at the arm. *Gangrene.* For a moment, he visualized Palan's stump. He began to panic, just a little bit. There were tiny signs that something was wrong—his toes were starting to clench and sweat was gathering in the small of his back. *Easy now. Don't go there.*

To focus his mind somewhere else, Line grabbed the candle and walked methodically around the room. He climbed onto the stage at the room's far end and was examining the stone pulpit when he took a bad step and slipped. He landed on a pile of cold, wet seaweed, and his arm felt as if it had been stabbed with red-hot needles. Line cursed loudly. He was about to get back on his feet when he noticed a latch attached to the top of a narrow metal drawer that was built into the pulpit. The drawer was so unobtrusive that, under other circumstances, he never would have seen it.

At first it wouldn't open, and when it finally did, there was an audible sucking noise—the sound of an airtight seal break-ing. The edges of the drawer were lined with crude rubber inserts. Line had seen seals like this before. People in seaside towns often kept their most valuable papers in airtight drawers to protect against the dampness and humidity; his own mother had stored jewelry and documents in such a compartment. Line reached into the drawer and pulled out a lone piece of paper, which was so old and thin that it was almost translucent in the candlelight. It was a diagram of the citadel, showing the main staircase, the chapel, and the roof with its grasses and trees. It also showed the second stairwell—the one that Marin was now exploring—which appeared to go all the way down beneath the tower into a vast, cavernous basement.

The diagram was etched in faded black ink, but someone had used blue ink to scrawl three crude X's along the very bottom of the back stairwell. There was also an arrow that started on the bottom of the back stairs and pointed into the great basement. Line studied the diagram carefully but couldn't puzzle out what the X's or the arrow meant.

At that very moment, Kana returned, silently emerging from the shadows.

"About time," said Line. "Hey, I could use more of that lekar."

"Sure," said Kana. He reached into his pocket, pulled out the wooden container, and handed it to Line.

There was very little left. Line spread a dollop of the oint-ment onto his forearm. Although it stung the wound and surrounding tissue at first, the sting was soon reduced to a tingle, and then the whole arm went cool and numb. Line re-turned the container to Kana.

"Where's Marin?" asked Kana. His eyes were bright and his cheeks were flushed—even without eating, he looked healthier than Line and Marin. The candle threw an arc of light onto his muscled legs . . . and onto a dark, spreading blot on Kana's right boot.

"She went down those stairs to look around," Line said. "Did something happen to your foot? Is that *blood*?"

Kana looked down and lifted the toe of his boot. "I slipped. Lucky it's just a scrape."

Line tilted his head and looked into his friend's blue eyes. "You *are* lucky."

Kana glanced at the darkened doorway.

"She'll be back soon," said Line. "How were the Dwarf Oak Islands?"

Kana shook his head ruefully. "No rescue ships, but at least I didn't see anything heading here from the island." He noticed the paper in Line's hands. "What did you find?"

"A diagram of the basement. It was in an airtight drawer built into the pulpit," Line replied, handing Kana the paper. "Take a look."

Seconds later, something scurried across the chapel floor. It was a rat. Line and Kana watched it with curiosity. Very occasionally he had seen rats by the town docks, but there were very few in Bliss. A second rat emerged and then a third. They were coming from the hallway that Marin had entered. More rats came—at least a dozen.

"What's with the rats?" Line muttered. He looked back at the diagram Kana was holding, then glanced again at the three rusted gates, which were lying on the floor of the chapel. "Wait a minute," said Line. "The three X's on the diagram—those are for the three gates."

"Huh?"

"The people who holed up here—they were going to use them to block the way up."

Kana still looked confused.

"Look at the arrow," said Line, stabbing his finger at the map. "The arrow must be pointing at a way into the basement—a way in from the outside—and the people here were going to use these gates to seal off the tower. But they never did."

"Why not?" asked Kana, glancing over at the gates lying on the ground.

"Who knows why," said Line. "The point is, there's a way to get inside the citadel from the basement."

A wave of fear swept across Kana's face.

"Marin!" yelled Kana. He ran to the doorway. "MARIN!"

CHAPTER 37

MARIN HEARD KANA YELLING, BUT BY THAT POINT SHE already knew that something was coming for her—pushing, shoving, and grunting through the darkness. And it wasn't alone. She raced up the stairs, only dimly aware that she was scraping her body against the jagged stone walls. Down below, she could hear the sounds of deadly struggle. A fight was taking place—grunts, running, bodies slamming to the ground—and then a loud, distinct groan. No question—it was somebody's last breath. *Was it the woman?* Marin almost stopped, almost turned around, but her desire to flee was overpowering. She climbed until she collided with her brother.

She nearly fell back, but Kana grabbed her by the arms and pulled her toward him. "Marin! What's going on?"

"They're coming!" she said breathlessly. "GO!"

Marin pushed past him and kept racing up the stairs, Kana close behind. Moments later, they found Line, who'd heard enough to understand that they had to get out, and fast. Marin grabbed his hand, and the three of them dashed across the room. Marin slipped and fell, but sprang back to her feet, and they all continued down the main staircase.

Marin slowed her pace just enough to avoid another fall. There was a steady rumble of thunder in the distance, as if a whole series of storms was passing over, one after the other.

By the time they made it to the ground floor, they were out of breath, but they dared not stop to rest. Instead, they climbed to the crumbling arrow slit and pushed through. They crossed the bridge of stones, and soon they were back on the exposed seabed. Only there did they pause to catch their breath. Clouds had parted, and the moon was the color of undyed muslin.

"Are they behind us?" she gasped.

Kana shook his head.

Line shouldered the sack that contained their possessions. It was distressingly light. *The candles.* The two they had brought along were in the citadel. Now, the sack held several half-rotten apples, a box of wooden matches, some rope, and a flint. That was it.

Thunder sounded in the distance, directly above the island. It was very regular, sounding at ten-second intervals. The storm seemed to be sitting on the island. But above them, the sky was clear.

"What did you see down there?" asked Line, still panting. He was bent over, his hands pushing against his knees for support.

"I—I didn't see anything," said Marin. "But I heard them—a lot of them."

"How many?" pressed Line. He moved closer to her, assessing for injuries.

Marin shook her head. "I don't know . . . but there was a woman down there, too."

Kana looked back at the citadel. "A woman? What did she look like?"

"Don't know," said Marin. "It was too dark. But she said we should take the path by the stone arch."

Kana frowned. "You had a conversation with her?"

"Not really," said Marin. "But she said at the end of that path there'd be a cave with a sea vessel." Marin took in Kana and Line's expressions and then threw her hands up in the air. "I don't know what else to tell you—the point is, that's the same path you were talking about, isn't it, Line?"

Line visualized the map. "I think so—but why does it matter? I thought we agreed we're not going back into the woods."

Kana ground his foot into the damp sand and then placed a hand gently on his friend's shoulder. "We don't have a choice."

Line stared at Kana in disbelief. *"Why?"*

Kana gestured up toward the Dwarf Oak Islands. "When I was up there—on top—I got a good look around," he said. "There are far too many canyons for us to be able to make it across the seabed. It's dangerous."

Line shook his head vehemently. "More dangerous than going back in the woods? You're not serious, are you?"

"Either way, we can't stay here," said Marin, cutting off the argument. "We have to get away from the citadel."

Line grimaced. *She's right. We can't just stand around.* "Okay," said Line. "But we're not done talking about this."

They walked quickly across a slippery mix of sand, pebbles, seaweed, and mud, then paused to get their bearings. Marin pointed toward a shallow stream of freshwater that wound across the old seabed, toward the citadel—just as the voice described. The reflection of the rising moon on the water made it look like a serpent.

It was hard scrambling over rocks to the stream, and at times, they had to crawl. Eventually, after what felt like hours, they reached the cliffs. Here, the stream continued inland, along the floor of a tight gully that cut into the cliffs.

Marin pointed up the gully and no one argued. It had been several hours since they left the citadel, and there was no sign that they were being followed. Once the fear faded, all their strength seemed to drain with it. Line, in particular, looked haggard. His face was flushed, his forehead covered with sweat, and his eyes burning.

"It looks like you have a fever," Marin said to Line. She laid the back of her hand on his neck and was shocked to feel how much heat was rising from his skin. Sometimes, particularly tenacious infections needed massive doses of lekar. *Is that what Line needs?* She glanced at Kana and saw the worry on his face.

For his part, Line was oblivious to their concern. He was focused only on each breath and each step.

"I'm fine," he said. "Let's just find some shelter."

They formed a line and Kana took the lead as they entered the gully. The path was the stream itself, and they had to walk in it, against the current. Within seconds, they were soaked to the knee. The rain had created dozens of small waterfalls that poured down on both sides and drenched the path they were walking along so that the stream underfoot became bigger and stronger. They were engulfed by mist and the sound of cascading water. The path narrowed.

"Tell me more about the voice," whispered Line as they splashed forward.

Marin described her encounter in the basement of the citadel with as much detail as she could remember. When she was finished, Line shook his head. "That's strange," he said as he continued to splash upstream.

"What's strange?"

"Just that, when I was down in the pit, I thought I saw someone. I was kind of out of it, but I could have sworn it was a woman."

Kana's mouth opened slightly, revealing his surprise. *So all three of us have met her. I'm not crazy. She's real.*

"This woman," said Kana. "Tell me again what she said about the boat."

Marin brushed droplets of frigid water from her face. "That it was in a cave," she said with a sigh. "And she didn't call it a boat—she called it a *sea vessel*. If it's a sea vessel, it could cross open water. That's better than what we'd find at the fishing depot. Right?"

"I've been on the Coil dozens of times," said Line. He slowed his pace to look at Marin, whom he could barely see through the darkness. "I've *never* seen any caves."

"But you have seen the hut with the fishing boat," replied Marin. She grabbed his hand, clasping his cold, clammy fingers. "And if she's wrong, we can still find it. The path will take us to the Coil—so we have both options. Right?"

"I guess," replied Line. Then he stumbled again and, this time, fell to his knees.

Marin and Kana helped him up. Line's skin was clammy now, and his teeth chattered. Marin turned to Kana. "We've got to rest soon," she said. "He's getting worse."

CHAPTER 38

THE GULLY WIDENED ENOUGH FOR THEM TO AVOID
walking through the ice-cold stream. Thanks to their knee-
high boots, their feet were relatively dry, but that wasn't
enough to keep out the cold. The ground ahead was filled with
pebbles and sand, and their walking became easier. After several minutes, the gully curved and they came upon a low-slung
overhang of rock, which formed a shallow cave.

They crawled underneath the overhang and collapsed onto
a floor of sand, which was remarkably dry. Marin sidled up to
Line and placed her hand on his forehead. "You're burning up,"
she said. "How do you feel?"

Line groaned and closed his eyes.

"Kana, I can't see a thing," said Marin. "I need you to look
at Line's arm."

Kana maneuvered closer to Line. "I can see enough."

"And?"

"It doesn't look good," said Kana. He exhaled heavily.

"How bad?"

"The arm is totally swollen, it's covered with blisters, and there's a lot of yellow pus," said Kana.

Marin was acutely aware of the sinking feeling in her stomach. "Do you think it's gangrene?" *If Line is that sick, how can we possibly get off the island?*

"I don't know," said Kana. "But we need to use all the lekar we have left. He should eat some, too. It'll help." Very gingerly, Kana slathered the ointment on Line's wound. Line winced. "Sit up," said Kana softly. "You've got to eat some." After some coaxing, Line sat up and swallowed the last of the lekar—about a teaspoonful.

Line lay back down, then raised his head. "Both of you should know," he said weakly. "If it comes time, I'll use the knife myself."

It took Marin a few seconds to register what he meant. Then she sucked in a sharp breath. "You'll be fine. Eating the lekar is going to help."

"Just saying . . . I'll do it myself," Line repeated. He closed his eyes. Marin and Kana watched his face soften as he fell asleep.

Marin rubbed her tired eyes. It was too much to comprehend. She turned to Kana. "How long will it take to work?"

"It should work right away, now that he's eaten it," said Kana. "But I scraped the container clean. There's nothing left."

"Will he need more?"

Kana looked away from his sister. He didn't want to give her false assurances, but he didn't want her panicking, either. "I don't know," he said finally. "Every person reacts differently. It healed my wound quickly—that's why I had so much left." He touched the scar on his face. There was just enough light for Marin to see him doing it.

"Can we find more?" asked Marin. Her voice sounded very far away.

"Doubtful," said Kana. "Line and I looked all the time, and we hardly found any. Let's just let him sleep for a few hours. That might be enough."

Marin shivered. It was very cold. Her mind felt slow and numb. She tried to settle in, but she couldn't seem to get comfortable. Eventually, she crept over to her brother's side.

"I can't even see you," she said, drawing closer.

"Careful," said Kana suddenly, jerking his leg away from his sister.

"Ow!" cried Marin. "Something just scraped me."

Kana froze. "Are you all right?" he asked, trying to keep his tone concerned but not alarmed. "What was it?"

"I don't know," she said. "But it's gone now." Marin leaned back against the wall of the cave and focused on her breathing.

"Are you sure you're fine?" Kana asked. He could hear her fidgeting in the darkness.

"I'm okay," said Marin.

Judging by his breathing, Line was in a deep sleep. Kana was genuinely worried for him. The jealousy he'd felt seemed so stupid now. So trivial. Line was very sick.

"Kana?" said Marin.

"Yes?"

"You know, Kana—I didn't want to leave this island," she said. "And now . . . now I'd give anything to be on the boats."

She paused. "Until I was in the citadel—in that stairwell, in the total darkness—I didn't really get how hard it was for you, not being able to see."

Kana dug his hands into the dry, cool sand. It felt soothing. "How could you?"

She lifted her head from the wall. "Were you dreading going to the desert?"

"A bit," he admitted.

"Because you'd be blind again? It won't be as bad as Bliss's years of noontime sun."

"I know," said Kana. "But I guess it wasn't just about being blind. There's something about this island . . . It just feels right. And I can't imagine the Desert Lands feeling that way."

Marin thought about this. "I get it," she replied. For a moment, she recalled climbing the cliffs with Line, when they discovered the hag. It felt like ages ago. "Really, I do get it."

No you don't, thought Kana. *And when do I tell you?* Kana stared at his feet. He could feel the pressure of his talons against the inside of his boots. It was growing more painful. Perhaps, if the forest was dark enough, he'd be able to take the boots off without anyone noticing.

"I can't get comfortable," said Marin. She was still fidgeting, wrapping her oilskin tightly around herself and then loosening it again. "My heart is just racing . . ."

"Marin?"

"Yes?"

"Do you remember when we were little—Dad would make me feed those sheep in the back pasture?"

"Yes," said Marin. She hadn't thought about it in a long time.

"I hated feeding those sheep," said Kana. "It was before I got my glasses, and I used to beg Father to—"

"Let me go with you," finished Marin.

"That's right," said Kana. "But he made me go by myself—to toughen me up, I guess." He paused before continuing. "It was awful. I couldn't see anything and I was terrified of getting turned around and wandering into the woods by accident. I remember I hid under your bed once, and you found me. Remember that?"

"I do," Marin replied softly.

"Do you remember what you told me?"

"Of course," she said, recalling his trembling shoulders and the way he'd gripped her hand so tight.

"Marin, it's just like that now, only I'm the one who can see. *I'll* be the lookout—for you and for Line."

Just then, Line groaned and shifted in his sleep.

Kana cursed under his breath. *It's inevitable. Line will need more lekar.*

"Marin, do you still have the knife—the one from the mayor's house?"

Marin sat up straight so fast that she nicked her head on a rock that jutted out from the cave wall. "Yes. Kana—you're not going to . . ."

"No," said Kana. "At least, not yet. Let him sleep."

CHAPTER 39

SEVERAL HOURS LATER, LINE'S FEVER BROKE. MARIN AND
Kana had been sleeping fitfully. There was a steady clamor of
thunder in the distance, which made it hard to remain asleep.
She didn't even realize that Line was awake—let alone feeling
better—until he spoke.

"It's really dark in here." Line said this casually, as if Night
was just a candle that had been blown out.

"Line!" said Marin excitedly. She crawled over to his side
and felt his forehead. It was cool now. "How's your arm?"

"Feels like I left it on a campfire overnight—but it's better."

"Kana, can you take a look at it?"

Kana crawled across the cool, dry sand. His waxed canvas
pants and wool sweater were caked in mud and dried bits of
seaweed. He brushed a lock of blond hair from his eyes, smear-
ing dirt across his pale face.

He studied Line's arm. "The swelling is down," he said.
"Now we just have to keep an eye on it."

"Finally some good news," said Marin, ruffling Line's hair.

A long roll of thunder came from outside the cave, followed

by another. There was something almost rhythmic to the sound.

After a reasonable amount of time had passed, Marin spoke up. "We should go," she said. "Line, are you up for walking?"

"I think so."

Marin crawled to the mouth of the cave. "It's not raining, and the moon is out," she announced. "Don't you find that weird?"

"Really?" said Kana. "Even with all that thunder . . ."

"It can't be thunder," said Line. He crawled from under the overhang and stood up straight next to the stream.

Marin and Kana joined him.

"There's no lightning," said Line. "Besides, thunder starts like a faraway rumble, then gets sharper—like a crack. Right? And like Marin said, it's not even raining."

He frowned. When he awoke from his feverish sleep, the thunder was the first thing he'd heard. It was steady, as if a great storm were drawing near but never arriving.

"What is it, then?" asked Kana.

"That's what I've been trying to figure out," replied Line. "The sound comes every ten seconds, right? It's almost like there's something intentional to it." He paused, uncertain whether he should continue. "Kana, remember back in the woods? Those slabs that were built into the side of the canyon?"

"Yeah?"

"What did they look like to you?" Line asked.

"I don't know," said Kana. He sighed and then rubbed his eyes savagely. "What do you think?"

"Doors," said Line. "They look like massive stone doors. There are lots of them—what if the thunder sound is them opening one by one?"

"Why would they be opening so regularly?" asked Marin, nuzzling her nose into her oilskin for warmth. "I mean, most doors just open at random, when people want to come or go."

"Maybe the doors only open at Nightfall," said Line. "They might open in sequence. Maybe it's all timed." He sighed heavily. "I have no idea. My point is, that's *not* thunder."

"We better go," said Kana, rising to his feet.

They left the cave and resumed their trek up the gully. As they splashed their way upstream, Line was tempted to insist that they return to the seabed, even though Marin seemed intent on following the woman's advice. *And we trust her why, exactly?* Line gritted his teeth but continued on.

After widening for several hundred feet, the gully narrowed again until it was nothing more than a tear in the cliffs. The tightness of the space was unnerving—a claustrophobe's nightmare—because the farther they went, the more the walls pressed in on them.

Kana led the way, with Marin and Line behind. They splashed through the stream, soaking themselves yet again. After about twenty minutes, the gully came to a dead end, enclosed by piles of stone boulders. Water poured down through crevices in the rocks and gathered in a deep black pool. The moon shone dully, as if there were several layers of translucent clouds obscuring its light. Nothing stirred. Marin walked silently to the pool and drank deeply. The water tasted sharp and fresh. It was a melancholy place—full of gurgling water but devoid of any other life. A mist of vapor hugged the dirt and swirled around their feet.

"So what now?" asked Line.

"We leave the gully and head for the white stone arch," said Marin. "She said it was just past the old walls."

"I'm having second thoughts," said Line. Going through that narrow part of the gully had crystallized his doubts. "We don't know anything about who was actually speaking to you. Why would we assume she's trying to help us?"

"I understand," said Marin. "But what's the alternative?"

"I'm just saying," said Line. "What if the voice you heard was one of the creatures?"

Marin shook her head. "If the creatures could speak, wouldn't they have said something at the mayor's house, when they were attacking us?"

"What did the voice sound like?" interjected Kana. "Did it sound like someone from Bliss?"

Marin thought back to the citadel. "No," she said. "But I had no trouble understanding it. At times her voice sounded harsh, but then it would suddenly go soft."

"She's spoken to me before," said Kana quietly, almost to himself. "I thought it was a dream."

"When?" asked Line. He lowered his head, trying to make eye contact with Kana.

"It doesn't matter," muttered Kana.

Line stood, suddenly alert. Something was up with Kana. *What isn't he telling us?* Line turned to Marin. "I have a bad feeling about this. Especially because she's telling us to go back into the forest. It could be—well—a death trap . . . don't you see that?"

Marin sighed. "Look, if you want to stay here, freezing to death and debating this—go right ahead. I'm in favor of finding a boat, and quickly. It's a risk, but it's also our best option." Her volume rose steadily until she was nearly shouting.

"Calm down," said Line. "We're just trying to think this through."

"We can't *think* our way off the island!" Marin snapped. Her sudden anger surprised her. She began walking around the pool of dark water, and hopped onto the nearby boulders. She found a narrow path leading away from the pool and into the meadow. "I'm going to find that arch. All right?"

This wasn't a question—it was a declaration. Marin punctuated her statement by jumping from a boulder onto the path. She walked on, and within seconds she was out of sight.

Kana stared after her. His face was paler and his jaw seemed more prominent than Line remembered. Line reached into his backpack, pulled out one of the last apples, and offered it to Kana.

Kana cringed and batted it roughly away with his hand.

"Kana!" said Line with shock, bending down to pick up the apple. *What's going on with him?*

"I don't want your apples," said Kana. His shoulders were hunched and tense, as if readying for a fight. "So don't shove them in my face."

"All right," said Line in a studiously even tone. "Do you want to tell me why you're angry?"

Kana glared at him, but then his features began to soften

and his shoulders relaxed. "I'm sorry," he said, shaking his head. "I'm . . . I'm . . . I'm just not myself."

Inwardly, Line felt a mounting sense of panic. They were all in terrible shape, physically and mentally. To make matters worse, their plan was going to pieces. The original plan had always been a long shot, but at least it was a *sensible* long shot, and one based on facts. There was a fishing depot on the Coil River. And it had a spare boat. This was certain. They had all agreed to go there, and this agreement had pushed them forward as a team. But now Marin had stomped off and Kana was having some sort of fit.

"Kana, you're not making sense," said Line. "What the hell is going on with you?"

Kana said nothing for a moment. At last, he spoke, and when he did, tears rolled down his cheeks and there was an unmistakable quiver in his voice. "Line, we've been friends for a long time, but I can't talk about it . . . not right now."

Kana took a step away from Line.

"Why not?" demanded Line. He watched Kana closely, searching for a clue in his body language, anything that might help him understand what was going on. Honestly, Line wanted to grab him and shake him. Instead, he waited.

"Listen," said Kana finally. "The two of you need to get off this island."

"Huh?" said Line. "You mean the three of us."

"Right," said Kana. And without another word, he started up the path after Marin.

CHAPTER 40

THEY WALKED SINGLE FILE ALONG THE NARROW PATH that hugged the cliff walls and meandered into open meadows. They went through thickets of waist-high undergrowth—hedgerows and bushes interspersed with prickly vines. Marin and Line were able to see fairly well here. Clouds dotted the sky, but the moon emitted enough light for them to discern the rough contours of the landscape.

It was easy enough for Kana to follow the trail, but he also followed the scent. He had first picked it up back in the gully, and it had been growing steadily stronger. It kindled a hunger that was so strong, he feared what he might do to satiate it. *Careful. Don't give yourself away. Not yet.* He thought about his outburst at Line. *Where did that come from?* It felt like he was losing control—of his body *and* his emotions. He needed to be the old Kana for just a little longer. *Get to the boat. That's the goal. The boat. Get there before the others wake.*

After an hour of steady walking, the rain returned. At first it was soft enough to ignore. Soon it increased in volume and power, and the raindrops themselves grew colder and colder until they changed into slush. The three of them were drenched and shivering, eyes fixed on the ground as they looked for obstacles that would trip them up. The meager consolation was that the rain washed away their footprints, and hopefully the smell of their bodies, which might make it easier to escape detection.

They stopped for a minute to regroup, crouching beneath some large glacial rocks. The rocks provided scant protection from the rain, but it was something. In front of them, the trail continued down a steep dip in the landscape. From their vantage point, it looked like a giant bowl depressed into the earth. Kana could see straight lines—walls—arranged in a grid. They were close.

He looked at Line and Marin. They were a sorry sight: bruised, cold, and hungry. Then something farther away caught his attention. He stood up. Marin started to rise as well, but Kana put out his hand to stop her.

"Wait," he said. He stared at the forest's edge, several hundred yards distant. After a long pause, he shook his head. "I guess it was nothing."

"You're sure?" asked Marin. "We shouldn't move until you're positive."

Kana continued to gaze into the woods, but nothing stirred. They continued slowly along the path, which led down toward the bottom of the bowl. The area here was more overgrown, with thick knots of twisted underbrush. Puddles of water and mud filled the path. Water dripped everywhere—from leaves, branches, and razor-sharp thorns. As the path made a final descent into the bowl, they came upon a fork. The main trail continued down, while a smaller path veered back up toward the cliffs and the old seabed.

Line stopped. "I'd rather go up than down into this mess," he shouted into the rain.

Marin nodded. She felt the same way but was reluctant to leave the main path. She looked at Kana. "What do you think?"

"The cemetery is down that way," he said, pointing into the bowl. "Those must be the old walls the woman was talking about. If we're following her instructions, then we have to go past the cemetery."

Marin turned to Line. "Are you okay with this?"

He shrugged wearily. "I guess I don't have a choice." Rain dripped all over his face—his chin, ears, even his eyebrows.

Within a few minutes, they arrived at the bottom of the bowl. Kana was right. The cemetery walls. They were set in an orderly grid, like a giant, sprawling maze that kept on going and going. Only certain sections were used as the cemetery; others were beginning to decay. Weathered but imposing porticos served as entrances to different parts of the grid.

"This is it," said Line grimly. He had last been here two years ago, at his mother's funeral. Those were the Evening years, with the sun low in the western sky. He remembered it vividly—the long shadows, the chill in the air, the sound of shovels scraping the earth, and the smell of burning incense. The vicar who gave the eulogy had carried a torch to shed light on her gravestone. Line remembered little of what the vicar had said. He had been focused almost entirely on Francis, who had sobbed unrelentingly.

Line carefully made his way through the dripping under-brush. He approached a portico that led into the grid, but stopped short of entering. Marin walked to where Line was standing. Despite the rain, she could still see the familiar con-tours of gravestones in a series of rows. She and Kana had been at the funeral, too. The entire town of Bliss had been there. She could still picture Line, wearing his black dress coat, holding his brother's hand. Her heart broke for him.

Kana joined them. He felt slightly faint, but he forced him-self to focus on the walls themselves. They were roughly twice the height of a grown man and thick, strong enough to support a hefty roof or to hold off an attack. And they certainly weren't the sort of stone structures built merely to enclose a graveyard.

"They use this place," said Kana softly.

Line frowned. "What do you mean?"

"We use this place during the Day and they use it at Night. It's a cycle. It's the same with the houses, the woods, everything."

Line stared at the gravestones. "But what would they want with this place? This is *our* graveyard."

Kana had a hunch, but he didn't dare say. Instead, he walked underneath the portico and approached the nearest wall. De-spite the rain, the scent was so strong, it made his head spin with hunger.

"I'll be right back," said Kana. He grabbed hold of the pebble-and moss-covered wall and began to climb. He had to see. Sec-onds later, he heard someone right behind him. It was Marin. She had that look of determination on her face. *I'm coming with you. I want to see, too.* Line remained where he was, staring at the gravestones.

Upon reaching the top, Marin and Kana looked down into the grid of stone walls. They formed square sections about twenty feet in length and width. The nearest sections were filled with gravestones. Nothing seemed unusual here. But something was happening in the more distant sections. They were filled with a milky liquid whose surface was bubbling, heaving, and undulating. Twice, Kana caught a glimpse of something humpbacked and fairly large breaking the surface. He could smell their fat and muscle. *What are they?* Food. That much was certain. And he couldn't put off eating. Not forever.

He glanced at Marin. *Does she know?* Sensing that he was looking at her, she turned to him.

She squinted and pointed to the distant sections of the grid. "Kana, what's in there?"

"I don't know," he said, struggling to keep his voice even in order to conceal the lie. "It's hard to tell."

CHAPTER 41

KANA APPROACHED THE EDGE OF THE WALL AND STARED at the creatures in the watery sections of the grid. He had their sour-ripe scent in his nostrils, and it took all of his self-control to stand on the wall and pretend to be revolted.

Luckily, Marin's attention was drawn by something else. She clutched his arm and pointed into the far distance, toward the forest. The rain had lessened and the moon had emerged. At the edge of the woods stood a stone archway.

"There it is," whispered Marin.

"Let's go," said Kana. "They'll be here soon enough."

They climbed down the wall to where Line was waiting for them. "What'd you see up there?"

"Graves," said Kana. "And beyond that, the grid was filled with water."

Line accepted this, in large part because of his eagerness to leave this place. They continued on the main path, heading toward the arch.

Heavy rains combined with the temperature drop had turned the path into a thick, muddy ramp. Pools of water lay everywhere, and around the edges Kana could see ice beginning to form. Fat worms wriggled from the earth. They were longer than usual, with divots and protrusions running along their segments.

They pressed on, with Kana in the lead. In places they had to claw their way up, sinking their fingers into the mud. As they emerged from the valley, Kana stopped so Line and Marin could catch their breath. It was still scrubland, a mixture of thorny bushes and windswept grass. The forest began a stone's throw away. The trees here were shrouded in vines.

"Get down!" hissed Kana.

They dropped into a crouch to avoid lying on the ground, which was covered with thorns.

"What is it?" whispered Marin.

"There," said Kana, pointing to several older trees growing on the hillside, no more than fifty feet away. They were small and scraggly, unprotected by the forest and therefore exposed to the constant wind from the cliffs. In the darkness it was impossible to see stationary objects, but movement was easier to track. Something was creeping through the trees, and as they watched, one movement became many. Several dozen tall, thin shapes were gliding down the hill, heading for the grid of stone walls.

"They're coming out of the woods," Line whispered. In a panic, he hugged the ground and felt the cold numbing his skin.

Kana grabbed Line's sweater and pulled. "Get up. We have to go," he whispered. Kana looked behind at Marin. She nodded.

They crept along the trail for several minutes, and began to run when they were safely away from the area. The trail curved back toward the cliffs, then turned again in the direction of the forest. Up ahead stood the arch. It was roughly twenty feet high and appeared to be made of a single piece of stone that had been carved into a perfect semicircle. It stood ominously at the very edge of the forest, a clear gateway into the woods beyond. They approached the arch, standing in its moon shadow, and eyed it warily. The trees beyond the arch parted and a narrow trail wound into the darkness.

Line peered into the forest and then looked back at the cliffs. "This doesn't make sense," he said.

Marin followed his gaze. "What do you mean?"

"The trail seems to head due north, away from the Coil, more into the center of the island."

Kana shook his head. "We don't know that," he said, sounding both patient and exasperated. "It's just the beginning of the trail."

Line's eyes flicked wildly to the left and right. "The point is—we start down that trail and we'll be walking into the thick of it." He held his injured arm out as if it were made of wood. "That's where those things are coming from."

"Line, we can't keep second-guessing ourselves," said Marin with a heavy sigh. "If the trail doesn't hit the Coil, we can always turn around."

Line squinted into the forest, willing himself to see even a little bit more. "This seems suicidal. We don't even have a candle."

Marin nodded at her brother. "Kana can see."

"But you and I will be blind," countered Line.

"So far, everything that woman has told us has been true,"

said Marin. "She said to follow the river, up the gully, past the walls, and through the arch. And there'll be a boat in that cave—I know it."

"Even if there *is* a boat, it won't do us any good without a sunstone," said Line. "I don't know the sky well enough to go by the stars. And with all this rain and the clouds . . ." He gestured up toward the sky but didn't bother to finish his thought.

"Let's get to the boat first," said Marin. "Then we can worry about the sunstone."

Line shifted his wounded arm—and instantly regretted it. The arm felt raw, as if the skin had been flayed off. His neck and shoulders ached, too, and pain radiated down his back.

"It matters," he said softly. "I'd rather die here—on this island—than out in the ocean, slowly, of thirst. Here, we can throw ourselves off the cliffs if we need to. At least it'll be our decision." He turned toward the vanished seabed.

"Line—NO!" Marin grabbed his good arm and drew close to him. "Why are you talking like that?"

"Don't you SEE?" he yelled. "Even if we make it through this forest and onto the boat, without a sunstone, we'll just be sailing aimlessly. It's not a plan—it's just a different way to die."

Marin bit her lip. *This is the moment,* she thought. *I can't stall any longer.*

"Line—listen—this is crazy," said Kana.

"No," said Line. He raised his good hand to cut off Kana. "I'm right—you know that. If I have to die, I want to control how and where."

"LINE!" yelled Marin. Line dropped his hand and turned

to her. "Line," she continued, more softly. "Listen! *We have the bloody sunstone!* I . . . have the bloody sunstone."

Kana and Line both leaned in slightly, staring. Marin reached into her pocket, pulled out the sunstone, and pressed it firmly into Line's palm. The sunstone was a small oval set in a perfectly circular gold pendant, with 360 small hash marks along the circumference—one mark for each of the degrees on a compass.

"I found it in my bag a few days after we got back from the woods and I was too embarrassed to say anything," said Marin. "I know—it looks really bad." She paused, and her voice became even softer. "But we have the sunstone now, so please—can we just go find the boat?"

Line and Kana stared at Marin in disbelief.

Line's face remained blank for several seconds, then his whole body began to tremble. "I went back into the woods looking for that sunstone!" he snarled. "I *abandoned my brother* for that sunstone. And you had it all along!" He balled his hands into fists, clenching them so hard, the knuckles turned white.

"I didn't want you to do that," said Marin. Tears filled her eyes and trickled down her cheeks. "I never asked you to."

"You said *nothing*!" He paused, looked around, and lowered his voice. "And all this time, I've been blaming myself!"

Kana put a hand on Line's shoulder. "We don't have time for this." He spoke slowly and calmly, taking care with each word. "I'm not defending Marin. I'm just saying we need to go. We have the sunstone. Now we just need to find the boat."

"Right," said Line. He took several deep breaths, as if to gather himself. Then he turned, spat violently on the ground, and began walking away from them into the forest.

Marin chased after Line and reached out to touch him, but he just turned and thrust the necklace back at her. "Take it. I don't want to be accused of losing it again."

His voice was so bitter—and in that instant, Marin wondered if things would ever be the same with them. She took the necklace and thrust it deep into the front pocket of her pants.

Together the three of them passed through the white stone archway and into the woods. The wind picked up—they could hear it whistling through the branches and gusting over the treetops. At ground level, however, all was still.

As he walked in furious silence, Line played over what had just happened. He should have trusted his memory of putting the necklace back in Marin's bag. He should never have gone into the woods looking for it. He should have boarded the furrier boats with everybody else, and he should—at this very moment—be sailing to the desert camp with Francis.

It was difficult to keep track of time while walking along the winding forest path. Line thought an hour had passed, then wondered if it was actually longer. His wounded arm was throbbing now.

Kana stopped walking and gestured for them to stop.

"What's wrong?" asked Marin.

"We're being followed," said Kana.

Line turned around. "Where?"

"It's not behind us. It's in front."

"What?" said Marin. She peered forward into the gloom. "How's it following us, then?"

"It's pacing us—matching our speed and staying out of sight," said Kana. "When we slow down, it slows down."

"What is *it*?" asked Line.

"I don't know," said Kana. "I can't tell." He looked at Line and Marin standing there, breathing in shallow gasps. They were exhausted and cold, and Line was grimacing in pain as he held his injured arm. He needed more lekar—that was obvious.

"I'm going to run up ahead," declared Kana. "You two stay here and rest."

Marin shook her head. "It's a bad idea to split up, especially since you're the only one who can see."

"I won't be gone long," said Kana. "We need to know what's ahead, and maybe I'll find the Coil." He nodded at Line's arm. "And we'll need more lekar before we go much farther—I want to look for some."

"You just want us to stand here, waiting for you?" asked Line. He was so tired that, unthinkingly, he began to lean against Marin, but then he remembered the sunstone and pulled away.

"The trees around here are huge," said Kana. "You can climb into the higher branches and rest until I come back."

"How is Line supposed to climb like that?" asked Marin, pointing to his bad arm. "It's crazy." They had come up with many different plans in the last forty-eight hours, but this one seemed to be the stupidest and most desperate.

"I can climb," said Line hotly. "That's *not* the point. The point is we'll be stuck here. Kana, what if something happens to you? What do we do then?"

"I won't be long," Kana said. "Besides, if there's trouble ahead, I don't want us to just stumble into it."

Marin placed a hand on Line's shoulder. "Can I have the vegetable sack?"

Line took the sack off his shoulder and handed it to her. She opened it, took out the small, rectangular flint, and gave it to Kana.

"Here," she said. "You don't need light, but you may need fire."

Kana nodded and took the flint.

"An hour," said Line. "No more."

"I know," Kana replied.

CHAPTER 42

KANA TOOK LEAPING STRIDES DOWN THE PATH, EACH one longer than the next, until it seemed as if his feet were barely touching the ground. He'd left his boots back down the trail, having taken them off while Marin and Line struggled noisily up a tree.

As he ran, Kana marveled at how much his reflexes had developed in mere hours. He knew where to step without even looking, as if he'd been sprinting through these dark woods all his life. The newly amplified sounds that poured into his ears—the sway of the branches, the rustle of pine needles, the chirping of bats—all fleshed out his sense of the forest. And above the din of the waking forest, he heard the creature just ahead. It was racing, moving quickly, and Kana was in pursuit.

Whatever he was chasing was the same thing, or woman, who had spoken to Marin back at the citadel. He was fairly confident about this. In fact, he suspected that *it* had been following him for a long time. Perhaps for weeks—long before the furrier boats had arrived. *It* had been there, lurking in the shadows, in his room, even. *It* had been waiting for him. *It* had been in his dreams, which, of course, weren't dreams or warnings that he was going mad. In fact, *it* had probably known what Kana really was long before Kana, himself, had.

At the moment, Kana was focused singularly on catching this thing. It wasn't a plan, per se. This was pure, hard-driving instinct. And he didn't fight it. He was giving in, and as he did, he could feel his former life as a weak, blind boy swirling away like water at the bottom of a drain.

Eventually, he came upon an opening in the forest. It looked as if a fire had killed a great stand of trees here and then quickly fizzled out. The remains of charred tree trunks were interspersed amid a sprawling field of waist-high grass. He could hear bats screeching from high in the surrounding forest. One thing above all was suddenly apparent to him: the creature had vanished. There was a chance that it had reacted to Kana's running by circling back and heading for Marin and Line. That was a possibility, but it seemed remote. The thing wasn't after Marin and Line. It was after him.

He took several deep breaths. The air seemed to alternate between warm and cold currents, reminding Kana of swimming in the ocean near shore. Even though he was deep in the woods, he knew he wasn't far from the sea, either. The Coil might be closer than expected. It might be very close.

When the trail entered the great clearing, it forked immediately. The main trail went back into the woods, climbing up steeply. The other fork, which was much fainter and clearly a side trail, headed across the clearing and down a gentle slope toward what seemed to be another meadow. For a moment, Kana was tempted to take the side trail and see where it led, but then he recalled what the voice had told Marin. To find the boat, they had to stick to the main trail.

The thought of the boat tugged at his consciousness, pulling him back to his old self—Kana, the boy with a family and a twin sister, the boy who was trying to escape the island. He had to find the boat. He had to find it for Marin and Line. For them. Because he would *not* be leaving this island.

He breathed in deeply, feeling the truth of this thought curl into his lungs. It felt good—and pure. For a long time, he had refused to acknowledge it. During all these long months of the town's preparation to leave, Kana had felt more torn than ever. To him, the forest was coming alive, and while everyone else complained about the growing dark, Kana felt more in his element than ever. He thought back to the moment on the Dwarf Oak Islands when he had finally surrendered to what he was becoming. *This is who I am. This is where I belong.*

Kana ran along the main trail, back into the woods, and up the steep slope. As he began to climb, the raucous squawk of far-off ravens broke the silence. Their shrill cries grew louder until it sounded as if they were right above him.

He arrived at the top of the hill and found himself at the edge of a bluff that dropped steeply into the forest below. There was water beyond those trees. He could smell it. He forced himself to picture Marin's face. *My sister is waiting for me,* he told himself. *How long ago did I leave them in the tree?* He didn't know. He'd lost track of time. *I have to go back*. He turned to go, but as he did, a loud crack came from the nearby trees. Startled, he looked up and heard a low-pitched growl. Kana reflexively stepped back several feet and fell into a mix of rocks and bushes, and in the next instant, he was tumbling down the bluff behind him. At first he tried to stop, but then he realized this was the fastest way to put distance between himself and whatever was up on that hill. He focused on controlling his slide and avoiding the trees that dotted the lower slope.

When he finally came to a rest, Kana was covered in mud. He looked back up the slope nervously—heart pounding. He saw no signs of movement. *What had growled? Is it still there?* Then he heard running water. It was close—very close. Kana jumped to his feet and soon came upon a fast-flowing but shallow stream. He splashed down the stream for several hundred yards, then knelt and drank his fill of the cold, refreshing water. He resumed walking, and eventually trees opened up and the stream merged with a wide, flowing river. It was the Coil—no question.

As he stood there, he remembered Marin in the gully, repeating the woman's words: *You will find the river—and a cave. Inside is a sea vessel.* "I found the river," he whispered, in a strange, hoarse voice that he hardly recognized as his own.

Just up ahead, another stream merged with the river. Here the water flowed over a series of flat rocks, which were streaked with red and black minerals, and gathered briefly in a deep pool. Kana walked over to the pool and surveyed the area. A clump of old, withered apple trees stood nearby. Bark peeled off the trees in ribbons.

A cold breeze flowed steadily through the trees. It smelled rich and musty, like handfuls of fertile soil thrown into the air. He saw a clump of tall zebra grass. Kana leaned in close. From this angle, he saw that the grass hid a wide, dark opening.

There it was—the cave.

CHAPTER 43

IT TOOK MARIN AND LINE SEVERAL MINUTES TO CLIMB the tree and settle into a comfortable perch. They were sitting above the canopy, which allowed them to see the moon and the stars. Silvery moonlight illuminated the landscape around them, which was an undulating terrain of treetops as far as the eye could see. Both Marin and Line had heard about the evil of the moon, and the madness that it caused, but it didn't seem especially frightening from where they sat. It looked beautiful, like a serene deity gazing down upon them. And everywhere else, the stars shimmered and twinkled in silence. It would've been a welcome rest, but for the fact that the cold made sitting there so uncomfortable.

They stared at the sky for a while, until at last Marin spoke.

"I never thought you'd go looking for the sunstone," she began.

Line looked at her blankly. He snorted and turned away. "Is that supposed to be an apology?"

"When I found it—"

"When you found it, you should have told me—right away,"

interrupted Line. "None of this was necessary. And for what? Why? Because you were too proud to say, *Sorry, actually, I do have my necklace after all.* And now look where we are." Line paused to let this sink in. He gestured toward the treetops with his good arm. "Marin . . . I don't even know what to say."

Marin shifted her position, trying to ease the aching in her legs. "You're right—I should have said something," she said finally.

"But you didn't," Line retorted. "You let me walk around for months thinking I had lost your family's heirloom. Of course I wanted to make it up to you." He paused and stared directly at her, his skin drawn tight against his cheeks. "I don't know what I was thinking."

Marin nodded and focused on a branch in front of her. The branch glistened, perhaps from the moonlight, perhaps from ice. She couldn't even look at Line.

"It seemed so stupid at the time," she said in a low voice. "I didn't know it would lead to . . . all this."

"I tried to find it because I wanted you to have that sunstone in the Desert Lands," said Line softly. "I wanted you to have it in the Cloister—when you were alone. I wanted you to think of me."

Marin stared at his face. He was so earnest—so sad. Suddenly she felt tears pricking her eyes.

"I should have known better—necklace or no necklace," said Line, his voice softening. He looked away at the distant clouds. He shook his head.

A minute passed, then two. Slowly, Marin reached out and

rested her hand on Line's shoulder. She expected him to shrug it off or push her away, but he didn't.

Eventually, they settled back into the tree and tried to rest. Whether it was warranted or not, it did feel safer up there—in no small part because the moon allowed them to actually see. Marin leaned back against the cold trunk.

Once, her eyes drooped and she caught herself just as she was beginning to slide off the tree. Momentarily panicked, Marin stood up on the branch. From this angle, she could see Line shivering. She reached over and touched his forehead. "Your fever," she said quietly. "It's coming back."

Line was curled up in a notch where two big branches joined. He brushed her hand away. "I'm fine."

"Line . . . ," began Marin. "You're sick—we should get down."

"No." Line shook his head. "I just need to close my eyes."

Marin looped a rope around the main trunk of the tree, and then around herself and Line. She drew the rope so that it was snug, but not too tight, then closed her eyes.

Sometime later, she bolted awake to the sound of Line cursing. He was sitting up, legs dangling over the branch, and peering downward.

"What happened?" she asked, trying to make out what he was looking at.

"The knife. *Damn*. It fell."

"What? That's our only knife."

"I know," snapped Line. He kicked his legs angrily. "It must have slipped out of my pocket."

"Maybe it's still on the branch. Look around."

"No—I heard it fall."

Marin was silent. Their only weapon was gone, and Kana still hadn't come back.

All around them the treetops trembled in the breeze. Wisps of fog and mist passed over them.

"I've got to go," said Line finally.

"Where?"

"To get the knife," he replied.

"What?" said Marin. She stared at him, incredulous. "That's crazy. You're sick. And what if you get lost?"

Line gripped the main trunk of the tree with his good hand. The sharpness of the bark helped clear his mind. "How could I possibly get lost?" he replied. "It's got to be sitting at the base of the tree."

"You have a fever and a bad arm!" said Marin.

"I know," said Line. "That's the point. I may need that knife . . ." He shifted his weight on the branch.

"Line—wait!"

But he had already swung off the branch and was heading down the tree, ignoring her frantic whispers. Marin peered down into the darkness below, wondering if she should follow.

She decided against it. They would only get in each other's way.

CHAPTER 44

THE CAVE OPENING WAS NARROW AND LOW, AND KANA
had to stoop to enter. As he ventured in deeper, however, the
walls flared out and the cave became large enough to stand
comfortably. Kana couldn't see the end, which tapered off
into absolute darkness. The ground was dry and pebbly, but a
nearby wall looked slick. He touched it, and his fingertips came
away wet. In the distance he heard a steady trickle of water.

He pressed forward carefully. The air felt close and thick,
but it didn't bother him—being in this enclosed space calmed
him down, made him feel more composed, more self-assured.
He reached out to touch a nearby wall outcropping. To his
surprise, it moved. He crouched down to examine it closer. It
wasn't a rock wall—it was canvas, expertly painted and cam-
ouflaged to look like part of the cave. He grabbed at it until he
found the edge, and flung the whole thing away. Underneath
sat a long concave shape made of wood. *The boat.* The hull was
made of smooth planks, and an elegant keel ran across the top
like a dorsal fin.

Kana took a deep breath. At last.

The boat was at least thirty feet long, likely much larger and sturdier than the canoe at the fishing outpost. The canvas was probably the sail, and underneath the hull he found some nautical equipment—including rigging, an anchor, and paddles. He wasn't an expert sailor himself, but Marin and Line would know how everything worked. It was, in fact, a sea vessel. It could handle open water. Line and Marin would have a chance, especially with the sunstone.

For a moment, Kana pictured them sailing off without him. He let the image settle in his mind. Then he imagined himself walking back into the woods, alone, surrounded by Night. It was sad to think of leaving Marin and his parents, but it seemed a divinely foretold plan. *This is when our lives diverge.*

Kana ran his palm across the smooth wooden hull. It felt warm, almost alive. He walked deeper into the cave and felt the ground turning cold and wet under his feet. A deep channel of icy water flowed along the cave floor. He stuck his hand into the water—it did not touch bottom—and brought it to his lips. The water tasted like rock and minerals, as if it came from the very bowels of the earth. Kana followed it for several feet until it plunged back under the rock. At some point, it probably joined up with the river. With a fresh water supply, someone could hole up in this cave for a long time.

He backtracked toward the entrance and found a collection of charred embers and bits of wood, the remains of a long-dead fire. From the looks of it, the cave had been unoccupied for many years. And then Kana came upon something wholly unexpected: a series of drawings that completely covered sections of the wall.

He moved to study them more closely. The drawings were incredibly lifelike. Closest to the entrance were tracings of boats racing across the ocean, full sailed, bows raised high in the waves. Kana could feel the movement just by looking at them. There was no doubt about what kind of ships they were—their yellowish, saffron-colored sails gave them away. They were furrier boats in formation, perhaps on the attack, perhaps fleeing. Fish seemed to jump out of the wall in desperate attempts to escape them.

Farther into the cave, the drawings focused on the nearby forest. Whoever drew these had done an exact rendering of the apple trees guarding the cave's mouth.

His eyes drifted across the apple trees and to a picture of two people standing close together, holding hands, their faces hidden in profile. They were gazing down at something that didn't appear in the painting. Kana wanted to keep looking around, but he knew that Marin and Line were waiting. Reluctantly, he forced himself to turn away and leave.

Kana retraced his steps. Outside the cave, several feet from the pool, was a long, rectangular mound of earth that he hadn't seen at first. A young cherry tree stood next to it, its limbs bare of leaves or fruit. The smaller branches were all encased in ice. Soon, the forest would be unrecognizable to Day-dwellers.

He had to hurry. Time was running out.

CHAPTER 45

EVER SO CAREFULLY, LINE CLIMBED DOWN THE TREE, limb by limb. It was tricky to do with one hand, but it was easier than the way up. Line knew his fever was back—the heat behind his eyes, the ache up his nose into his forehead, and the dull gnaw on his brain. It wasn't too bad, though. Not yet. But it was back and that was bad news. If Kana didn't find lekar, he would need to . . .

No.

That is not a helpful thought. Or is it?

There came a time when the need for truth trumped the value of denial. Because it *might* come to that. And if he had to cut off his arm—*there, I said it*—then he would need a way to stop the bleeding. He would need to cauterize the wound. He would need to do this with fire. He would need to apply the fire to his arm. Searing hot flames. And if—*when*—he blacked out, it would be Marin or Kana's turn to pick up the knife and finish the job.

Line shook his head. That was enough truth for the moment. It hadn't yet come to that. And it might not. Maybe Kana

250

would find the Coil. And since woodfern often grew near water, maybe he'd even find some lekar. Line wiped his sweaty brow. *Enough hoping.* Too much hope could make it harder to accept reality when the time came.

He needed to find that knife. *That* was useful. And so he descended the tree, branch by branch, until he reached the forest floor. Then he stopped and listened.

Nothing.

Not even a faraway chirp. The forest was still, though he sensed there was something more. Moonlight slanted down to the forest floor, creating crisscrossing shafts of light. Line knelt down and patted the ground around him. He just needed to find the knife, grab it, and get back up the tree. Simple. He rummaged through crinkly leaves, pine needles, dirt, and moss, but it wasn't there. It was cold enough for the ground to be covered with a very thin layer of frost. Even so, he felt hot and half expected to see steam rising off of his body.

He widened his search. He crawled forward two paces, and then two paces to his left and right, and repeated this on the other side of the tree.

Line searched for several minutes—pausing occasionally to listen—but came up empty. The wind began to blow, making leaves flutter and branches sway overhead, and allowing moonlight to pierce the canopy. Something gleamed on the forest floor. It was close, no more than twenty feet away, but far enough for him to get lost trying to find it. Line hesitated, then began crawling toward what he had seen.

Before long, he encountered a tree. Line felt around the trunk, trying to gauge its dimensions, and soon came upon an opening. He gave the hole a wide berth, not wanting to encounter what might live inside. As he crawled onward, he felt something hard underfoot. He reached down and grasped polished wood—the handle of the knife.

Line let out a sigh of relief and ran his finger across the flat side of the blade. It wasn't much—hardly the key to their salvation—but still, they needed that knife, and he had found it.

Crack.

Line froze. It was the sound of a branch breaking in the distance. It was a perfectly normal sound, but it wasn't *just* the sound of a branch breaking—it meant that something was here. Then he heard footsteps coming fast. No human being could possibly move with that kind of speed in the dark forest. It was something else. And it was headed this way.

Line's immediate impulse was to retreat into the tree, but that would just give away Marin's location. He turned to the tree next to him and climbed inside the hollow trunk. No other option.

It was just large enough. Cobwebs draped thickly across his face. Even after he wiped them away, he could feel torn-off strands stuck to his skin. He waited and listened—but heard nothing. A curious insect began crawling across his arm. He was about to crush it when something passed in front of the tree. Line felt the disturbance of heavy air and the slight scent of the creature. He held his breath.

The creature continued along, now only a stone's throw away from the tree with Marin in it. Line heard a faint scratching. It sounded like the creature was climbing. Maybe it was Marin's tree, maybe not.

Line couldn't take that chance. Especially now that he had the knife.

He stepped out of his hiding place, took a deep breath, and plunged toward the sound of the creature. Seconds later, he collided with it. Line yelped in agony as his bad arm banged into the creature's body, but he pressed on. The creature reeled backward and Line jumped after it. His hand grasped the creature's lower leg—which was cold and leathery—but he lost his grip when something sharp protruding from the thing's ankle cut into his shoulder. In a heartbeat, the creature was back on its feet. It flung itself at Line, knocked him over, pinned him down, and grabbed him by the neck. Line struggled madly but couldn't get loose.

Tears came to his eyes and his oxygen began to give out. Line wrenched his entire body in one powerful movement. It was enough. The creature fell to Line's side. Line sprang to his feet. Still holding the knife, he pinned the creature's chest with his knee. This was the moment. Line raised his knife for a killing blow.

"No! It's me!"

Line heard this only dimly, through the fog of his rage. Still, it was enough to make him pause with the blade suspended over the creature's body.

"LINE! NO!"

That cry broke through. It was Kana's voice. Keeping the knife in one hand, Line used his other hand to feel Kana's face. It *was* him. Slowly, he lowered the knife.

"You were about to—"

"I thought you were one of them," gasped Line.

"I know," said Kana, also panting for breath.

"I cut myself on your leg," said Line. His eyes widened. "Your leg. It's . . ."

Line reached down for Kana's leg. Although he felt Kana's boot, above that there was no mistaking the talon sticking out of Kana's ankle.

At first Line felt confused, unable to process this information. Then slowly, it came together. Kana's strength, his night vision, his taloned feet—they were all part of the same fact.

Kana was one of *them*.

"Don't tell her," said Kana. His voice was low but pleading. "Listen . . . I found the boat. I'll take you and Marin to it. And then you'll never see me again."

CHAPTER 46

KANA, MARIN, AND LINE WALKED THROUGH A SPARSELY treed stretch of forest. Moonlight washed the landscape, bathing everything in a milky light. They moved quickly, and for a while, none of them spoke.

As she walked, Marin strained her eyes to look for any signs of lekar. More than once, she fought off the temptation to stop and search more closely. Line might die if they didn't find lekar soon, but they could all die if they stopped to look for it.

"What kind of boat is it?" asked Marin finally. The silence had become oppressive and she wanted to know more about what, precisely, Kana had found.

"It looks like an old furrier's longboat," said Kana. His voice sounded strained.

Marin turned toward Line with a forced half smile.

"And you found the knife—well done!"

Neither Line nor Kana replied, but she saw them glance at each other. Clearly, something had happened between the two of them, but neither wanted to talk about it.

"How long was the boat?" asked Marin. She rubbed her face

and felt the cold on her nose and lips, then tightened the scarf around her neck, hoping to eke out a little more warmth.

Kana noted Marin's adjustments and curiously touched his own face. His skin wasn't cold at all—in fact, it felt warm. "I don't know—maybe thirty or forty feet," said Kana. "Big enough."

"Which is it—thirty or forty?" asked Line tensely. He was walking in the back of their procession, slightly hunched over and cradling his bad arm. "Ten feet of hull makes a big difference when crossing the open sea."

Kana glared at Line. "I don't know," he replied. "I didn't have a measuring stick with me."

"Does it matter?" asked Marin. "It's not like we have a choice of boats."

They continued walking in silence. Soon it began to rain and then the rain quickly turned to sleet. The pieces of sleet grew larger and harder, until they became pebble-size balls of solid ice. It stung their exposed skin, but it hurt even underneath their clothes. They bent down as if struggling under heavy loads.

"What's happening?" Marin asked. She was breathing heavily, trying to prevent panic from taking over. Every time she couldn't imagine it getting any worse, it did.

"I don't know," shouted Line. "Keep going. Stay under the trees."

And then, as quickly as it began, the sleet ended. It was exactly like a wave, rolling through, punishing in its power, then gone.

They pressed on and soon arrived at the large meadow that

had been cleared by a forest fire. Kana came upon the fork in the path. The main path turned back into the woods and climbed up a steep slope. On the far side of this slope was the cave. The other trail, which was fainter, cut through the meadow. Beyond the meadow, in the moonlight, was the distant glimmer of the seabed. They lingered on the edge of the meadow for a few seconds, in the shadows just outside the moonlight. Kana and Marin started up the main path, but halted when they realized Line had stopped walking.

"Line—let's go," called Kana. "We're close."

Line did not respond. His face was impassive, and he stood rigidly, almost at attention. "Tell me why you're headed back into the woods," he said.

"Because that's the way the trail goes," said Kana. He read Line's face and posture, and tensed. It was clear that the encounter at the base of the tree could not be ignored. Could he postpone the inevitable, until they reached the boat? *Doubtful*.

"The other path leads to the sea," said Line. His eyes narrowed as he peered at Kana. "Even I can tell that."

"I know," said Kana, trying to modulate his voice so that it was as reassuring as possible. It was probably too late to convince Line, but he had to try. "I almost went that way myself, but I'm telling you, the boat is up this trail. Please—Line—let's go. Now."

Line didn't move. "No," he said firmly.

Marin stepped forward. Somehow this had turned into a confrontation. *Why is Line doing this?* They couldn't afford to waste time. Not when Kana had found the boat and they were about to leave the island.

"Line," said Marin in a calm, direct voice. "We need to follow Kana."

Line ignored her. He drew himself up and confronted Kana. "I'll follow you, but first you have to *tell* her. I'm not going to pretend it didn't happen." His eyes blazed.

"Tell me what?" Marin demanded. "LINE?"

"Right now, the only thing to know is that I found the boat," said Kana. He put out his hand in a subconscious gesture to mollify Line. "Nothing else matters. Nothing."

Slowly Line pointed to his shoulder, which was spotted with fresh blood. "Why is my shoulder bleeding?" he asked. "You cut me—with your . . ." He jerked his head toward Kana. "Go on, tell her."

Kana's eyes were steady, but his lips and mouth twitched.

"We don't have time for this . . . ," said Marin.

"Kana," said Line. "No more secrets."

"I've had about enough of you," said Kana. He took a step toward Line and his hands curled into fists. A small tremor started at his jaw. They were separated by two feet, perhaps three. Marin took a step sideways and again inserted herself between them. Kana was scaring her—she'd never seen him like this.

"This is not happening!" said Marin fiercely. "Turn around, be quiet, and start walking up the hill."

"I'll go," said Line finally. "As soon as Kana shows you what he showed me."

Marin grabbed Line by the shoulder. "Will *somebody* tell me what's going on? Right now!"

"Fine!" said Kana, his voice trembling with anger. "I'm sick of this."

Kana sat on a nearby boulder and began unlacing his boots. It took him a while—they were made of thick leather that clung to his feet. Finally, Kana wedged them off, and his legs dangled freely, catching the glow of the moon. The three of them stared at his feet. They were streaked with blood, and had obviously grown too large for his boots. His talons were long and thick and curved. Protective ridges had formed above the bones in his feet. His previously thin ankles had expanded with sinew and muscle. Midway up the back of each ankle, a full-size talon emerged. It was like staring at the feet of an overgrown bird of prey.

Marin's gasped. She glanced over at Line, who was steely faced.

"Are you happy?" asked Kana. He stared at Line as he spit out the question.

Line's face was a mask. Kana had been a friend—that was true—but now, clearly, he was a threat.

Marin lifted her head and looked at her brother. Other things about him seemed suddenly different. *How did I not notice before?* His skin seemed rougher. He'd been scrawny his whole life, but now his shoulders and arms were strong. The muscles that connected his neck to his back were visible. *Even his ears look different—could they be larger than I remember?* Her mind raced, trying to put together when all these changes had occurred.

"I wanted to tell you," said Kana. He got up from the boulder and stepped toward Marin. "I know I should have told you, but you have to believe me about the boat. I wouldn't lie."

Marin backed up, away from the exposed meadow and deeper into the shadow of the trees. Her mind whirled with confusion. "I don't understand," she said. "What—? Who—?"

"Stop," interrupted Kana. "There's a boat. I promise. For the two of you."

Marin put her hand to her mouth. "The two of us . . . ," she whispered.

"Yes," said Kana. "You and Line."

"You're my brother," said Marin. "Why is this happening to you?"

Kana grimaced. He just wanted to get them on the boat. Right now, that was all that mattered. "I don't understand, either," he said. "But I know that you and Line have to leave the island."

"Not without you," said Marin. Tears were streaming down her face. She looked at his talons again. They were horrifying.

"You have to trust me," said Kana. He took another step toward Marin. Instinctively, she backed up again, tripping over an exposed tree root and falling. Kana went to help her, but Line quickly stepped between them, blocking Kana's way.

"Give her some space," said Line. He put his good hand firmly on Kana's shoulder. His intent was unmistakable. *You will not touch her.* All three were in the shadow of the trees, on rocky ground.

"Get your hand off of me," said Kana, pushing Line away.

Line shoved him back. Kana absorbed the blow easily and stood his ground. In a sudden whirl he grabbed Line's good arm and twisted it sharply, then flung him toward the meadow.

Line smashed into a tree stump and fell limply into the tall grass. Kana crossed the distance between them in a single jump and picked up Line by his shirt. Line writhed in front of Kana like a hooked fish. Blood trickled freely from a gash in Line's face.

"Get away from him!" Marin screamed as she tugged at Kana's elbow. "Stop!"

Kana glanced back at her, shrugged free of her grip, and returned his attention to Line. He brought Line's face forward so it was only inches from his own. Kana's free hand rose and folded slowly around Line's neck. Kana's mind was empty of everything but white-hot anger.

A moment later, excruciating pain blossomed across Kana's skull and radiated down his back. He dropped Line and toppled onto his knees. Groaning, he grabbed the back of his head. His hands came away slick with blood. He felt dizzy, and instinctively began to crawl. *Reach the trees.* It was an ancient order, coming from somewhere deep inside his subconscious brain. Bushes reared up around him, and he stopped, feeling the branches sheltering his head and back.

"KANA!"

He raised his head slowly. Above him stood Marin. She gripped a long, heavily knotted tree branch. Just ahead he sensed plunging terrain and the forest.

"Hurt him again and I'll hit you even harder," said Marin. "Do you understand?" Her voice cracked, but there was no mistaking the blaze in her eyes.

Kana rose slowly to standing. His lips moved, but it was several seconds before he managed to speak.

"Marin, I'm sorry," he whispered, reaching out for her with both hands. As he stared at Marin, he felt momentarily drawn back to his senses—to his old self. In the distance, he saw Line lying on the ground, face bloodied. Kana shuddered. *Did I really just do that?* "The boat . . ."

"Get away!" she shrieked, clutching the tree branch. Kana took a step closer. She pursed her lips tightly and raised the branch above her head.

Kana nodded wearily. His body teetered back and forth, as if buffeted by a fierce wind. His vision blurred and, for a moment, he saw the cave wall, alive with drawings. He reached out for them, tripped over a bush, and fell into the underbrush. The terrain here pitched down steeply. Kana clawed at the earth for purchase, but it did no good. He picked up speed and slid into the darkness below.

CHAPTER 47

MARIN STARED INTO THE FOREST, UNBLINKING, DIMLY conscious of an ache that blossomed up her arm. She looked down and with sudden horror dropped the branch she was holding. *What the hell just happened? What did I do? And where is my brother?* Clarity rushed back to her, and with it, a kind of wild remorse. Her mind flashed back to the time Kana fell into the canyon near the pond. In that moment, she feared that she had lost him forever. Now the same danger—and the same fear—seemed to have been realized.

"*Kana?*" she called.

No reply.

"*Kana? Please. Answer me.*"

Again, nothing.

"Marin," whispered Line. He was behind her, halfway sitting up, still in the meadow where Kana had thrown him. He seemed groggy but not seriously injured, even though the blood on his face made him look rather gruesome.

"I saw him tumble down that slope into the woods," said

Marin, frantically pointing into the forest. "I don't know where he is."

Line hesitated for several seconds. "What do you mean?" he asked. He spoke slowly and seemed disoriented. "Where . . . where did he go?"

"I don't know," said Marin, a tremor in her voice. "KANA! Come back!" Her voice was as loud as she dared. She looked around as if lost. "We have to find my brother," she whispered.

Why did it take me so long to realize that something was wrong? The clues had been there for months: his sudden strength, his ability to see in the dark, his loss of appetite, his nightmares, and so on. She had seen all of this, and yet she hadn't questioned any of it.

Suddenly, a massive tree limb fell nearby. Marin jumped. Then a second limb fell. It cracked deafeningly and seemed to explode as it hit the ground.

She ran into the meadow and helped Line to his feet. Another loud crack echoed through the forest. It was closer this time, and it sounded as if a tree canopy had just snapped in two.

"Something's coming," said Line. He turned toward the smaller side trail that cut through the meadow. This was the path that led away from the cave—the one that Kana warned them not to take.

Marin grabbed his arm. "Stop!" she whispered. "What about the cave and the boat? And Kana?"

"We need to—"

Suddenly, the forest exploded in noise. It was a mixture of animal grunts, branches tearing, and rocks smashing against each other—and it came from the main trail, the one leading to the cave. Line pulled on her arm, but he need not have bothered. Marin was already running down the side trail and across the meadow. The meadow sloped downward, which helped them run blindingly fast, but then it ended abruptly at a thick line of trees. Line cursed.

The side trail continued into the woods, and they had no choice but to keep following it. As they ran, the path grew even fainter. Branches stung their faces and arms. They tripped over roots but stayed upright. The side trail dipped and climbed but none of that mattered to Marin. She welcomed it all: the burn in her lungs, the painful tingling in her fingers, heat crawling up her neck and across her scalp. It was simple and primal. She ran until her legs buckled and she collapsed.

Then blackness.

Sometime later, she revived to the sound of her own gasps. Then she began to hear other noises—a strong wind, the creak of long-dead trees . . . and something else. It was a voice. Line's voice.

"Get up. MARIN. Get up."

She lifted her head. Dirt and pine needles clung to her lips. She wiped them away and rose unsteadily to her knees. Line helped her to stand.

"What happened?" she asked.

"I think you fainted," whispered Line.

"Where are—"

"Shhhh." Line stood up tall, straining to listen . . . or to see. They were standing in a copse of smaller trees, which allowed some moonlight to filter down to them. Shadows—of leaves and branches—danced across their frightened faces. Just

then, Line sensed a presence nearby. He whirled around and glimpsed movement—something powerful and slow-moving. He shoved Marin behind him.

The beast advanced. It seemed cautious, yet interested. Two dull yellow eyes blinked open. It stood as tall as a man, but had four legs, was as long as a horse, and had a wide, squat body. Instead of fur, its body was lined with interlocked black scales. Two tusks bordered a long, fleshy snout. At the tip of each tusk sat a cluster of foot-long spikes that looked like bouquets of daggers.

"The rat," Line whispered. He recognized the creature from the mounted heads he'd unpacked. But the creature on his wall was far smaller than the one before them. It also lacked the spikes that this one had on each tusk.

The creature moved toward them, sniffing the air and bobbing its head back and forth in a wide arc. Moonlight caught the tusks and spikes, making them shine. Its small eyes remained fixed on Line and Marin. *How good is its sight?* It was hard to tell.

"Is there a tree we can climb?" Line whispered.

Marin looked around. The trees were too small to hold them, and likely they'd be too short to provide any protection against the creature.

"Not nearby."

Line nodded as they slowly backed up. "Then we'll have to run."

"We did that already, and it followed us."

Marin wondered whether perhaps, finally, their luck had

run out. They would have to face this thing. It was the only option.

"Do you have the knife?" she asked, holding out her hand.

Line carefully extricated the knife from the sack. He'd wrapped it in vines and leaves to avoid getting cut.

"What are you going to do?" he asked.

"You'll see," she whispered. "Give it to me. The sack, too."

Line handed them over. Marin exhaled sharply.

"Line—I need you to run. It doesn't matter where. *Now.*"

Marin backed away quickly from Line and crouched to the ground. She had an idea. It was a trick that she and Kana had once used to catch a particularly ornery rooster with a burlap sack. It was the only thing she could think of.

Marin backed away, her movement catching the attention of the creature, but when Line began running, the creature forgot about Marin and followed Line through the woods. The giant rat moved awkwardly, and its flexible snout undulated as it used its tusks to destroy branches and smaller trees that had the temerity to be in its path.

Now it was Marin's turn.

She started after the rat. Timing was important, but being able to see was even more so. It had to be done quickly, while there was still moonlight. She followed them as quietly as possible. It wasn't difficult. The creature and Line made enough noise to drown out everything else.

She sped up until she was an arm's length away from the creature. At this point, her plan was pure improvisation. The creature was no rooster. It could not be stuffed into a burlap sack. It had a long, whiplike tail that trailed behind it, but thankfully it was only muscle and skin. Marin leapt onto its back and gripped the scales as the creature lunged from side to side, trying to rid itself of the sudden weight on its back. Marin was flung forward but hung on, the weight of her body centered on the creature's head. She could feel her back being lashed by the tail, and the snout arched up as her left hand released the scales and plunged the knife into the creature's eye, forcing it deep into the skull.

It hissed and yowled and bucked into the air. Marin lost her grip and landed heavily nearby. The creature's tusks whipped blindly from side to side. One of the tusks scraped across her back. Marin grimaced but was determined not to scream. She rose to her hands and knees and crawled away along the forest floor. The creature flopped onto its back and turned over again. It was writhing now, cutting nearby trees into shreds with its tusks. A mix of blood and foul-smelling yellow mist sprayed from its injured eye. Finally, the giant rat slumped to the ground and lay motionless.

After waiting a full minute, Line crawled over to the rat, pulled the knife from its eye, wiped the blade on the ground, and wedged it into his belt. He ran to Marin and helped her up.

"Are you okay?" he asked.

Marin nodded wearily. She looked at her arms, which were covered in the creature's blood. With a stifled cry, she wiped them against her jacket and pants, hunched over, and threw up.

Line put a hand on her back and waited. Several minutes later, she wiped her mouth, looked at Line, and nodded.

"Come on, then," he said. "Let's retrace our steps—we need to find the trail."

They set off quickly and came upon what appeared to be a trail. But after a few minutes, it faded away. They tried to return to where they killed the rat, but in the thick forest, there was no landmark to hold on to, nothing to point at with certainty and say *yes, we passed this place*.

Thin shavings of ice started falling from the sky. Unlike the sleet, these specks were so small that they seemed to float. Marin and Line had both seen hail during bad storms in the Afternoon years, but never this.

"I think it's *snow*," said Line, brushing the flakes off his brows and cheekbones.

"Yes," she replied. "Strange that it's so . . . peaceful." She shivered—and was reminded that they had to keep moving. "Do you have any idea where we are?"

Line looked around in a vain attempt to get his bearings. Darkness lay everywhere, a thick blanket that encircled them. They could still see a little—there was ambient light from the moon, light refracted from sky to cloud to forest—but details were wiped away. The forest closed in, blurring away distinctions, individual trees, trails.

"We need to get back to the meadow," said Marin. "To find Kana." She said these last words looking at the ground. *Does this even make sense?* Of course they needed Kana to show them where the boat was. And she clung to the hope that perhaps, somehow, Kana was fine—that it was all a mistake, a nightmarish hallucination. But that was wishful thinking.

She was suddenly aware of the sound of Line's breathing. She could feel his presence, and it was reassuring. At least she wasn't alone. Again her mind returned to Kana, who was alone, *left behind*, somewhere on the island. It didn't matter what made sense or what didn't make sense. There was only one right course of action. To find her brother. To find Kana.

Line stared into the labyrinth of trees. He touched Marin's face. It was cold, as cold as his. "I'm sorry, Marin," he said. "I don't know where we are. I think we're lost."

CHAPTER 48

KANA WOKE IN STAGES. AT FIRST, HE WAS AWARE ONLY of movement, a deliberate, rhythmic swaying of his body. His head pulsed with pain, a deep fatigue had settled in his limbs, and it was only with great effort that he was able to open his eyes and take in his surroundings. He was staring downward and the ground was moving.

In his state, it took him a while to realize that he was being carried over someone's shoulder. Kana opened his mouth and tried to yell. A tiny sputter came out instead. Immediately, something cold and leathery covered his mouth. The musty, humid smell of it. The same as in his dream. Kana struggled, but it did no good. The object covering his mouth was clenched like a vise, and slowly, Kana realized that it was a hand. Not a human hand, but a hand nonetheless. Then a voice spoke to him. It was harsh and guttural, though undeniably feminine. He recognized it almost at once.

"If you make noise—you will draw them to us," purred the voice.

Kana tried to reply, but his mouth was still gagged.

"I will set you down," said the voice, "but you mustn't make a sound."

The hand released his mouth. His body slid downward, and a moment later, he was resting with his back against the trunk of an enormous tree. He blinked, trying to take in the scene. He was in a part of the forest where the ground was carpeted in moss and the trees were spaced well apart. All around him, great shafts of timber rose up like the columns of a long-forgotten temple. Wisps of fog hung in the air, curled together, and drifted past.

At first, he did not see who had been carrying him. He felt certain that it was the woman from his dream, but he had not managed to get a look at her. As soon as she set him down, she seemed to vanish. But then a silhouette emerged from the fog-shrouded gloom. It moved quickly, fluidly. The figure had a delicate face, pointy ears, large feline eyes, and long, flowing red hair. She was dressed in plain, unornamented animal skins, but around her long neck she wore several tight copper necklaces. Her arms were muscular but elegant; her hands and fingers seemed longer than a normal person's. She was tall, at least six feet, and her legs were toned and lean. Her brown skin shimmered as if sprinkled with tiny shards of glass. The color seemed to change as they walked—getting lighter with the moon, darker without. Her feet—like his—were clawed and covered in scales. She was equal parts beautiful and frightening.

Kana was so startled when she first emerged from the fog that he lurched backward and smacked his head against the tree, triggering a fresh burst of pain. He put his hand to his head and felt the mix of sticky and fresh blood. He remembered it clearly now. Most of all, he remembered his sudden murderous rage. Would he really have killed Line if Marin hadn't intervened? He had never been that angry before. And yet, in the moment, it all felt so easy and right: the anger, the aggression, the violence.

"Your friends have left you," said the creature, as if she could read his thoughts. "Your chances are better without them."

"It's *you*," said Kana. These were his first words and they came out sounding strained. But he didn't need to elaborate. "You're the one. Before you spoke to Marin, you spoke to me." His voice cracked with fear. "You warned me to stay away from the woods."

"I did—and you didn't listen," said the creature flatly. She drew close to him in a blur of movement that left him no time to react. She was crouching now, just feet away. Her long, sinewy muscles twitched, as if tensing, but her large eyes—which were streaked with iridescent rays of amber—were as still and lifeless as two glass paperweights.

"Your friends won't last long," she said. "They smell powerfully of fear—it will bring out the hunters, especially the ones that like to play with their prey. That little rat chasing them is the least of their problems."

It took Kana a few seconds to understand what she was saying. But when he did, his eyes widened and he struggled to sit up. "I need to find them," he said. "I need to help . . ." But he didn't finish this thought because, all at once, he sensed the futility of it. *Help them how? Marin just hit me over the head—hit me because I had my hands around Line's throat.* It wasn't that he didn't *want* to help them. It was the realization that they were now probably running from him as much as anything else. And for good reason.

It was the sound of the knife that broke him away from his thoughts. Kana heard it being unsheathed and, an instant later, saw the long, curved blade. She tilted the knife toward him casually. He tried to retreat, but she had backed him into the trunk of a tree. "I took you to the cave," said the creature quietly, with her calm, glassy, unblinking eyes. "I tried." Then she thrust the blade toward him, pressing its tip against his throat.

"Don't," gasped Kana. He struggled to keep his neck still to avoid being cut. All the while, he tried to think. *Why is she doing this? Why now? Why wait until this moment?* He had to stall her. "Y-y-you were carrying me somewhere," he stammered. "You're still trying—to help me."

"Not so, child," said the creature. "I was looking for a place to bury you." As she said this, she pressed the blade more firmly against his throat, drawing a pinprick of blood. "It will be a mercy. I should have done this long ago."

"Wait," said Kana desperately. "I'll go with you to the cave."

The creature remained still, showing no indication that she had even heard him. Kana felt his hopes sink. Her eyes were so lifeless. "Please," said Kana. Tears welled in his eyes. His legs began to shake and he fought to keep still. "You don't want to do this. Or you would have done it in my bedroom—weeks ago."

The creature hesitated.

"That is true. I am weak." Her long fingers twitched fast as

274

insect wings, and suddenly the blade was back in the sheath that was buckled to her belt. "But know that I will kill you before I let the hunters see you."

Kana wiped the fresh blood from his throat. The creature bent down, tore a swath of moss from the earth, and rubbed it roughly against Kana's throat.

"To hide the scent," she said.

Kana let out a deep breath and began to think. He could not be surprised again—he wouldn't survive it. "How far are we from the cave?" he asked. He thought of the cave drawings, of the woman and man standing there. *Does she look like the woman on the wall?*

"It is very close." For a moment, she flicked her head to the right, moving it so quickly that it looked more like a muscle spasm than a gesture.

"What about my sister?" asked Kana.

"You have no sister," the creature replied. "But, of course, you know that already."

Kana began to say something, but she cut him off with a hiss.

"Whisper or keep your mouth shut!"

Kana gritted his teeth and let out a deep breath. "But how can I just leave them?"

"You must," she retorted. "And if you don't, you will die by their sides. You still have the scent of Day."

Kana slowly struggled to his feet. The creature took a step backward, giving him some space.

"How many of you are here?" whispered Kana.

"Thousands," replied the creature with the slightest of tremors in her voice.

"And they all live in our town?"

"There isn't enough room," replied the creature. "Our numbers have grown. Now only the hunters are allowed to live in the town. And it is ours now—not *yours*—or is this still confusing to you?"

"I understand," said Kana. He moved his hands to his face and massaged his temples with his fingers, as if to goad his brain to process everything that she had said. All around them now, snow was falling, covering the ground with a thin layer of white. Kana did not notice the cold, even though his feet were bare.

"You shouldn't be here," said the creature. "You should've left on the boats with the other Day-dwellers. That has always been the understanding."

"The understanding?"

"Yes, at sundown you leave the island. Everything must be left as you found it. This time, your people left later than usual. Even when we carved the markings on your door—our door—you stayed. You and that old man."

"You killed him," said Kana.

"Not me." Her eyes showed nothing, not a trace of thought or feeling.

"But one of the hunters?"

"Yes—and they will gladly do the same to your friends."

"And me?"

"To you," said the creature, "they will do much worse."

"Why? I'm one of y-you," he stammered, pleading at her with his eyes.

"You will *never* be one of us," replied the creature. She drew closer and narrowed her eyes. "Look at me and then look at yourself. Are we the same?"

What she said was true. Some of Kana's features were similar to hers—the fingers, the feet, the eyes—but overall, he looked more like Marin and Line. Kana felt hollow in his chest.

"But I'm still changing . . . ," began Kana.

"And so am I," she replied. "It happens with the rising of the moon. You may change a little more, but we'll never look the same. You cannot survive the Night."

Kana looked away. A deep feeling of loneliness came over him—heaviness, like a weight pulling him down to the bottom of a dark well. *I belong nowhere. And I never will.*

"So if I'm not one of you . . . and I'm not one of *them* . . . what am I?"

"Isn't it obvious?" she asked, and her voice seemed to falter.

Kana was about to ask what she meant, but the creature sharply jerked her head to the right and growled—a deep, full-throated growl—like an animal that sensed an imminent threat. It took a moment for Kana to see what she was growling at because, at first, he saw only wisps of swirling fog. But then he saw two suspicious eyes and the contours of a tall, muscular body.

It was another creature. It eyed Kana, grunted with surprise, and leapt instantly onto the trunk of a nearby tree. Its talons gripped the bark and it circled up the side as if the trunk were a spiral staircase. Then it vanished. Seconds later, the amber-eyed creature leapt onto the same tree.

She turned back to Kana.

"Follow me up the tree!" she barked. "I'll hunt him back to you." Then she grabbed her knife, pulled it from its sheath, and flung it toward Kana. Without thinking, he caught it by the handle as it whizzed past.

CHAPTER 49

THEY WERE COMPLETELY AND UTTERLY LOST. MARIN clasped Line's good hand and led him forward through the trackless forest. The interlocking of their fingers was the only scrap of comfort left to them. It was impossible to measure time, but Marin figured they'd been walking at least an hour since fighting off the rat. They climbed, descended, followed animal trails that petered out, but they were always in the forest, always surrounded by trees. Every so often, Marin would stop and press her hand to Line's burning forehead. The situation was bad—they both knew it—and it would only get worse.

Line, meanwhile, tried to ignore his fever and the raw throbbing in his hand. In fact, he tried to ignore everything and focus on Marin's hand in his, and their breath turning into mist as they exhaled. He dreamed of blankets, hats, gloves, a fire, and—most of all—light. He remembered the way the sun felt on his skin and the way it made him squint his eyes. He wanted only to see daylight again. He wanted to feel the warmth of the sun as he and Francis ran bare-chested on the beach.

It was Line who first heard the sound of water flowing. *Please,* he thought. *Please be the Coil.* They grasped each other's hand tighter and pushed toward the sound. Line became acutely aware of his loud, ragged breathing. *Can the things hear me? Are they nearby? And what of Kana?* For a moment, Line saw Kana's pale face, lurking in the shadows. Then he shivered. *What happened to Kana? And why isn't it happening to me and Marin?* One thing was clear: they had left Kana to die. Line could still recall the viselike grip of Kana's hands on his throat. *How could I not run?* And yet hadn't all this started because Kana had risked his own life for him, venturing back into the woods instead of boarding the boat? And now Line was running, abandoning him. *What kind of friend am I?*

Again, Line heard the sound of flowing water. It was growing louder. *The Coil. Let it be the Coil.*

The ground turned mushy and soft; trees gave way to bushes; and suddenly, open skies were above them. They had come upon a clearing filled with waist-high grass. A fast stream flowed through the middle of it, gleaming silver in the moonlight. Snow filled the air—softly but steadily, without remorse.

"The Coil," Line whispered. His lips were cracked, his hair was matted wetly to his skull, and he trembled uncontrollably. He opened his mouth, tried to speak, but started coughing instead. Marin wrapped an arm around him, waiting for the spasms to stop. In the moment, she was also keenly aware of the cold. They couldn't last much longer in these conditions. They had a few hours, at most, before hypothermia set in.

"You may be right," replied Marin. She squinted into the darkness. The ground was now white with snow and reflecting the moonlight. Marin could see the flowing water, but for some reason, it didn't give her confidence. "It looks awfully narrow to be the Coil."

"I—I—I need water," he said. "Just a few sips."

He pushed forward, but Marin pulled him back.

"*Stop*. Something isn't right." She listened intently and realized that she heard water flowing in *several* places—by the stream, but also nearby, almost at her feet.

Marin knelt on the ground, groping with her hands until she found a hole that was roughly two feet in diameter. She thrust an arm inside and felt only cold air. She scooped up a handful of dirt and flung it into the hole. It vanished, as if swallowed. Several seconds later, she heard a faint *thwack*. The drop must have been at least fifty feet.

"Another stream is flowing underground," she said, looking at Line. "If we had fallen into that hole . . ."

There's no point in finishing that thought.

"Stay here," said Marin. "I'll come back with water." Line collapsed into the snow-covered grass. Marin crawled toward the stream. Along the way, she had to maneuver around two more sinkholes. When she finally made it to the stream, she drank deeply, greedily. After she drank her fill, she looked around for something that would hold liquid.

Nearby, the trunk of a downed tree lay decomposing in the fast-flowing water. Marin grasped at it, and it came apart in her hands. She did, however, find a stub of a branch that was nearly intact. It wasn't large, perhaps six inches in diameter and a foot long, but it was hollow and didn't crumble to pieces. It would hold water as long as Marin plugged up the bottom end with her hand.

She filled it to the top and walked carefully around the sink-holes back to Line. He was still lying in the grass, and for a split second she was afraid he might have gone unconscious. But then she whispered his name, and a sound gurgled from his cracked lips. While holding the branch in one hand, Marin helped him sit upright. She carefully tipped the branch and dribbled water into his mouth.

After drinking, Line rested there, his eyes tightly closed. Marin sat by his side in silence.

Eventually, Line opened his eyes and peered at Marin.

"I'm not feeling very well," he said. It was a simple state-ment, but the way he delivered it brought tears to Marin's eyes. She looked away so he wouldn't see.

She bent close to his face. "You'll be fine," she whispered. "I'll get you more water."

Before he could say anything else, Marin took the hollow branch and returned to the stream. As she went, she visualized Line's pained face. It was coming soon—his arm and the knife. *I can't do it.* She shuddered. *Yes, I can. And I will.* Unless she found lekar first.

Back at the stream, Marin paused to splash water on her face. It was so comforting that she had to tear herself away to focus on the task at hand.

The moon lit up a broad area and she spent several minutes looking for the tiny woodfern plant: a cluster of soft, round leaves surrounding three thumblike, red-brown stems. Lekar. That was what she needed right now.

Marin ranged up and down the stream, at least twenty paces in either direction. She didn't find even a hint of woodfern. In the distance, she could hear Line coughing weakly and calling for her. Marin's heart broke. *What if he dies?* As that thought surfaced, she returned to what Line had said—his terrifying suggestion—that they simply throw themselves off a cliff. End it all, quickly. Anything would be better than this: *Kana gone, Line dying, me alone.*

The simplicity of this thought shook loose another. What if she just ran? *Get up, abandon Line, run toward the sinkhole. Leap. Headfirst. Fall. The End.*

Once in her mind, it was hard to release the seductiveness of the idea. She stood still and felt her muscles tense for the final sprint. But then her mind fought back, and images of Kana as a child, and climbing with Line, formed a bulwark against any further thoughts of suicide. *No. I will keep moving—always keep moving.*

Marin turned back to the stream and knelt to fill the hollow branch again. She began walking back toward Line. She was so focused on not spilling the water that her foot came down too close to the edge of a hole, which crumbled under her weight. She fell, and grabbed at the grass, pulling herself onto more solid ground. Her pulse pounded in her ears. She choked back a sob. Her branch had fallen, and seconds later, she heard a distant *plop* far below.

Marin buried her head in the grass. Her arms and legs trembled. She rubbed her face into the icy ground so hard that it scraped her cheeks. But the pain helped bring her back. She peered down into the sinkhole. A shaft of moonlight partially illuminated the distant water rushing by, along with the hollowed-out earthen walls dotted with rocks, roots, and tiny plants. As her eyes adjusted to the murky light within the sinkhole, she saw a recognizable clump of round leaves surrounding small, red-brown stems.

Woodfern.

It was about twenty feet down, nestled around a series of embedded, fist-size rocks made slick with the constantly trickling water. She wanted to throw herself into the hole, grabbing at the woodfern as she fell—such was her eagerness. But she had to be careful. She had to think this through. Getting in was easy—getting out would be much tougher.

She extended her legs in both directions, burying them into the tall tangled grasses around her. This anchored her—a little. She then leaned her shoulders, head, and arms farther into the sinkhole.

At ground level, the hole was only two feet wide, but it steadily expanded as it went down, so that—at the level of the woodfern—the walls were about five feet apart. Marin reached in and tugged experimentally at a rock embedded in the wall of the sinkhole. As soon she touched it, the rock came loose and tumbled down. Marin scanned the walls of the sinkhole again, until her eyes fell upon a network of stringy roots that looked like a spiderweb. Marin stretched a bit farther, leaning deeper and more precariously into the hole, to get a better look. The roots appeared to continue all the way down to the water.

Suddenly, she realized she hadn't heard Line in several minutes. She closed her eyes against the fear. *It doesn't matter now. I can't help him without lekar.*

Very carefully, Marin set her sack down on the ground beside her. She didn't want it dropping down the hole. Then she prepared herself. She rolled away from the sinkhole and rotated her body so that her feet entered first. She grabbed handfuls of the tangled grasses with her arms, bunching together as many as she could to lessen the weight on any one strand of the thick growth. She descended slowly, bracing her legs against the walls. Just as she was about to fully enter the hole, the walls widened. Her feet lost contact and swung freely. *I need to grab the roots. Now!*

She let go of the grass with one hand and reached frantically for a root just as she heard and felt the clump of grass—which she was still clinging to with her other hand—begin to tear. Her free hand grazed a patch of roots and clamped down, followed by the other hand, which captured a nearby web. The roots were just strong enough to hold her weight for a few seconds before tearing. They formed a kind of rope ladder that disintegrated soon after it was used. As she climbed down, Marin became aware of her breathing—it was fast and shallow, and it was proving difficult to get enough oxygen into her lungs. Her hands became sweaty, and her grip on the web of roots began to waver.

CHAPTER 50

SHE STRUCK FURIOUSLY AT THE WALL, TRYING TO FIND something solid. *Anything—a root, a rock, something that won't fall away.* With her left hand, she clung to a single clump of stringy roots, but she could feel them tearing. Marin reached out with her feet. Her left foot brushed something solid that felt like a large rock, maybe even a boulder. There was no time—she had to commit. With a deep breath, she shifted her weight to her left foot and stood on the rock. It held, and it was wide enough for her to stand on with both feet. In fact, she was soon able to crouch down and gingerly sit on the rock. The woodfern was just below, and she could almost touch it with her dangling feet.

Marin took off one of her sturdy leather boots, scooted to the edge of the rock, and extended down her bare foot as far as she could. She could feel her toes brushing the plants. Gently, she tore at them with her toes and, over the span of several minutes, methodically took as much as she could and crammed it into her pockets.

Marin laced up her boot and began to contemplate her exit

strategy. As she looked up at the snowy moonlight, one thing became clear—she couldn't return the same way she'd come. The stringy roots were all torn.

How do I get out? It's only twenty feet, but if there's nothing to hold me . . .

She sensed the fear coming back, worming its way into her limbs, into her brain. But she had lekar with her, and there was no way she would give in to that fear, not when she had the means to save Line's life. She forced herself to examine the sinkhole walls as methodically as possible. Then something caught her eye. To the right of the rock, she saw the nub of a root protruding from the earthen wall. This root was different from the others. It looked much thicker and stronger. This root was her way out.

She reached into her pants pocket and took out the copper box that her mother had given her—the one containing the scalpels. Using the corner of the box, she began chipping away at the dirt surrounding the root. The dirt came away easily, in chunks, revealing that the root continued up toward the ground, just as Marin had hoped it would. The root was sturdy and knobby, with dozens of smaller roots radiating deeper into the ground.

Marin continued to dig, chipping away at the earthen wall, following the root upward. Because the soil was so crumbly, it was easy to expose the root and shimmy up. After about twenty minutes, she had made her way almost back to the surface. When she extended her arms, her hands were about two feet away from the mouth of the sinkhole. And then the root changed course, and dove back down. Two feet. Grass hung over the edge. Thick grass. *Will it hold?* There was only one thing to do. Marin gathered her breath and lunged for the top of the hole.

She grabbed handfuls of the grass and yanked herself up. Wriggling her way forward, she didn't stop until her entire body was out of the sinkhole and resting on solid ground. She tried to control her frenetic breathing, but this was no time for rest. *Line.* She had to check on him.

Line was unconscious and wheezing faintly. Marin took a handful of the woodfern from her pockets. It was so caked with fungus that Marin could feel it coating her fingers. She crammed the whole handful into her mouth, chewing on the leaves and turning them into a soft, slimy poultice, which she then slathered onto Line's arm. It seemed like the only way to make an ointment.

Marin's hands were cold from the sinkhole, and she caressed his cheeks and forehead to wake him up. His eyelids moved but did not open. She took another handful of woodfern from her pocket and placed several of the leaves in Line's mouth.

"Lekar," she whispered. "Swallow it down. I'll get you water."

Line's jaw began to clench as he started chewing. Marin rushed back to the stream and returned with more water, cupped in her hands. For the next fifteen minutes, she ferried water to Line, and he drank greedily. His eyes were still closed, but the way his chest rose and fell gave Marin hope. Lekar worked fast.

Marin still had a great deal of it—in all likelihood, more than he would need.

She settled next to Line and tried to catch her breath. What they both needed now was rest. They huddled against each other for warmth. An hour passed, and the gently falling snow reminded Marin that they couldn't stay like this for long. They had to keep moving, as soon as Line could manage.

At some point, Marin decided to go to the stream for another drink, and when she returned, Line was sitting up. His eyes were open and it was clear that his fever had broken. He looked at her, shook his head, and chuckled softly to himself.

He reached out and squeezed her hand. "Thank you, Marin," he whispered.

She brought his hand to her lips and kissed it.

"Line," she said a few seconds later. "We need to get back to that meadow. He'll be waiting for us—I know it."

Line nodded, then pursed his lips, as if he wanted to speak but was holding back.

"What?"

"What do we do if he's not there?"

"He'll be there," said Marin flatly.

Line was unconvinced. It wasn't just a matter of whether Kana was there or not. The question was whether Kana would even *want* to go with them. The Kana they knew was gone, perhaps forever. It might be pointless, but Marin was right— they still had to try and find him.

Sometime later, Line felt strong enough to stagger forward. It was a good moment—he was feeling better, and the snow had stopped. They set off together at a slow pace, heading in a direction that he believed—and hoped—would lead back to the meadow where they had left Kana. Their path followed the stream, but it eventually disappeared underground. It was not the Coil. Marin and Line pressed on. The ground sloped upward and they began to climb. The trees grew taller and taller and soon they were back in the dark forest, making their way toward an unknown ridge.

When they reached it, the forest ended abruptly. They were on the cusp of a chasm and, far off in the distance, they could see a great clearing. For a moment, their hopes soared, because it seemed they had found their way back to the meadow. But it wasn't the case. Instead they saw moonlight reflecting off the surface of a pond.

Marin made the connection first. "This canyon . . . We've been here before." She pressed the heels of her hands into her eyes, as if to block out what she was seeing. "On the other side of the canyon. Me and you—and Kana. It's where we left the sunstone."

Line cursed softly and covered his mouth with his hand.

Marin looked into the canyon. Although she couldn't see the bottom, there were a series of perfectly rectangular openings along the walls. When they had been here last, the openings had been covered by stone slabs. Now those slabs had either fallen or somehow rolled away.

"You were right," she whispered, almost inaudibly. "They opened. They all opened."

It began to snow again and the canyon became a soft blur of white. Clouds gathered overhead while Marin and Line watched each other's faces fade into black as the moon vanished. A frigid wind picked up.

"I don't know what to do," said Marin, more to herself than to Line.

"Let's wait for the clouds to pass," Line said, taking Marin's hand in his. "It's not safe for us to walk without *some* moonlight."

Seconds later, they heard a loud crack—the sound of a branch being intentionally broken.

"Kana?!" Marin whispered.

Another loud crack, this time much closer. Marin flinched.

Line took the box of matches from the vegetable sack Marin was holding. He counted the matches—three left.

Grabbing one, he held it between his thumb and index finger and slid it sharply across the striking surface. It sputtered once, twice, and then died.

"Try another," said Marin.

"We only have two."

"It doesn't matter," she said. *"Do it."*

Line grabbed a second match and struck it. This one flared and then caught. The flame lit up his face and hands. It lit up Marin's face—she looked stricken with panic.

"Behind you," she whispered.

Line turned around so quickly that the motion blew out the flame. They were plunged back into darkness. He turned back toward Marin.

"What was it? What did you see?" he asked.

"Them."

Line fumbled with the last match. It flared to life. Line turned, more slowly this time. The tiny match threw off enough light to reveal dozens of shadowy figures, watching him quietly. They were only feet away, close enough for him to see their powerful chests rising with each breath. They towered over Line. Their faces were human in appearance, although the skin was mottled and gray. Their large, unblinking eyes reflected the tiny, quivering flame.

Line turned back to Marin. He could feel the fire crawling down the match. The heat was beginning to burn his fingertips.

"Marin—they're behind you, too," he whispered. "They're everywhere."

CHAPTER 51

KANA SAW THE CREATURE FOR JUST A SPLIT SECOND longer before she disappeared into the tree. He stared at the knife in his hand. The creature had told him to climb the tree. *I'll chase him back to you,* she had said. What he did next was more instinct than a decision—he simply leapt at the tree trunk. Without boots to constrict his feet, he felt his claws catch onto the bark and grab hold. It wasn't easy—he still wobbled—but he held on. He gripped the tree trunk lightly with his hands and began moving up the trunk.

Kana climbed slowly, one foot over the other, straight up. At first his leg muscles burned, but that soon faded and he moved faster. The upper trunk was covered in patches of ice, but it made no difference because Kana's talons pierced it easily, sinking deep into the bark. With every step, his movements became less awkward. The wind picked up as he neared the upper half of the tree. He looked down and saw that the ground had disappeared below the low-lying mist.

In the distance, Kana began to discern the sound of the two creatures as they moved across the treetops. He wanted to follow them, but it seemed impossible. The gap between the tree he was standing on and the branches of the nearest tree was at least twenty feet. Even if he *could* jump this distance—the outermost branches of the pine were thin and unlikely to hold his weight.

Kana knew what he wanted to do, but it seemed ridiculous. Still, he lowered himself into a crouch, held it for several seconds, then exhaled and exploded upward, springing off the tree with tremendous power and speed. He soared into the air. The pine loomed quickly. Kana overshot the branch he was aiming for and slammed into the actual trunk. At the last minute, he tried to cushion his impact with his arms, nearly impaling himself with the knife he was holding.

He gasped for air, but recovered quickly, flinging himself onto the next tree and then the next. With each movement, he became quicker and more adroit. There was a rhythm to it. He had to run lightly across the branches, leap across the gap, catch another branch or trunk, and then run again. By the time he became adept at this, however, he lost the two creatures. Kana came to a rest on a sturdy branch and took in his surroundings.

He was standing on one of the uppermost branches of a wick tree. It was older and taller than the one in Bliss, and it dominated the surrounding area. *Bliss.* A face flickered into his mind—a woman's face—and he struggled to place it. She was standing in a large room next to an old player piano. She had tan-colored skin and her arms were covered with strange markings. He knew her. And yet he couldn't say how exactly. Everything felt so foggy in his mind. He felt the way he sometimes did when he was drifting in and out of sleep—torn between two states of consciousness. "Your name is Kana," he whispered to himself. "You are from Bliss."

Suddenly, Kana was aware of the sound of feet jumping quickly across branches. Something was angling through the treetops toward him. *I'll hunt him back to you.* The two creatures were coming. Kana dropped into a crouch and waited. He heard a grunt and the rush of air. He held the knife tightly and prepared to thrust it. The branch that he was standing on shook violently; a darkened figure reached for him, its long fingers only inches from his face. But at the last minute, Kana heard a sickening crunch, and his would-be attacker fell from the branch and plummeted toward the ground.

Kana looked around, sensing the amber-eyed creature nearby. Then he saw her standing on the branch directly next to him. She had appeared as silently as a ghost.

"What happened?" he asked, keeping a tight hold on the knife.

"I got to him first," said the creature. She gestured to the ground below.

"He's dead?"

"Yes," she replied.

Kana remembered that other creature's surprise. The memory enraged him. He wanted to jump down and kill the creature himself.

"You are an abomination to us," the female creature continued. "The Day-dwellers would feel the same way if they knew what you are. Neither world can tolerate your presence." She spoke to him without emotion, as if these were ordinary and incontrovertible facts. "It is very simple. Go to the boat, and go on living."

Kana stared at her impassive face, trying to understand. "The boat—it's a furrier's boat, isn't it?" he asked. "It's one of the small boats that they lash to the side of their ships."

"If you say so," she replied. She was a full head taller than Kana, and she craned her neck downward to meet his eyes.

"What's it doing there—in that cave?"

"It will work on the sea—if that's what you're asking."

"That's not what I'm asking," replied Kana. His voice had become sharp. *She's toying with me.*

She sighed, as if in irritation. "There was a shipwreck and a man landed here in his lifeboat—many years ago. It happened some months before Dawn. Somehow, this man paddled up the river in the cold and darkness. He took refuge in that cave."

"About fourteen years ago?"

The amber-eyed creature stared at Kana.

"Yes."

Kana recalled his brief encounter with the furrier on the cliffs above the sea, just before everyone boarded the boats to leave the island. The man had been right. Kana *did* have the watery-blue eyes of the furriers. And his eyes had not changed with the rest of his body.

Kana exhaled and leaned against the trunk of the wick tree. "The man who was shipwrecked—he was my father."

She nodded.

"And the drawings on the wall of the cave?"

"His."

An image rose in Kana's mind. The rectangular mound with the apple tree.

"Is that *his* grave near the cave?"

"Yes."

Kana hesitated. He needed to know, but he was afraid of the answer.

"And my mother?" he asked, straining to keep a tremor out of his voice. He looked into her amber eyes, knowing the answer and daring her to tell the truth.

She looked away, toward the ground. "One of us."

"Who?" he pressed.

"A despicable woman," the creature replied. "She left you for dead at the edge of the woods. At Dawn, when you were still an infant."

"So how . . ."

"Two Day-dwellers found you on a rock, took you in, and cared for you," said the creature. She raised her hands in a gesture of impatience. "No more chattering. You must leave."

Kana ignored her command. *Day-dwellers*. That word let loose a torrent of other memories. *Other parents—from the Day.* An image appeared in his confused brain. Table Rock, by the edge of the woods, where his mother came each day to do her needlework. She always looked at him in a particular way when they were there, with a smile that surfaced almost as if she couldn't help it.

"And Marin?" he asked.

The creature shrugged indifferently. "An ordinary Day-dweller. Nothing more."

"There's something else," pressed Kana. "Why are you so scared that they'll find me?"

"Enough!" snapped the creature. "We must go—now."

"Where are Marin and Line?" demanded Kana, and as he spoke, he balanced on the tree branch and pointed the knife toward the creature's chest. The creature's eyes narrowed. She was stronger than Kana, no doubt about it, but all Kana had to do was thrust forward. He held the knife steady, without the slightest tremble. He would do it. And he readied himself for the thrust.

"Where are they?" Kana repeated.

"They are lost—and they have been found, by the hunters. As I said they would."

Kana's knife drew closer to her. "Where?"

"The canyon—our entrance to the underground." She nodded her head to the north. "That way. But it's too late to help them."

"I don't even know your name," said Kana.

She blinked, then looked away. "Soraya."

"Soraya," said Kana. "Thank you."

Kana made his next move so quickly and impulsively that he almost surprised himself. He tossed the knife toward Soraya, throwing her off balance as she reached for it. Then he dropped into a crouch and leapt spectacularly through the darkness, soaring through eddies of mist onto a faraway tree. He landed and jumped again—heading north.

He half expected Soraya to bring him down, but it didn't happen. Kana leapt from treetop to treetop, and soon he felt his mind emptying of words and thoughts. Action—reaction. That was all. He would not remember anything when thinking back on this particular moment. A powerful force welled up inside: pulsing, burning aggression.

Kana continued on through the treetops until the forest ended rather abruptly. He perched on the top of another wick tree, whose trunk was shrouded in a spiraling tangle of vines, and peered down into the darkened canyon below. It was at least three miles long, wide at both ends and narrowed dramatically in the center. Where the canyon was wide and open, Kana could see its walls clearly, along with the great stone doorways that were carved into these walls. He recognized the place immediately. He had passed close to it with Marin and Line when they were racing back to town to catch the furrier boats. At the time, Kana had felt something strange and mysterious about the place, and now he understood. This is where they slept, where they hibernated when the sun loomed high in the sky, and where they crawled out when the sun set and the ice began to form.

He heard very little, but felt motion and life below in the canyon, as if it were a cauldron of pent-up energy. He knew what he would find before he even saw it. And somewhere in the canyon below were Marin and Line. He was certain of it.

CHAPTER 52

MARIN OPENED HER EYES. AT FIRST THEY DIDN'T SEEM to work, so she blinked and tried again. And again. And again. Still she saw nothing—only a vast, empty, dreamlike darkness. In that moment, she was overcome with a deep, visceral longing for the Desert Lands. It was as if she remembered the place, from another life, and ached to return. She pined to feel the hot sun on her face and the warm sand beneath her feet. She imagined the caress of the dry winds, the taste of sweet dates in her mouth, and the sound of her mother's voice. That's what surprised her most of all. She had never missed her mother so fiercely in her life. Her mother had wanted nothing more than to bring Marin to the desert, and Marin had railed against her. *I didn't want to leave this island,* Marin thought. *And I got what I wanted.*

With effort, Marin tried to move. She opened her mouth and was reassured to taste something granular, bitter, and metallic—perhaps pebbles and dirt. Her body was working and she was alive. That was something. She rocked slightly back and forth. Her upper back and neck erupted in pain. She massaged the inflamed tendons. They were swollen and tight, and extremely tender. Nevertheless, the pain became tolerable as she grew accustomed to it. Like the pebbles and cold dirt, it told her she was alive. She was also warm. Wherever she was, the place was protected from the wind and the cold. This was, at the very least, something.

"Line," she whispered. *"Line."*

There was no reply.

Marin groped around with her hands, searching for Line, but felt only compacted earth and cold rocks.

Quietly, she pushed herself to sitting and realized her sack was no longer on her shoulders. Panicked, she searched the ground but found nothing. The effort made her short of breath, and it took a full minute until she was able to calm herself. Breathing deeply made the problem worse; it caused shallow coughs that she had difficulty stopping. The air felt pinched and dusty. Suffocating.

"I'm glad you're feeling better."

The voice was relatively close by—how close was impossible to say. It echoed in the musty air.

Marin said nothing. Her mind churned, trying to place the voice. She came up empty.

"Help me," she replied. As if to emphasize her need, Marin erupted in an avalanche of coughs. She wheezed and tried to breathe, but it felt like a losing battle.

"Help you?" came the reply. "But I have helped you. You would have frozen to death if I hadn't brought you down here." This remark was followed by a buzzing sound—almost like the hum of cicadas—which drifted down from above. She sensed she was being watched by many eyes; but the speaker—the voice—was much closer.

"I never realized until now how frail you are," purred the voice. "Every time I returned to my house, I found bits of your skin and hair embedded in the cracks. I suppose I should have known . . ." The voice trailed off into silence.

The darkness was total. Marin raised her hand in front of her eyes but saw nothing. "Who are you?" she asked.

"Yes, of course, I shall explain," said the voice. "But first, tell me . . . where is *she*?"

Marin wasn't sure how to answer.

"Where did she try to take you?" asked the voice. "Where is she hiding?"

"I don't know," said Marin as she slowly sat up and leaned back against a rock wall. She felt tired and sore, but otherwise okay. "Who are you talking about?"

"Soraya," said the voice.

"I don't know what you—"

"This is useless," bellowed an impatient voice from far above. "Take her to the wall—then she will speak."

"Yes," called a third voice. "To the wall!"

"To the wall!" came a cascade of voices, repeating it like a mantra.

Marin heard the sound of relentless scampering, as if a great many things were moving toward her all at once.

"Enough!" boomed the voice that had been asking her questions. Instantly, the area was silent. For a moment, it was so quiet that Marin could hear only the sound of her own breathing. She struggled to think clearly. She was surrounded by a horde of these things. A mob. And it seemed as if the only thing holding them back was the one asking her questions. He hadn't killed her yet, seemingly because he wanted to know where Soraya was. *But who was she?*

"Where's Line?" Marin finally said. She had to stall. And she had to find Line. "My friend . . ." *Is he still alive? He has to be. Why would they kill him and not me?*

"Where is Line?" said the voice, mimicking her words and the exact sound of her voice with the skillfulness of a ventriloquist.

"Please," said Marin.

"First tell me where my daughter is."

His daughter. His daughter, Soraya, is missing. That's something—a fact to build on.

"I-I'm not sure exactly," stammered Marin. She wiped a hand across her face. Her skin was warm. *What should I say— what will keep us alive for a little while longer?* "I might know," she said. *Hope. Everyone needs it.* Her voice strengthened. "But first tell me where Line is."

"He hasn't woken up yet," said the voice matter-of-factly.

Marin shivered suddenly.

"Tell me, why are you even here?" asked the voice. It was coming closer. "Did your father and mother leave you behind?"

At the mention of her parents, Marin felt for the copper box. To her relief, she found it nestled in her pants pocket. She envisioned the sharp blades, and it calmed her.

"If you could just let me see Line," said Marin. "I'll help you find . . . your daughter."

Suddenly, a high-pitched voice cried out from far above: "She's lying—the cockroach is a liar!"

"Make the cockroach climb," shrieked another voice. "TO THE WALL!"

There was a loud snarl and, once again, all was silent.

"Forgive them," said the voice. "That was rude, but don't you see . . . You stay in our houses and eat, and sweat, and breed, and shed your hair." The voice seemed to come closer and closer, until Marin sensed that it was now just a few feet away.

"We wanted to leave . . . ," began Marin.

"But. You. Didn't." The voice enunciated each word slowly, as if explaining something to a very small child.

Marin felt a sharp, curious fingernail run along the contour of her cheek, as if testing the elasticity of her skin. Her heart hammered inside her chest. *Keep stalling. Find Line.*

"You must see matters from our perspective. This town is ours. Of course, we understand that others may want to use our homes in the Day, which is why we have rules."

"Rules," said Marin slowly. *Yes, that's right. Of course there are rules, like the ones we saw on the statue of the sea hag. There's no point in playing dumb.* "That's true," said Marin as calmly as she could. "We have no right to be here."

As she said this, she could hear someone groan nearby. *Line.* It had to be Line. She inched toward the sound, keeping her back to the stone wall and scooting steadily.

"Yes," said the voice. "The rules you ignored. It wasn't enough that you stayed in our homes. You had to defile everything—even burying your dead in the very place from which we gather our food."

The voice paused for a moment, and then asked quietly:

"Would you like that? If we buried our corpses in your little vegetable gardens?"

"No," said Marin softly.

For several seconds, there was no sound. Then the voice returned, this time more tired and frustrated than angry. "And now, my daughter has gone missing—my most vexing daughter ran away to help *you*."

To help us.

Suddenly it clicked in Marin's head. The voice in the citadel. That was Soraya. That was *his* daughter. She was the one who had helped them. *But why?*

"Do you or don't you know where she is right now?" asked the voice.

Marin thought for a moment. She was tempted to lie, but something told her that this would be unwise. It was in the voice's calm, serious tone. This was no time to play games.

"No," said Marin. "I wish I knew—but I don't."

"As I thought," said the voice.

Just then, there was movement to the right of Marin. "Marin . . . ," a voice called out groggily from the darkness. It was Line. "Marin, where are you?"

"Line—I'm here," Marin said. "Stay where you are."

"No, that's all right," said the voice in an almost kindly manner. "Stand up if you like. We'll be leaving shortly. Or at least *you* will be."

"Leaving?" croaked Marin.

"Yes," said the voice. "In fact, we've all gathered to see you go."

"But where . . . ?" began Marin.

Marin felt something take her wrist. It was coarse and leathery and it held her in an iron-like vise. Together they proceeded through the darkness. As she walked, she tried to plan her next move, but she didn't know what was going to happen. Attacking them with the scalpels would be a useless gesture. She'd be killed within seconds. *What can I do?* A faint light glowed in the distance. They were heading toward it.

CHAPTER 53

"LINE!" CALLED MARIN.

"Behind you," he said. He was moving slowly, shuffling his feet.

Marin's heart sank—he sounded hurt. "Line—what happened? What did they do?"

"I'm fine," Line said. He started coughing, but strangely it comforted Marin. *He's hurt, but he doesn't sound weak. He's not going to die.*

The creature squeezed Marin's hand so tightly, she winced in pain. "Be careful of the *witches' fingers.*"

Marin had seen witches' fingers while exploring caves along the coast. They were spearlike rocks that rose from the floor of caves; the ones she encountered were only a few feet tall. They formed when water and minerals dripped down from above. The creature guided her through what appeared to be a vast maze of these. Marin couldn't see the witches' fingers, of course, but she could feel them with her free hand as she walked. Some were only waist high, while others seemed to be as thick and tall as pillars on a large building.

At some point, they emerged into the open. Marin could tell because it was sleeting, slowly and thickly, showering icy granules on her head. The creature came to a stop and released her hand.

"Look up," he commanded. She could hear the disdain and relief in his voice. He no longer had to touch her hand.

Marin did as she was told. She was able to discern a band of dark gray clouds. Slowly she came to understand that she was standing at the bottom of a very deep, narrow crevice and that she was actually looking up at a sliver of the sky above. They were somewhere in the canyon.

"Here's your chance," the voice said.

"My chance?"

"Yes, you know how to climb—don't you?"

"You're asking us to climb *that*?" asked Marin. It looked like a wall—the vertical rock wall of the canyon.

"Not asking," said the voice in a smooth, matter-of-fact tone. "Telling."

She felt Line's presence next to her and reached out for him. His fingers touched hers—and her heart heaved a great sigh of relief. Marin took a tentative step forward and pressed her palms against the wall of the canyon. The surface was smooth and wet; the wall itself was completely vertical.

"I can't do it," said Line. His voice was soft, defeated. "No way."

Marin looked toward the sound of his voice. She was about to reply but suddenly realized how the copper box might be useful. And it did *not* involve stabbing the creature. It was something else altogether.

She pressed closer to the wall and bent down, as if examining it more closely. She was conscious of the box in her pocket, its subtle weight tugging on her pants. *How did it unlatch?*

Marin heard Line breathing. She reached out for him with her free hand. His clothes were wet and dirty and his forehead felt cool.

"How's your arm?" she asked.

"Better," said Line. "Swelling is down."

"Good." Then she leaned in close and whispered in his ear, "Stay close—I have a plan."

"Marin—"

"We can do this," interrupted Marin. "Trust me—it's just like the cliffs after a rainstorm."

The creatures had backed away, giving them room to begin their climb. Marin took off her jacket and then her sweater, cinching them tightly around her waist. She reached into her pants pocket, pulled out the copper box, and slid it between her body and the wall of the cave. Conscious of the seconds ticking away, she fiddled with the latches and opened the box. Immediately she saw the small glass bottle that was glowing faintly. *That's the one.*

Everything depended on whether she could pull off the next move. Marin removed the bottle of glowing ink and screwed the top of it into the handle of one of the rods. It worked— locking into place—just as it had in her bedroom days before.

"What are you doing?" asked the voice. It sounded a good twenty feet away. Marin quickly slid the box back into her pants pocket and held the scalpel at the ready. Now came the real test. She didn't know how to use the scalpel, but she had a hunch. Holding it in her right hand, she extended her left arm and made two long cuts through her shirt and into the skin—from the shoulder all the way to her wrist. Her skin stung momentarily, then began to glow.

"Stop her!" called a creature from above.

Steady now. Marin hastily extended her right arm and marked it in the same manner, with two quick slashes. Again the sting, and now that arm also radiated two bright bands. It wasn't a powerful light, but it cast a muted radiance against the cliff wall, allowing her to see some of the minute cracks and crevices.

"I don't believe it . . . ," gasped Line.

"Your turn," she whispered. Line took the rod, but at that moment, something hit him hard in the arm. The scalpel fell and glowing ink skittered across the floor of the canyon, leaving a ragged line on the ground. Marin was struck across the head. She fell heavily and tasted cold dirt—but she had enough presence of mind to push the copper box farther down in her pocket.

"Enough of this!" boomed the voice from close by. The canyon fell quiet. And then the voice spoke again in a soft, almost sweet whisper. "Now *climb*—before I throw you onto the witches' fingers myself."

CHAPTER 54

THE WALL WAS SLICK, VERTICAL, AND NEARLY SMOOTH.
Still, tiny holds were scattered throughout and, therefore,
it could be climbed. Starting at the base of the cliff, several
cracks in the rock zigzagged up the face. Along with the
cracks, a few scalloped divots were enough to balance a finger
or a tiny portion of a foot. As she drew close to the wall, Marin
could see all this. The markings on her arms were not as radiant as a torch, or a candle, or even a matchstick. The reach of
its light was several inches at most, but was useful even so. It
gave her hope. Most important, it allowed a weakened Line to
follow her lead.

Marin began to climb the wall. She blocked out the darkness,
the rain, the cold. *It's just another climb.* She repeated this over
and over, pausing only to make sure that Line was behind her.
Every one of her movements was deliberate, because she knew
Line needed it. He needed the certainty that she was climbing
well and making the right choices. Line could rely only on one
good arm and infrequently on his wounded one.

About twenty minutes into the climb, they had made sub-stantial progress. But this did not give Marin or Line any re-assurance. It made sense. The creatures wanted a show, and it wouldn't be exciting if they failed too early. When they were high enough—when falling meant certain death—the wall would likely become more difficult.

And so it happened. At a certain point, the crack narrowed and became so tiny that Marin could barely squeeze the tip of her pinky into it. However, alongside the crack—in the faint glow created by her skin markings—she saw a series of shallow divots. This was all she needed.

"It's still climbable," she called down to Line, who was star-ing up at her. "Feel around for the divots along the crack and then you can just pinch your way up."

"Marin—I—I . . ."

She knew that he was about to say he couldn't, but she in-terrupted him before he voiced that thought.

"It's like the splintered rock at the edge of Bliss," she said, forcing her voice to radiate calm. "You have to dig in hard with your toes. You can do this. You're a better climber than I am. Wedge your fingers in." Her voice rose and she struggled sud-denly to control it. "You can do this," she repeated. "But it's going to hurt. Make them bleed if you have to."

"Yes," whispered a voice from the darkness. *"Bleeeeed."*

And so they crept up the wall. Marin waited for Line to crimp his way up the crack, ascending the wall ever so slowly. Before long, the waiting for Line became painful. Marin's fin-gers were raw and her legs kept seizing up as her calves and thighs jittered with muscle spasms. But the most ominous sign was that her forearms were beginning to tire. Once she lost the power to grip, it'd be over.

It was difficult to tell where they were. Marin kept looking up, hoping to see the top of the cliff. After all, they had made it this far.

Early in the climb, Marin had glanced back over her shoulder and seen a galaxy of faint lights; she soon realized that these were the eyes of the spectators who had come to witness her climb and, presumably, her fall. However, as she climbed and steadily weakened, she sensed that the throng of creatures had closed in around her. She could hear them nearby, ascending with her, reacting to her every move. The sensation reminded her of walking on Bliss's nearby beach and stepping carefully as sea crabs scurried underfoot.

As they approached, Marin's heart sank. She understood what this meant: an insurmountable challenge loomed in front of them. Perhaps an overhang or loose rock. The creatures could see it. They knew it was just up ahead, which is why they were drawing nearer. These were the same creatures who shared their town, their houses, their beds. And they wanted to see them fall, up close.

Line and Marin had drawn even and were climbing within inches of each other. Just a minute or two later, they came upon it. Ice. They could feel it with their hands. Whatever cracks and nubs there may have been had vanished under the smooth layer of ice. They stopped climbing. Neither of them spoke—they didn't have to.

In those days before the sun disappeared, before they were left behind, ice was an oddity. Nothing more. But now the cold shimmered off the rock in thick waves, and it chilled Marin so deeply that she felt numb all over. It made her want to let go.

Line's breath was coming in ragged gasps. She knew he was flailing, searching in panic for a hold in the ice.

Marin didn't dare speak for fear of losing her focus. She took her finger out of a nub and tried to wiggle out a cramp.

"Let go," whispered a nearby voice. "Make the pain go away. Let go."

"Fall," murmured another.

And then it caught on. All around her, the creatures began to chant softly, in unison: *"Fall, fall, fall . . ."* Their raspy whispers reverberated through the canyon, like a great wind rustling dead leaves.

"My legs are locked," gasped Marin. "Line! LINE!"

"Fall, fall, fall . . ."

"Don't listen to them!" shouted Line.

"Fall, fall, fall . . ."

"I'm losing my grip!" called Marin, struggling to suppress a panic.

"Fall, fall, fall . . ."

Marin felt herself tilting backward. Her arms weren't strong enough. She was going to fall. She was going to die climbing. She was going to fail at the one thing she was best at—and that would be the end. And Line would die, too—because of her and the mess that she had gotten them into. And in this moment, more than anything, Marin felt . . . not fear, but a deep regret.

Kana. She imagined his face, in the sunlight, squinting—the way he used to as a boy.

And then, seconds later, she heard Kana's voice calling to her. "Kana!" she screamed back at him. "Kana!"

A blinding flash of light came from above. Her muscles clenched and she pulled herself flush to the wall of the canyon. She looked up and saw a long, swirling cord of blazing-red flame—like a burning serpent descending on them. She could hear the creatures around her skittering away. The light was so bright that she couldn't see the creatures at first, only their shadows. Then a creature fell, dropped right past her, and screamed as it hit the witches' fingers below. All the while, the burning snake was plunging toward her. It was only when it shot past her that she saw what it actually was: a long, spiraling vine whose end had been lit on fire. So far, just the last ten feet of the vine was burning; the remainder was unlit, like the fuse on a firecracker. The vine continued to drop, for perhaps another twenty feet, and then it stopped moving.

An instant later, Marin heard a voice calling from above.

"Grab the vine and climb!"

It was Kana's voice.

Marin and Line needed no persuading. They each grabbed hold of the vine and—bruised and battered—began to pump and pull themselves up as quickly as they could. Below was utter chaos—clearly the fire panicked the creatures. The wall was alive with movement; bodies were pushing, clawing, and colliding. Marin glanced down and saw immediately that the flames were gaining on her, ascending the vine faster than she was.

Line, who had always been very good with ropes, was already nearing the top of the canyon. Marin, however, couldn't keep pace. After hours of exertion, her legs obeyed her brain only fitfully.

Meanwhile, at the top of the canyon, Kana was struggling with all his might to hold on to the wick vine. Initially his plan had gone well, better than he could have hoped for, but now Marin was stuck at the bottom of the rope and the flames were about to overtake her.

Kana cursed to himself. There was no place to anchor the rope. That had been his plan from the outset, but the top of the canyon was bare of trees, boulders, or roots. So he had to hold the rope himself. Line was getting closer, but he was still a good ten feet away, and he knew Marin couldn't wait that long.

"Go on—get her!"

Kana jerked his head back and saw Soraya staring at him with her large, lifeless, amber-colored eyes. She was already holding the vine.

"Go!" she commanded.

Seconds later, Kana was rushing down the vine at full speed. When he came upon Line, he yelled at him to hold tight. Then he vaulted over Line and briefly plummeted down in a free fall. From afar, it looked as if he was dropping to his death, but Kana reached out, grabbed at the vine again, and continued his descent. By the time he reached Marin, the flames had begun lapping her feet.

"Kana!" she cried, reaching for his outstretched arm. Kana seized her hand and pulled her up. She clutched him fiercely with one arm and tried to beat out the flames on her pants with the other.

"Just hold on!" he yelled as he climbed with Marin hanging on to his shoulders.

"I tried," she said. The words came tumbling out in a mad haste. "I tried to find you in the forest . . ." But the shrieking from below drowned out the rest of what she said.

Kana put all of his might into ascending the rope until, completely spent, he pulled himself across the upper lip of the precipice and eased Marin off his shoulders. She was yelling incoherently. The fire had caught on her pants and was burning her legs. He threw himself across her and extinguished the flames with his body. Trembling, he rolled away and struggled to his feet. At that moment, he saw the jagged, glowing slashes across Marin's arms.

Marin muttered something unintelligible. Her hair was singed and her face was swollen with fast-rising bruises. She looked around, suddenly aware of Soraya.

"It's all right," said Line. "She's the one who saved us."

"No," said Soraya coldly. Then she pointed a long, elegant finger at Kana and said, "He's the one who came back for you."

"I waited nearby, in the tops of the trees," said Kana. "I waited for hours—I knew you were down there." He was aware of Line looking at him. For a moment, Kana panicked. *They won't come with me. They're too scared.* But then Line stepped toward him and placed a hand on his shoulder.

"Thank you," said Line, squeezing his friend's shoulder.

Kana thought of taking Line's hand but stopped abruptly when he thought of how leathery his own hand had become.

"We found each other," replied Kana tersely. "That's what matters."

"We leave now," snapped Soraya. She tossed the vine she had been holding over the precipice.

They heard screams from below. Moments later, a lone voice thundered up from the depths.

"SORAYA!"

CHAPTER 55

THE SLEET RETURNED IN FORCE—AND AS THEY RAN, IT
became a maelstrom of ice, slush, and snow. It stung and
drenched them all at once. Visibility was low, so they formed a
ragged line and ran together into the woods.

Line was last, and as he stumbled across the uneven terrain,
he could hear a cacophony of noise erupt from behind him. It
was high-pitched and so powerful that Line couldn't help but
wince. It was not one shriek but hundreds, and they reverberated through the woods, melding together like a chorus of demons from the underworld.

Line charged forward, errant branches cutting and tearing
at his face. It didn't matter—he was so filled with adrenaline
that he felt nothing. He was focused entirely on Marin, who
was directly in front of him and running just as fast as he was.
Occasionally, his hand slipped out of hers and—in those brief,
terrifying moments—he would have been hopelessly lost if it
weren't for the glowing lines on Marin's arms. Together, they
pressed on. Kana was ahead of Marin, and all of them were

following the creature that Kana had called Soraya. It must have been Soraya who spoke to Marin at the citadel. She had been helping them all along. *But why?* Because of Kana, of course. *What was between them? Did it even matter?*

The woods soon began to thin and they emerged into an open area covered with clumps of ice-encrusted grass, some as tall as Line's shoulders. Wind and sleet were blowing sideways now, causing the grass to whip madly about. They all ran together until Line took a bad step, twisted his weak ankle, and fell. By the time he rose to his feet, Line had lost sight of Marin and the others. He was about to call out to her when he heard something behind him. It was very close.

Line knew he couldn't outrun this thing. Not in the darkness. He had to strike first.

He sidestepped into the tall grass and knelt down. With his good hand, Line searched madly for something—anything. Buried under the mud, he found a fist-size rock. For a second, he marveled at how natural it seemed to be holding this rock, waiting to bludgeon his enemy. *Who have I become?* No matter. He would ponder such questions later, if he lived. Line gripped the rock and waited for several long seconds. The sound of movement grew louder, and when he felt it rush past, he leapt from the grass and struck the darkened body with all his might. He brought the rock down again and again, hoping to hit its head. At first the creature merely growled, as if angered, but then Line heard a sickening crack, and all went quiet. Line fell next to the creature and kept hitting it, well past the time when it was dead.

"Line!" called a voice.

It was Marin.

Line pulled himself off the ground. He stood and looked around, wild-eyed, half expecting hordes of creatures to descend on him.

"Line!"

He pushed himself through the grass, moving toward the sound of her voice.

"Line!"

He followed the glowing lines in the distance. When he finally found her, Marin didn't even react to his blood-covered arms or to the rock he was holding. She just grabbed his hand and led him through the grass, then up a steep, rocky slope. In front of them, Line could see two figures: Kana and Soraya.

"What happened?" asked Kana, staring at Line's blood-covered arms. For a moment, suspicion clouded his face.

Line was about to answer, but suddenly they heard a leathery flutter of wings, and his face erupted in pinpricks of pain. His hands closed around a warm, furry, plump body. Bats. He grabbed the bat that was clinging to his face, ripped it off, and threw it to the ground in disgust. They were everywhere, swarming.

"Up the hill!" commanded Soraya.

Line bent low to the ground and focused on covering his face. Somehow he still remembered to keep climbing. All four of them sprinted, jostling each other as they fought back against the attack. The bats were so densely packed, it seemed as if they were interconnected—one giant, writhing, living thing. The sound of their wings filled the air. And then they were at the tree line and back into the forest. The bats stayed in the open area, circling in a thick cloud.

They paused for a second to regroup. Behind them, the rising chorus of shrieks was drawing nearer. Soraya led them into a stand of pine trees. The ground, which was soft and covered with pine needles, absorbed much of the surrounding noise. They ran for a short while until Soraya came to an abrupt stop and bent down to the ground.

Half a minute later, she grunted in satisfaction, tore at a thick layer of pine needles, and hoisted up an armful of branches caked with mud. It looked like a large bird's nest that had been flattened. When Soraya lifted the branches off the ground, they heard the sound of rapidly flowing water.

Line knelt down next to Soraya and felt the outline of a small sinkhole. He stuck his arm in and felt the earthen walls.

"What's down there?"

"A river," replied Soraya. She stood up. "Can all of you swim?"

"You mean for us to—" began Marin.

"We'll never make it through the woods," she said. "But there is another way." She paused and easily ripped a large branch off a nearby tree. "Quickly now—come here."

They moved toward Soraya. Marin tripped in the darkness, but Kana caught her. Soraya hissed at her. "*Quiet*. Someone's coming."

Then a deep, gravelly voice spoke—from behind them.

"Soraya."

Marin and Line turned toward the voice but saw nothing. It didn't matter. They knew who it was—the creature from the canyon. They couldn't see him, but the sound of his voice was unmistakable.

"Stay where you are!" yelled Soraya. As she said this, she began pulling Line, Kana, and Marin backward—ever closer to the sinkhole. She then raised the branch that she had ripped off the tree and brandished it menacingly. The jagged end resembled a bayonet.

"Put that down," said the creature in a calm, almost bored fashion. He took a step closer, into a shaft of moonlight that illuminated his body. He was over seven feet tall, with the same features as Soraya—the elongated ears, narrow face, and large eyes. However, his face and throat looked tight, as if the skin had been pulled back across his skull. And this was precisely the case. A tiny dark bud protruded from the top of the creature's head—it was a tuft of his own skin, tied off with coarse twine. His eyes, which were entirely black, were fixed on Kana.

"So, this is the boy . . . ," said the creature, eyeing Kana appraisingly. "Soraya, do you really think that you showed this child mercy by allowing him to live?"

"Father!" said Soraya. Her hand tentatively folded around Kana's arm. "This child is—"

"Yes, I *know* who he is," whispered the creature. Then, from behind his back, he brandished the glittering battle-ax with the two-foot-long cutting edge—the one from the mayor's house.

"Soraya, this isn't my doing," continued the creature. "It's yours."

Soraya eyed the ax and then her father. "No," she whispered. "Don't."

"Then you do it!" snapped her father.

Marin sucked in a breath of air.

"It's okay," Kana whispered. "It'll be okay."

"All right," said Soraya. She dropped her stick, stepped forward, and extended her arms. The creatures looked at each other for several seconds. Clearly, he didn't know whether to trust her. But then he came to a decision, nodded solemnly, and handed her the massive battle-ax. Soraya took the weapon, ran her fingers along its blade, and turned to face Kana.

Kana stiffened. Marin tried to move between them, but Kana pushed her back. There was no point. He was done running. In a way, he knew that this moment was coming all along—from the very first time that Soraya had visited him in his room, weeks before. In fact, he suspected it might end like this: deep in the woods, in the darkness, at Night, with his sister at his side. And he was strangely at peace with it. Soraya and her father were right. He didn't belong anywhere—and he never would. The inevitability and certainty of it all washed over him and deadened his sense of fear.

Kana looked directly into Soraya's eyes. "Help Marin and Line get to the sea," he whispered. *"Please."*

Soraya took a step closer and raised the battle-ax high over her shoulder. Then there was a quick whir of movement, followed by a loud crack. Soraya had spun around and swung the battle-ax at her father. He managed to avoid the blow, and the battle-ax glanced off a nearby tree and clattered to the ground.

Her father recovered quickly, but not before Soraya had pulled Kana, Line, and Marin toward her.

"Hold your breath!" she commanded. She wrapped her arms around them and fell backward into the sinkhole. Together they plummeted through the void: emptiness, rushing wind, and the cold, dark shock.

CHAPTER 56

KANA PLUNGED INTO THE WATER AND HUNG THERE, several feet below the surface, until finally he popped up, gasping for air. He panicked, swallowed water, and flailed about. The river's current whisked him through a roaring void of blackness. The numbingly cold water deadened his senses, making his legs heavy and useless. Time seemed to stop. He lost track of where he was and his thoughts faded to a flicker.

Then he saw a faint glow in the distance and a silhouette. Someone gesturing to him. He floated toward the person rapidly, which was an indication of the power of the current. A muffled voice called out. It was Soraya.

She grabbed Kana, clasped him by the shoulders, and yanked him out of the water. There was just enough light to make out Soraya's features. Her eyes were eerily still and calm, as always, but her voice betrayed a hint of anxiety.

"Prepare the boat!" she ordered. "I'll get your friends."

Kana rose to his feet, teeth chattering, and moved toward the mouth of the cave. For the first time in days, he felt cold. Behind him, Kana could hear her pulling Marin and Line out of the water. Kana knew he should turn his attention to the boat, yet precious seconds passed and he just stood there, staring at the cave paintings in front of him—the swirls of blue and green paint forming vivid depictions of the sea and the forest. His father had made these.

My father.

Kana didn't know his father's name. He knew only that he had lived here and had painted on these walls.

And what of my mother?

Kana knew the truth, and still, it was hard to fully grasp it.

Moments later, Soraya appeared with Marin and Line in tow.

"What are you doing?" demanded Soraya.

Kana held up his hand, a gesture for patience. "I know we have to leave," he said.

Somehow, Soraya understood.

"There's the boat," she told Marin and Line brusquely, pointing in the direction of the smooth wooden hull. "Drag it outside and get it ready by the river."

Line nodded and left, but Marin stayed. Her face was terribly bruised, but her eyes were the same as ever—fierce and determined.

"Kana, I'm not leaving you here," she said. "You are coming off this island with us."

Kana looked at the ground. "Marin, go to the boat—please."

"Promise you're coming with us," said Marin. She took his hand. *"Promise me."*

Kana felt her cold fingertips and the warmth of her palm. "I need to speak with Soraya," he whispered. "Please."

327

"All right," Marin replied. She left to help Line with the boat.

Soraya faced Kana and leaned in toward him. "You need to leave," she said. "He will be here soon. And others will follow. He didn't jump in right away—he doesn't like the water—but he'll swim after us when he realizes he has no other choice."

Kana nodded. His eyes were drawn to the furrier boats painted on the wall. "How did he die—my father?" His voice wavered.

"It's not what you think," replied Soraya with a shake of her head. "He was older when he came, and something was wrong with his heart."

"I feel like I have memories of this place," said Kana quietly, almost to himself.

"I understand," replied Soraya.

Kana nodded and looked down. *Of course she does. She was here, too.*

"What happened?" he whispered.

"I was young," she replied softly. "And I was scared. By the time that you were born, your father had died. By then it was almost Dawn. I knew what was expected . . . But I could not . . . I left you on that rock instead."

Kana looked past Soraya, at the painting of two figures staring down at something. That something was a baby—him.

"I regret many things," said Soraya. She reached to touch Kana's cheek. It was tentative and soft. "But there was no taking you back to this cave. They would have killed you."

"Why didn't you tell me sooner?" he asked with a trace of anger. "We could've . . ."

"We could have done nothing," she replied. "There is no life for us together, just as there was no life for me with your father. Just a few moments." She breathed heavily. "Now only one thing matters . . ."

Behind them, from the darkness, they heard the faintest splashing sound.

"Go now," said Soraya. Her body stiffened and her voice became intense, almost guttural. "He's coming."

"Come with us," pleaded Kana.

Soraya shook her head. "Impossible." She grabbed his hand and pulled him toward the cave opening. Tentatively, she placed her long fingers across his shoulders. Touching him like this seemed to affect her in a profound way. Her eyes glimmered for a moment—as if briefly coming to life—and then she staggered as if she'd lost her balance.

"Take the river downstream," she continued. She leaned into Kana and breathed his scent.

"Kana—do not go ashore. The woods along the river are waking."

Kana couldn't move.

There was a second splash and then a third. The air in the cave grew pinched and close.

Soraya touched two fingers to his forehead. They lingered there for a second. Then she spun around and retreated into the darkness of the cave. Kana ran down to the water, where Marin and Line were waiting for him. They had the boat in the river and were already sitting in it, Line at the stern, Marin in the middle of the boat. Kana hopped in at the bow.

"Where is she?" asked Marin.

"Just go," said Kana. His voice cracked, and Marin could tell he was crying.

Line and Marin both hesitated.

"GO!" Kana yelled.

Line nodded. With a powerful thrust, he dug his oar into the riverbed and shoved off, guiding the boat into the fast-moving current of the Coil. The river took hold of the boat quickly, pushing it downstream, beneath a thick canopy of trees and into the inky blackness beyond. Kana tried in vain to catch a last glimpse of the cave, but it had vanished.

CHAPTER 57

LINE SAT IN THE STERN OF THE BOAT, SHAKING WITH
cold, his good hand on the well-polished tiller. Sleet battered
him, and at times he could barely see the rear of the boat, much
less guide it down the river. His fever had subsided, thanks to
the lekar that Marin continued to give him, but his wound still
ached. It felt good to be at the helm of a boat—it gave him a
sense of confidence and purpose.

"Kana!" he yelled. "Get to the edge of the bow—we need
your eyes."

Kana leaned over the edge and immediately called out a
warning: "Two rocks off starboard bow!"

Line cranked the rudder violently and the boat lurched to
port. The hull scraped the rocks, then slid.

"There's a sharp turn to port ahead," said Kana. "I'll tell you
when."

"How far?"

"Five boat lengths!" He paused. "Four lengths, three lengths,
two lengths. Now!"

The boat turned and continued downstream. With Kana

guiding him, Line navigated through several more rapids. Meanwhile, Marin used her oar to shove floating branches out of the way. Rocks thumped against the hull, but the boat was ruggedly built. The Coil deepened and the trees crept closer to the water's edge. Then the river narrowed a little more, forcing Line to maneuver the boat sharply. Kana glanced back at Line and Marin.

"We're fine," said Line in a terse voice. "Just keep telling me where to turn."

They cleared another bend and Kana let out a shout. Just ahead, a massive tree had fallen across the river, leaving an opening only a few feet high for them to squeeze under. A curtain of moss, glistening with ice, draped across the gap and extended down to the water.

"Slow down!" Kana ordered. "Hard to starboard—get over and hug the far bank!"

Line threw the rudder into position, but it wasn't nearly enough. Seconds later, the boat careened headlong into the tangle of moss. At their angle and speed, the impact spun the boat sideways. It stopped perpendicular to the current. Water began crashing over the gunnels.

"We're stuck!" yelled Kana. "Hold on!"

Marin and Kana tore at the moss, but within seconds, the force of the water against the boat had pushed them through. It looked like they were free, but then they heard a great cracking sound overhead, followed by an explosion that shot a geyser of water into the boat. The tree had been rotten inside, and the impact of the boat had caused it to weaken and crash into the water, narrowly missing them. Just then, something small bit Kana on the neck. Then it happened again.

"They're dropping everywhere!" Kana shouted, swatting at his neck.

"What's dropping?" demanded Line. His question was answered when he felt something land in his hair and wriggle furiously. He pulled out a caterpillar-like insect that had jagged ice crystals embedded in its fur. It rose up in his palm and thrust a curved pincer deep into his thumb. Line yelped and the thumb blossomed in sharp pain. Soon he was being stung all over.

Line forced himself to keep hold of the rudder, ignoring the stinging along his scalp and arms. He felt the current grab and spin the boat, careening it toward the opposite bank, where the branches of a fallen tree were sticking out like spikes.

"Kana!" Line yelled. "Behind you!"

An instant after Kana saw the sharp branches looming, something threw him to the bottom of the boat. Line had grabbed both Kana and Marin and yanked them down with him. Seconds later, the boat spun around again, although this time they were pushed downstream. Line scrambled back to the rudder.

A rising swell of noise filled the forest. It was a deep, bass pounding, as if drums were being played all around them. The trees beyond the cover of shoreline vegetation began to sway. Kana recalled Soraya's final warning: *The woods along the river are waking.*

"We have to flip the boat!" said Kana.

"WHAT?" shouted Marin. She stared at Kana as if he were insane. "We'll freeze to death."

The thrumming continued to rise from the riverbanks, as if the entire forest was converging on them.

"We don't have a choice," Kana yelled. "We have to get under the hull—it's our only protection."

Dark objects began whizzing past. The sounds of the forest rose from every direction.

"Lean to starboard!" yelled Kana.

Together, they lurched to starboard. The port gunwale rose up out of the water, wobbled precariously for a moment or two, and then flipped. Marin, Line, and Kana plunged into the water. Moments later, they resurfaced, grabbed for the hull of the boat, and hid underneath.

"W-where are you?" Marin sobbed. The cold was deadening her senses. "I can't see anything."

"Here," shouted Line. "KANA?"

"HERE!"

"Grab the wooden slats and hold," Line ordered. "Hold on tight."

On the other side of the hull, they could hear the sounds of bodies—large and small—thudding against the hull. The onslaught continued over the course of several minutes; it sounded, at times, as if it was being pelted with stones. They clung tightly to the boat, their arm muscles frozen into position.

It was hard to gauge time, but eventually Line realized that the outside world had grown quiet and the boat was no longer being bombarded. And then his feet began to drag along the river bottom. It was running shallow. A jolt of water splashed onto his lips, and it no longer tasted like freshwater.

"It's brackish," he called out. "We're probably near the old seabed. Marin, Kana—hold on a little longer. We're almost out."

They floated downstream in silence for several more minutes, until the cold numbed Marin's arms so completely that, without warning, she lost her grip and sank down into the water. It happened in an instant, and it took Line several seconds to realize she had disappeared.

"MARIN!" screamed Line. "Quick, Kana—beach the boat."

Line let go as well, leaving Kana alone underneath the boat. Kana dug into the riverbed, and slowly, the boat turned. A moment later, he heard the overturned hull grate against rock. Kana swam out from under the boat and looked around. The island was behind them. They were situated on the edge of the Coil as it cut across the old seabed. Line had found Marin about twenty yards upstream and was struggling to get her out of the water. Kana shoved the boat farther onto shore and ran to them.

Marin lay on her back, her arms and legs covered in mud. Her eyes were closed and her face was as pale as the moon. Only the glow from her skin markings seemed alive.

"Marin!" shouted Kana. *"Marin!"*

Her lips pursed and shifted, as if she was trying to speak. An arm twitched, then Marin's body began to tremble all over. With great effort, she opened her eyes. Line helped her to a sitting position. He was trembling, too—the cold had seeped into every pore of his skin and sapped away his last reserves of energy.

Kana was far less affected by the cold. Marin and Line huddled on the rocks while snowflakes landed steadily on their hair and shoulders. Then he remembered the flint. It was still there, in his pocket. It took only a few minutes to build a small pile of driftwood and pine needles for kindling. Soon, the sparks and smoke turned to fire. Kana and Line carried Marin as close to the fire as they dared and set her on the ground.

It was risky, building a fire this close to the island, but Marin would die of hypothermia if she didn't get warm. Once the fire was going strong, Kana searched the boat from top to bottom. In a small, inset compartment, he found an empty leather flask and two wool blankets. He draped the blankets around Marin and Line. With the blankets and the fire, they finally stopped shivering. Soon, they were warm enough to proceed. Line made sure to apply more lekar, and afterward, he and Kana pushed the boat back into the water.

They floated downstream through the darkness. There was little work or steering involved. The current would carry them to the sea, and only then would they need to worry about which way to go.

An hour passed and then another. Marin had been huddled on the boat's floor, drifting in and out of sleep, when suddenly she stirred to life with an awareness of something she needed to do. She crept to the bow of the boat, where Kana was perched, looking downstream. He had been studying the river ahead and occasionally warning Line of obstacles in their way.

"Are you all right?" asked Marin. She placed a tentative hand on his knee.

Kana shrugged. His mind had been churning—with thoughts about Soraya, Anton, Tarae, Marin, Line, the sea voyage, life in the Desert Lands, and countless other things. "Honestly," he said, "I'm not sure how I feel."

Marin put her hand on his arm. They sat like this, motionless, for a while.

At one point, Kana turned to look at Marin's luminescent markings. The blanket had loosened, baring her arms.

"You did that?" he asked.

Marin nodded, and briefly described the climb up the cliff. Kana leaned in to study her markings. After a moment's reflection, he sat back.

"They suit you," he said quietly.

CHAPTER 58

THEY FLOATED THROUGH THE NIGHT, AS IF RIDING THE
current of an endless dream. To slake their thirst, they collected
melted snow and rainwater in the leather flask. For food, Line
tore off a slat of wood from the boat and made a rudimentary
harpoon; it was good enough to catch migrating eels. Thanks
to the lekar, Line's arm healed steadily. The swelling subsided
and his fevers ceased.

Each of them took shifts at the rudder, guiding the small
boat along the river's serpentine bends and between the many
gravel shoals that emerged. In places, the Coil itself widened
enormously, fanning out to cover great expanses, so that it was
just several inches deep. On these occasions, they hoisted up
the keel and the rudder, and pushed the boat across the rocks
and dried kelp. Elsewhere, the river narrowed into tight chutes
and then dropped down into craters where river water had
pooled to form small lakes. It didn't matter—they simply followed the current.

Marin spent hours staring at the horizon, which seemed to

be growing lighter. The air warmed to the point where fog was common. Oddly enough, she didn't worry about all the things that could still go wrong. She was too tired and too numb to worry. Right now she was safe and she needed to rest. Her thoughts wandered, to the desert camp and the two-humped horses from the storybooks. She pictured the sand dunes, and the mountains, and the warmth of the sun on her face.

If they made it to the Desert Lands, they would remain there for fourteen years. Marin would spend the rest of her childhood there, would become an adult there, would get married there, might even have a child there. She tried to envision Line as her husband but couldn't quite see it. And then she imagined Kana in the blinding sunlight—and the thought filled her with sorrow. Of course he had to leave the island, but still, life in the desert would not be easy for him.

Marin would be twenty-eight years old when she returned to the island. Twenty-eight. It was hard to fathom. Back before all of this happened—before she knew what lurked deep in the woods of the island—she had loved this place. But how could she sleep in her bed, walk by the edge of the woods, visit the old cemetery, and sail to the Dwarf Oak Islands without feeling a current of fear? Could these places possibly feel like home again? The dark would be with them forever—even in the brightest hours of Day.

As Marin considered this, she was suddenly more sympathetic to the possibility that her parents—and other adults— may have chosen wisely *not* to know what lurked in the woods.

Not that any of this mattered now. Those worries were years

away. When—or if—she returned, she vowed to do so only if Line and Kana were with her. They knew the truth. And the knowing bound them together.

At one point, when the Coil poured into a newly formed lake along the seabed, they stopped for several hours. Kana and Line worked together to chase fish into the shallow areas, where they caught half a dozen flatheads with the makeshift harpoon. The boat was several hundred feet away, and they walked slowly, pleased with their catch. Walking together like that reminded Line of the times when he and Kana were in the forest together. They had been such good friends then.

As they walked back to Marin, Line turned to Kana and smiled. "You still have that flint, right?" he said. "I'm getting tired of eating stuff raw."

"Sure," Kana said. "We'll just grab some driftwood and dried seaweed. It'll smoke a bit, but that might make it taste better."

Line took in Kana's features—his body somehow seemed smaller, leaner, and frailer. *Is he already changing back? It's hard to tell.*

He clasped Kana's shoulder. "You're a good man to have around."

Kana stood there awkwardly.

"Line," said Kana finally, with a trace of a stammer in his throat. "Back there in the forest—for a long time—I wasn't myself." He paused, trying and failing to find the right words to describe the way his mind had transformed. "Something was pulling at me . . ."

"It's okay," said Line. "You don't have to explain."

"But I want to."

"And you can," said Line. "Sometimes it takes time, though, to figure things out. It was like that after my mom died." He paused and smiled. "You know—you were there."

Kana nodded.

"Are you . . . back to the way you were?" asked Line. As he said this, he glanced at Kana's feet.

"Kind of," replied Kana. "Physically I'm pretty close to how I was before . . . but I don't think I'll ever really be the same. Truth is—I don't know if I'd *want* to go back to being that person. Maybe I knew, even back then, that something wasn't right. I just didn't know what."

Line looked toward the horizon, where they could see the sky lightening. "What happens next, do you think?"

"I'm not sure," replied Kana.

"Well," said Line with a determined nod, "some cooked flat-heads will help."

Kana nodded. "Sounds good."

An hour later, they were on their way, continuing down the now wide and slow-moving Coil River. Kana saw a deep purple on the far western sky. It might be a while yet before they saw the sun, but if they made it, Kana knew it would mark a shift within himself. He had told Line the truth. He was changing. As time passed, his eyes weren't quite as sharp as they had been and his breathing was less rapid. More strikingly, his feet seemed smaller—as did his talons—and the skin along his ankles and lower calves began to grow back while his greenish scales dried and peeled off. To Kana, these changes were bittersweet. He remembered the exhilaration of speeding through the treetops, alive with powers he never imagined he

341

might possess. That strength was fading now, and he hated to lose it. Perhaps in the Desert Lands, during the three days of Night, he'd get some of it back.

They continued downstream, past great, twisting chimneys of dying coral that had been abandoned by the sea. Once they saw the skeleton of a massive whale, propped up vertically on a series of boulders. Its rib cage looked like the scaffolding of a great, half-built tower. Later, they saw an old barnacle-covered shipwreck that had probably been on the floor of the sea for centuries.

In idle moments, Marin speculated about the life that was waiting in the Desert Lands. It made Kana uneasy. Even before Nightfall he'd been an outsider among what Soraya had called "the Day-dwellers."

Soraya.

Kana didn't let himself contemplate what had happened to her—whether she was still alive. Everything was still so raw and unresolved in his own mind. However, he happily recalled the cave with the drawings on the wall. He pictured his father, standing there in the flickering light of a campfire, carefully etching the paint onto the slabs of smooth stone, and he imagined Soraya with him in the darkness.

"You'll see her again," Marin said at one point, unprompted, as if she had been reading his thoughts. "She's strong . . . she'll survive."

Kana sighed heavily, obviously unconvinced.

"Marin," he said after some time. "You know who she is—right?"

Marin nodded.

"And that means that we're not really . . ."

Marin scoffed. "We'll always be twins," she said before he could finish. "Nothing can change that. You're stuck with me." She paused. "And at Dawn, when we return to the island, we'll look for her."

Kana raised his eyebrows. "When we return to the island?"

"Don't," said Marin with a smile.

"Don't what?"

"Don't assume we're never going back. Or that, if we do, nothing good will come from it," said Marin.

"What makes you so certain that's what I'm thinking?" he asked.

"Because I know you," Marin replied. She reached through the darkness, and her arms—which still glowed from the markings of her hastily drawn tattoos—encircled him. "I know you better than anyone else in the world."

Kana said nothing, but he hugged her back. Line sat quietly in the stern of the boat and smiled.

EPILOGUE

THEY SMELLED THE OCEAN BEFORE THEY SAW IT, AND they felt the salt from the air on their faces. In time, they heard the distant caw of seagulls and the muted, far off rumbling of the surf. Soon the boat began to accelerate. They could feel the pull of the sea as the vessel was buffeted by the chop. Seawater began to spray around them. Waves rocked the boat. And then, in an instant, the Coil had faded away and they were at sea—surrounded by an expanse of water that stretched toward the horizon.

"We did it!" shouted Line above the noise of the surf. He was sitting in the stern of the boat with his hand on the tiller. "Kana!" he yelled. "We need to raise the mast and the sails!"

"Got it!" Kana bellowed. Marin helped him, and within a few minutes, they had put up the mainsail and were moving at a steady clip, farther out to sea. As they sailed, Marin climbed back to the stern on the boat and sat down next to Line. She then reached into her shirt and took off the sunstone that hung around her neck. She felt its weight in the palm of her hand, and then handed it to Line.

"It's yours," she said. "I want you to have it."

Line stared at the sunstone, then at her. A moment later, he grinned.

"Are you sure?"

"Yes," said Marin. "Now use it."

Line nodded. "Take the tiller."

Marin grabbed it as Line climbed toward the bow. He passed Kana along the way, held up the sunstone, and smiled. Kana smiled back. When he reached the bow, Line raised the sunstone to the western sky, which was shimmering with the effervescence of Dawn. The stone glowed and cast a thin slice of light on one of the 360 hash marks that lined the circumference of the pendant.

"We're at two-oh-five," Line called out. "Bring us slightly to port. We need to be at two twenty-one." Marin nodded and turned the boat. Line studied the markings on the pendant as the stripe of light moved slowly, finally settling at 221. "All right!" hollered Line. He felt the wind at his back and pointed straight ahead.

"Are we good?" asked Kana.

"Yes," said Line, gazing out across the trackless ocean. "I think so."

ACKNOWLEDGMENTS

Before we had a title or characters for *Nightfall*, we talked about how it should feel. We talked at length about darkness and about night. There was a time, not long ago, when darkness evoked a primal fear. Before the advent of electric lights, night was something very powerful for humankind. Crimes committed at night, for example, often carried stiffer penalties. In the evening, as the sun dipped below the horizon, a tinge of worry would creep up people's spines. Night was something to fear. And this was the feeling that we hoped to conjure.

This book was a powerful lesson in collaboration: despite throwing everything we had into it, the two of us still came up short. What pushed this book across the finish line was the help we received from so many. We shared our very first drafts of *Nightfall* with Tina Bennett and Svetlana Katz at WME, and our gratitude for Tina's advocacy and advice, and to Svetlana for her wise counsel, is profound. They never, ever gave up on this book—or on us. We are grateful to others at WME who improved this book, especially Kathleen Nishimoto, as well as Laura Bonner and Janine Kamouh for their assistance on foreign rights. To Alicia Gordon and Erin Conroy, who represent the book for movie and television rights, we're thrilled to be working with you!

Family and a few closest friends gave crucial input as we prepared the book for submission. To Tamar Halpern, Micah Nathan, Dan Kujawinski, Nancy Kujawinski, Brian Zittel, and Paul Zuydhoek, thank you for being there at the beginning, and for your advice and help throughout. You were truly our first editors.

It was an uncertain and turbulent road to publication, but that all changed when we signed with Penguin. From the very first phone call with Putnam publisher Jen Besser, we felt at home. Jen's expertise and confidence was exactly what we needed—and what we continue to rely upon. As for our editor, Ari Lewin: WOW. You were *exactly* what we needed, at perhaps the most critical moment in the book's evolution—your creativity, talent, and superb editing skills were a wonder to behold. We hit the jackpot with you as our editor, and we can't imagine this book—or other future books—without you.

To Katherine Perkins—Perkins!—assistant editor and Ari's muse, thank you for your creativity and for being part of this incredibly impressive Putnam team.

Penguin's competitive advantage became crystal clear when we met with the marketing and publicity groups. The marketing group's intellect, passion, and energy made our day, thanks to Emily Romero, Erin Berger, Lisa Kelly, Anna Jarzab, Rachel Cone-Gorham, Leah Schiano, and Carmela Iaria. To our publicity gurus, Lindsay Boggs and Shanta Newlin, we owe HUGE thanks. Your enthusiasm encouraged us to double down. To designer Kristin Smith, who created our cover, we couldn't have imagined a better introduction to the feeling we wanted the book to evoke. . . . To art director Cecilia Yung and map creator Martin Sanders, thank you for turning our awkward scribbles into something beautiful.

After spending some time with Penguin executives, it's clear how fortunate we are to be with this incredible group. Their leadership, intelligence, and passion are a wonder to behold. Don Weisberg, Felicia Frazier and Jen Loja are the best in the business—and we're hoping to work with them for years to come.

Peter: To my mom, Jo Kujawinski, your strength and laughter keep me going. To my dad, Frank Kujawinski, thank you for teaching me how to write—I miss you. To my brother, Dan Kujawinski, you teach me how to live. To my sister, Liza Kujawinski-Behn, you're the ultimate role model. And to my mother-in-law, Arlene Weinsier, thank you for your encouragement and your talent with the camera. *Nightfall* is dedicated to my children, Blaze, Alina, and Sylvie, who fill my life with the purest joy imaginable. To my wife, Nancy Celia Rose, from that moment decades ago when you entered my life, you have been my everything.

Jake: To my sons, Sebastian and Lucian, this book is for you. Someday, I hope you will take it off the shelf, dust it off, read these words, and remember just how dearly your father loved and loves you. Special thanks goes to my mother, Tamar Halpern, for her endless devotion and encouragement on this book. I am also grateful to a number of other friends and family members, including Stephen Halpern, Betty Stanton,

Paul Zuydhoek, Barbara Lipska, Mirek Gorski, Greg Halpern, Ahndraya Parlato, Roya Reese, Lila Kleppner, Brian Groh, Brad Collins, and Emily Bazelon. I am also indebted to Aaron Poach, Amanda Zapatka, and Ralphie Sylvester for keeping me fit and sane. Finally, to my wife, Kasia, thank you for reminding me in so many ways that I must always "Hold on to what you believe in the light / When the darkness has robbed you of all your sight."

MUSIC FROM BLISS

"Hand over Hand" is a traditional climbing tune sung by the men and women of Bliss as they traverse the cliffs. It is usually begun by the lead climber, and is continued by those sharing the same rope line. The words on this sheet music are the basic text, but there are countless variations among the many towns in the northern islands.

"The Other Side of Me" is a ballad meant to evoke Marin's and Kana's thoughts as circumstances begin to push them apart.

A recording of both songs can be found at
www.celiarosemusic.com.

Hand Over Hand

Celia Rose

© 2015

The Other Side Of Me

Ballad ♩ = 80

Celia Rose

© 2015

B'' w/ male *8vb* Are you com-ing now to save ___ me __ or do I have to save my - self

you're my eyes when I can't see you're the oth-er side of me you're the oth-er side of me ___

Are you com-ing now to save ___ me __ or do I have to save my - self

you're my eyes when I can't see you're the oth-er side of me you're the oth-er side of me the oth-er side

A'' my hands are cold my grip is fail-ing too much load - der and I will fall

To listen to the music recording, go to www.celiarosemusic.com